GW00492990

Fran O'Brien and Arthur McGuinness
established McGuinness Books
to publish Fran's novels to raise funds
for LauraLynn Children's Hospice.

Fran's thirteen novels, *The Married Woman*,
The Liberated Woman, The Passionate Woman,
Odds on Love, Who is Faye? The Red Carpet,
Fairfields, The Pact, 1916, Love of her Life,
Rose Cottage Years, Ballystrand and Vorlane Hall,
have raised over €600,000.00 in sales and donations
for LauraLynn House.

Fran and Arthur hope that *The Big Red Velvet Couch*
will raise even more funds for LauraLynn.

www.franobrien.net

Also by Fran O'Brien

The Married Woman
The Liberated Woman
The Passionate Woman
Odds on Love
Who is Faye?
The Red Carpet
Fairfields
The Pact
1916
Love of her Life
Rose Cottage Years
Ballystrand
Vorlane Hall

Buy now online <u>www.franobrien.net</u>

THE BIG RED
VELVET COUCH

FRAN O'BRIEN

Fran

McGuinness Books

McGuinness Books

THE BIG RED VELVET COUCH

This book is a work of fiction and any resemblance
to actual persons, living or dead is purely coincidental.

Published by McGuinness Books,
15 Glenvara Park, Ballycullen Road,
Templeogue, Dublin 16 RR71.

A catalogue record for this book
is available from the British Library.

ISBN 978-0-9954698-4-6

Typeset by Martone Design & Print,
Celbridge Industrial Estate, Celbridge, Co. Kildare.

Printed and bound in Great Britain by
CPI Group (UK) Ltd, Croydon, CR04YY.

www.franobrien.net

Chapter One

Claire looked at her phone. Apprehension crept through her. A tidal race. She pressed her fingers to her neck and could feel her pulse. A drum beat. Marking time. Dum. Dum. Dum. She walked to the window, and pushed back the white voile curtain. Sun splashed through the high trees which grew at the edge of the pavement. Blue shadows cast sharp angles underneath leafy green branches. The road outside was empty. No one around. No-one taking a walk. No children playing. Just a few parked cars in driveways. The second car in the family unrequired after they had all gone to the beach, or the hills, or into town for the day.

Her ex-husband, Dr Alan Wang Li, had taken their thirteen-year old son, Neil, to visit his grandparents in Beijing as he had done for many years. Claire had never objected as she wanted Neil to know his Chinese heritage which was very important to Alan. They were due to return this evening but they were late and she assumed that perhaps the flight had been delayed. On checking the arrivals at the airport she discovered that it had actually arrived on time, and when eight o'clock passed and then nine, she began to panic and called Alan. But she couldn't get through. She drove over to his apartment and found neither he nor Neil were there, and Alan's car wasn't parked outside. She rushed home then and waited. Desperately worried.

Her phone rang.

'Claire?'

'Alan, where are you?' she screamed.

'Calm down.'

'Where is Neil?' she demanded.

'We are both in Beijing.'

'What are you doing there?' Her knees buckled. She couldn't stand. And had to hold on to the back of a chair for support.

'My son needs to know the place of his ancestors.'

'But he has lived in Ireland all his life, not China. This is his home,' she insisted.

'His family are here in China.'

'Fifty per cent of his family.'

'That's as may be. For now, he will grow up here.'

'But you can't do this. You're not entitled.' She was in tears.

'You have given me permission to take him back to China for the last few years. He just wants to stay on here for a bit. He loves it. He will be really happy.'

'I agreed to holidays, but not a permanent move to Beijing.'

'I have made the decision. It is final.'

She was silenced. Choking. Incoherent. Tears rolled down her cheeks.

'And Claire, don't ring the police. Don't accuse me of abduction.'

'But that's just what you have done,' she blubbered.

'If you take any legal steps at all, you will never see him again. China is a large country. We are a powerful family and I can simply disappear. He can disappear.' There was a distinct threat in his voice.

'But why must you take him from me? You know how much I love him. My heart will break if I lose him,' she gabbled.

'Listen carefully. I want him to grow up here with his Chinese family, it is important for the dynasty. He is my only son.'

'But I want Neil back,' demanded Claire.

'We can discuss that in the future.'

'I want him now. How is he? Put him on to me,' she demanded.

'He's with my mother.'

'When will I be able to talk to him?'

'Soon, I don't want to upset him by telling him that he isn't going back to Ireland for the moment.'

'I'm coming out there.' She made up her mind immediately.

'Don't.'

'Why not?' she grew angry.

'Because Neil will want to go back with you, and I can't have that.'

'Please, Alan?' she implored.

'You must see what that would mean.'

'I promise I won't upset him.'

'That isn't possible.'

'You're treating me as if I'm a child.' She couldn't believe this was happening. It was like some sort of a nightmare. She stared out through the window, expecting to see them at the door waiting for her to answer. Laughing at her as they played this crass joke. But no, it wasn't a joke and there was no one outside.

Chapter Two

Claire didn't know what to do. How was she going to force Alan to let her see Neil? She looked in a drawer for an address book. Her most recent records were on her mobile phone and computer, but now she went to that old book and found Alan's home address. She didn't know where it was in Beijing. Although she knew they were a wealthy family and owned a large home in Chaoyang Park. Their country estate was in a rural area outside of Shanghai. Alan's father was a wealthy property developer and had business interests in many parts of China. In such a family, if Alan wanted to hide Neil from her he would have no difficulty. But still she felt that she had to make an effort to find her son and not just accept her ex-husband's threats.

She searched for a flight to Beijing, and booked a room at the Holiday Inn for a few days, having just enough money to cover the cost by using her credit card, although there wasn't much credit left. She would have to repay the amount before the end of the month. And in addition she had to apply for a visa and pay extra so that she could be sure it would come through quickly.

'I have a problem,' she explained to her boss, Liz. 'I need some time off.'

'How long?'

'I'm not sure, perhaps a week?'

'You are due some holidays but I'll have to check how much.'

'I don't have enough, I know that. But I can take some time off

4

at my own expense if that's all right with you?'

'Can I help in any way,' Liz asked, a concerned look on her heavily made-up features.

'Thanks for asking, but it's to do with my ex-husband's family,' Claire explained.

'If it's that important,' Liz said, picking up her phone from the desk and pressing the key pad. 'I'll check the roster, someone will have to cover for you.'

'I'm sorry.'

'I'll pitch in myself as well,' she grinned ruefully.

'Thank you so much. I do appreciate it.'

'When are you leaving?'

'I'm not sure yet, but I'll work up to the day.' Only employed for under twelve months in the company, she was doubly grateful to Liz who was an amazing boss really. When Claire had noticed a job advertised on line at an upmarket fashion store, she had dismissed it at first. Fashion wasn't her thing. Her career up to that point had been in pharmaceuticals. Marketing medications all over the world for many years. Then she was headhunted by another company in the same field, with a very attractive offer and all the perks. But to her utter shock, without any warning that company was taken over, and she was out of a job. And because of the short time she was employed, there was no redundancy. She was distraught. Quite unable to cope with the fact that she had nothing to do each day. No meetings or travel to arrange. No targets to fulfil. For the first time in her working life, she felt as if she was drowning. Drifted down into the depths. Unable to breathe. Hands reached upwards and feet kicked furiously as she tried to burst through the surface of the sea. Feel the sun on her face, take deep gulps of oxygen and know that she was alive.

Immediately, she signed up with employment agencies. And sat back to wait. But she was impatient by nature and as the days passed without any job interviews she began to wonder would she ever get another position. But at the same time, in those first weeks she was able to spend so much time with her son she had drifted into a dreamlike state. She took him to school every morning and was there in the afternoon when he finished, and the happiness she experienced when he appeared out the school gate was something else. She couldn't believe how elated she was. But that euphoria was short lived. As soon as she had found a job, she would be leaving her boy once again.

'I'm sorry, my love.' She cupped his face in her two hands, and kissed him. What a situation. Since their divorce Alan had not supported Claire and had only given her a small amount every month for Neil's expenses. She hadn't wanted anything for herself, but now, with very large mortgage repayments she certainly couldn't be out of work for a long time, and those last few weeks without a salary had put quite a dent in her bank balance.

Her parents had looked after Neil every day since he was born, and she was glad to give them a break until she managed to get another job.

'We don't mind looking after him, love. Neil is our only grandson and deserves everything we can give him.' Her grey-haired mother insisted. 'If we didn't have him, we wouldn't know what to do with ourselves.'

'We love him,' added her father, looking up from reading his newspaper. 'He's ours.'

'I know you do.'

'When Neil was young we often used to worry that you would move permanently to China with Alan,' her mother had murmured.

'And that didn't happen,' Claire laughed.

'But we're sorry you're divorced.'

'So am I, for Neil's sake,' Claire admitted.

'You need us all the more, and we need you.'

6

'Thanks Mam.' She hugged her mother. She couldn't have managed without her parents.

When the job in the fashion store came up Neil was disappointed.

'Why do you have to work?' he asked, kicking the kerb as they walked up the driveway.

'If I don't work, we'll have no money.'

His face was sullen.

'Imagine what that would be like?' she asked him.

He didn't answer.

She put her arm around him. Beating herself up for not being the right sort of mother. Perhaps she should have been around every day, as Alan had expected. Back then she didn't have to work. There was no need for extra money. Alan earned enough and more for them as a family. Maybe their break-up was caused by the pressure under which they both worked. A wave of guilt swept through her. Perhaps she had let the achievement in her working life mislead her into thinking that she couldn't survive without a career. A foolish conclusion. As far as she knew, he hadn't been unfaithful. And she hadn't been either. They had simply forgotten how to know one another. Forgotten how to love. How to touch. To whisper words which would remind them of how much they had loved at one time. At night as they lay in bed, their bodies had been close but there had been no spark to ignite. Both so exhausted their eyes closed immediately, clouding any awareness that there was another person there. Sometimes, she said his name softly, or perhaps he may have murmured hers, but neither heard the other, and sleep sapped. Love had no chance.

Chapter Three

The plane slowly descended. It came through a cloud of smog which drifted quite low and prevented her from seeing the city itself. She knew that the air pollution in Beijing was quite high and had brought some masks to wear, as did many of the Chinese. A few more metres and the wheels thumped on to the runway. Claire gripped the top of the seat in front of her and closed her eyes for those last minutes until finally the plane came to a halt.

It was very slow going through Customs and Passport Control, and eventually she took the lift down to the ground floor and out to the taxi rank. In her handbag she had a sheet of paper which showed a translation into Mandarin Chinese of her request to the taxi driver to take her to the hotel. He understood and pulled out into hoards of traffic which travelled on a ten-lane highway into the city. This part of Beijing was modern, and on the sky line she could see numerous cranes, a sign of development in this ever-expanding city, with tall skyscrapers, and the most amazing architecture. She was blown away by the innovation, although in between she caught glimpses of ancient Chinese pagodas and temples, brightly coloured roofs, red and orange, which gave her a sense of the real China of the past. Alongside, she noticed huge shopping malls with English signage as well as Mandarin. There were many bars and restaurants which were thronged with people, and hawkers selling their wares from stands at the roadside.

The taxi dropped her off at the hotel, and she showered and

changed, anxious to go over to see Alan and Neil as quickly as she could. She took another taxi and directed the man to where they lived. It was more scenic. She had read up on this area of Beijing on the flight, but she didn't see herself as a tourist, although she would have given anything to spend time with Neil and explore this mysterious city and culture with him.

It was beautiful. A green oasis which had once been a palace. Lakes spanned by decorative bridges were surrounded by beautifully tended trees and plants. Ornate temples, and pavilions. She watched a group of people perform the slow movements of Tai Chi. Fishermen cast their lines from steps leading down into the water. People used the running track which she could see nearby. There were colourful children's play spaces. Apartments and houses built along the edge of the lakes, many with boats docked on marinas, and further out, yachts sailed. It looked like a holiday resort.

The driver turned off the main road, and drove through some of the more luxurious villas, eventually stopping outside a high walled enclosure. She paid him and climbed out of the car. She walked across and opened the gate of a narrow pedestrian entrance and followed a road which led towards the lake. She checked the numbers of the houses, and eventually arrived at Alan's parents' home. It had high metal gates which were locked and through them she could see a very large house with a beautiful formal garden. A waterfall sparkled in the sunshine and cascaded into a circular pool in front, reflected in the glass doors and windows. The house and outer walls were built of white stone with tiny glinting flecks of silver.

She rang the intercom.

A voice spoke rapidly in Chinese.

'I am looking for Alan Wang Li?'

There was another spate of Chinese.

'Does Alan Wang Li live here?' she repeated.

There was silence after that.

She stood for a while, unsure of what to do. There was obviously someone there, and if it was Alan's parents then she could talk to them, she knew they both spoke fluent English.

She rang the intercom again, and was becoming irritated when suddenly, her phone rang. She rooted in her handbag for it. 'Yes?'

'What are you doing in China?' It was Alan.

'I'm looking for my son.'

'I told you not to come out here,' he rapped angrily.

'I want to see him.'

'But you can't see him. He isn't in Beijing anyway.'

'Where is he?'

'With my parents.'

'Where are they?'

'That is none of your business.'

She tried a different tack and softened her tone.

'Alan, can't you just let me see him? It's cruel of you to prevent me from seeing him. He's my only child.'

'I told you why.'

'But he must be missing me, as I'm missing him.' Claire was blubbering now, and her voice was indistinct.

'He's happy here.'

She took a deep breath.

'When will you let me see him?' she begged.

'In time.'

'When will that be?'

'He must be settled first.'

'Can I talk to him on the phone at least?'

He was silent for a moment.

She could feel her heart beating rapidly as she waited.

'That might be possible.'

'Oh, thank you, thank you. Can you put him on now?' She was so relieved.

'No, not at this moment, but maybe tomorrow perhaps, if I can.'

'You promise?'

'If I agree, then I agree. There is no need for a promise.'

'I'll keep my phone open, but I can't ring you, the number is blocked.'

'I have a different number now.'

'Can I have it please?' she beseeched weakly. Like a bold child.

'No, I'll call you.'

'What time?'

'Probably in the morning.'

'Thank you so much,' she murmured.

He didn't reply.

'Alan?'

He had gone.

Anger swept through her, *bastard,* she thought. But she put it aside as a thrill flew through her heart. She would have to be glad that he had agreed she could talk to her darling boy tomorrow. 'Thank you, God,' she whispered, her prayers had been answered. It was only then Claire noticed the CCTV cameras positioned around, and decided to leave. If she didn't, then he might change his mind about letting her talk to Neil. She walked out of the gated estate, hating the thought that he was spying on her.

She went out later that evening to have something to eat. Beijing was an enormous arc of lights. Every colour of the rainbow flickered and sparkled like a fireworks display. By now the streets were very crowded. Chinese voices rose and fell. Argumentative. Excited. Lanes of congested traffic. Taxis pulling in and out to pick up and set down fares. And what seemed like hundreds of cyclists, whizzing mopeds and scooters threaded their way through the vehicles.

She wandered along, gazing vaguely into bright shop windows.

Some sold designer labels, and others sold cheaper brands. On one occasion, feeling uncomfortable because of the high level of humidity, she stepped into one of the shops glad of the air-conditioned interior, but saw nothing there which appealed to her. Even though she worked in a fashion store, she wasn't a *shopper* really. If she needed an item for a particular event, she could never find what she had in mind. So she bought things on the *spur of the moment* although sometimes she didn't wear them for months. Now she couldn't afford to buy anything for herself, but she was looking out for unusual designer brands which might interest Liz for the store. And there certainly were some very unusual designs which she knew would appeal to her boss.

She went into a restaurant near the hotel which was quite full, and had to check her online dictionary to understand the extensive menu, but eventually she ordered *Peking Duck* although it was a very different dish compared to the version she was used to in Ireland. Relishing the original, she sipped a glass of chilled white wine, glancing at her phone every now and then just in case Alan had texted or emailed. She paid her bill and left the place. Wandering down side streets among throngs of people who pushed past her. If she left the slightest gap between herself and the person in front it was quickly filled by a body, and it seemed she wasn't going to get anywhere, and only hoped she could find her way back.

She turned down an even narrower street. The buildings here were not much more than hovels. Such a difference to the main thoroughfares. An old woman squatted in an open doorway mixing something in a black cooking pot over a small fire and gazed at her curiously. Inside a dark hallway she could see a group of children sitting on the floor playing with a small ginger kitten, their pale faces peering out of the shadows. An acrid aroma of urine drifted out, mingled with smoke from the fire.

She awoke early after a disturbed night. Only sleeping on

and off. All the time, her mind was full of Neil. Smiling at her. Hugging her. She glanced at her phone. It was after six o'clock now and she wondered when Alan would call. Imagining her boy climbing out of bed too. Sleep in his dark brown eyes. Straight black hair tousled. Waving goodbye as he ran in the gate of the school. Her heart ached for him, longing to hold him close to her. Tears drifted down her cheeks. But just in case Alan phoned early and put her on to Neil, she didn't want him to notice her upset, and dabbed her eyes with a tissue, trying to control her emotion.

She showered and dressed quickly then, and went down to the dining room. She was very tense as she waited for Alan's call, and although she wasn't hungry, she felt it would be better to eat something to keep her going during the day. There was a very wide selection of meats, rice, noodles and other food available, and always adventurous with her choices when in a new country, she ordered *Mu xu rou* or *Moo Shu Pork* - made with pork, vegetables, and scrambled eggs, rolled into small thin pancakes. After that, she sampled some Douhua which was tofu pudding. She was sure that the flavours were delicious but surprisingly couldn't taste them. It was food. Simply that.

She returned to her room, sat in an armchair and waited. It was hard. Watching the time on her phone. Hoping that it might ring at any moment and she would hear Neil's voice. But what to say to him? If he asked where she was, should she say Beijing? Or lie and tell him she was still at home. Or maybe a soft enquiry if he was happy here? Enjoying himself? She was in a quandary. Wondering whether Alan would allow her to talk to him for long, or would he cut her off after a couple of minutes? Or ring at all?

Chapter Four

Claire was nervous. Walking up and down the bedroom. She had considered sitting in the lobby to wait but was reluctant to be in a place where it might be difficult to hear a call because there was always such a high level of chattering voices from the many people who passed through. And when at last the phone finally rang around lunchtime, she almost leapt out of the armchair.

'Neil?' she burst out.

'Talk to your Mum.' She could hear Alan say.

'Mum?'

The voice of her son echoed, and she could barely utter a word herself for a few seconds.

'Hallo, my love?'

'I was at the play space today, playing computer games on big screens.'

'Was it fun?' she asked.

'Yes, and tomorrow I'm going fishing with Yeh Yeh.' He was excited.

'That's going to be great, you'll really enjoy that.'

'We're going to catch lots of fish and eat them for dinner,' he giggled.

'I'm sure you will.'

'Can you come?'

'I don't know. I'm really busy at work,' she struggled to find an excuse.

'You're always busy, Mum,' he said. A dullness in his voice.

Immediately she could sense how he felt. His disappointment merged with her instant guilt. It was something he often said to her at home and now she wondered how good a mother she was. She remembered the rows she had with Alan when they were together about the long hours she worked.

'I'm sorry but ...' Tears flooded her eyes. She wiped them away. 'I wish I could see you, but it's probably better if you stay with your Dad for a little while.' She didn't want to upset him. This situation was all about her and Alan and she couldn't drag Neil into it.

'How are Gran and Grandad?' Neil asked.

'They were asking for you.'

'How's Rusty?'

'He's grand,' she reassured.

'Is Grandad still taking him for walks?'

'Yes, he is.'

'Neil, come on, we'll be late,' Alan spoke in the background.

'Bye Mum.'

'I'll see you soon, Neil,' she said to him. 'Very soon.'

Alan said something in Chinese to him.

Immediately Claire felt excluded.

'Love you, Neil,' she said.

'Love you Mum.'

'Go into Nai Nai,' Alan said. Once again in English.

'Bye Mum.'

'Take care,' she whispered and waited to hear his voice again, her heart trembling. But he didn't speak.

'Neil? Are you there?'

'He's gone,' Alan said.

'Let me talk to him again?' Claire begged.

'Perhaps in a day or two,' Alan said. 'But be careful what you say to him. Do not mention you are in Beijing.'

'I want to talk to him again today, see him.'

She felt she was losing her grip. 'I'm going over to the house now.'

'He's not here, I told you that.'

'Where is he?'

'With my parents.'

'But I thought that was their home?' she demanded.

'They're in the country now. Go home, Claire.'

'No, I want to see my son,' she wailed. 'I need him. He's due to start secondary school in Dublin next week.'

'He'll go to school here.'

'But I want him, he's mine, mine,' she screamed, pressing the phone tight against her ear. 'Do you hear me? Alan, answer me?'

There was no response.

'Alan?'

She stared at the phone but the call had ended. In floods of tears, she flopped on to the bed and buried her face in the pillow.

There was a knock on the door.

She rushed to it and dragged it open.

A young boy stood outside and for one crazy moment she thought it was Neil and stared at him.

'Housekeeping,' he said.

'No thanks.' She closed the door and stood there, her hands hanging. Only now regretting that she had lost her head with Alan. Would he let her speak with Neil again? Or would he disappear with him as he had threatened?

Her knees crumpled and she sank to the floor like a limp silk scarf. She lay there, holding herself with shaking arms, knees hunched up, until the choking sobs eased a little. Then she crawled into the bed and huddled under the duvet, thinking back to when Alan had accused her of being a bad mother. Guilt resonated and pierced her heart. She thought of how she had given all her love to her baby, her child, her boy, as he grew up. Although she had not been there all the time, and her own parents took her place, they loved Neil too. Should she have given up her job to look after her child? Had he suffered because of her own selfishness. Her own need to succeed in a career as would any man. She always enjoyed her work. And had never wanted to be at home all day, craving to be her own independent woman out in the market-place.

She fell into a routine. Afraid to move too far away from the hotel in case she wouldn't pick up Alan's call because of a weaker phone signal somewhere else. She had to wait. That's if his *next week* proved to be Monday. Or even Tuesday or would she have to wait even longer. She had booked her return flight and she was tied into that date. There was so much to see in Beijing she wished she could have visited the Forbidden City to see the wonderful architecture which dated back hundreds of years. Ancient temples. Imperial palaces. Even the Great Wall. She had picked up some brochures in the lobby of the hotel just to have something to glance through. And while she had her Kindle, she couldn't concentrate on reading a book. But that didn't matter to her. All she wanted was to see her child and hold him close.

Alan did call on Monday, and to her great joy, put Neil on to her.

'Are you having a good time in the country,' she asked.

'Yes, I like it here.'

'That's great.' She forced herself to be happy for him.

'Will you come over for a holiday and then we can go home together?'

'I'm sorry, love, I can't.'

'It's very nice here.' He tried to persuade her.

'I'm sure it is. I'll try and come next time.' Tears flooded her eyes.

'When will I be going home?' he asked.

'Dad will bring you.'

'He said he doesn't know.'

She was silent.

'Will you tell Tommy and Calum that I'm here?' His voice was faint.

'I will of course.'

'I miss them,' he said.

'And they miss you, they are always asking for you.' She changed the subject sensing his upset. 'Did you catch many fish the other day?'

'We caught a lot of fish.'

She could see him smiling. Happy. Dimples in his cheeks.

'Were you in a boat?'

'A little boat.'

'And did you have a fishing rod?'

'Yeh Yeh gave me one and we put worms on the hooks. Wriggly things,' he giggled.

'Were they big fish?' she asked, enjoying this time to chat with her boy, loving him so much.

'Three big ones and lots of small ones as well.'

'What else will you be doing?' she asked, curious.

'Yeh Yeh said he would let me ride his horse.'

'That's going to be great fun.' She was delighted he seemed to be so happy.

'What's his name?'

'*Ma.*'

Among her very few words of Chinese she knew that meant *horse.*

'I wish I could go with you,' she tried to control her emotion.

'Do, please, you can ride *Ma* as well.'

'I look forward to that.'

'Dad says I have to go now.'

'Enjoy the country.'

'Bye Mum.'

'Put your Dad on the phone.'

'Dad, Mum wants to talk to you.'

Alan came on the line. 'Yes?' he was abrupt.

'When will I see Neil?'

'I can't say. And I don't want you to come to the house again or I'll call the police.'

She was silent for a few seconds, unable to believe what he had just said. She swallowed the words which she very nearly uttered and softened her tone.

'Can I talk to Neil again?'

'I don't know.'

'Please?' She hated being in this position. 'Why are you being so mean to me?'

'I'm not, I just want to take a bigger role in the raising of our son.'

'You had every chance of that when you were living in Dublin.'

'My job was too demanding, and I have resigned.'

'You're not coming back at all.' She was shocked.

'No.'

'What about your apartment?'

'It's rented.'

She couldn't believe the finality of what she was hearing.

Chapter Five

Claire returned from Beijing, desperately disappointed that Alan had not called again and she had no chance to see or even talk to Neil. Since Alan would only allow her talk to her son on the phone, she realised that it made no difference where she was. Dublin or Beijing. And she had to return to work anyway, having taken a week off.

The first thing she had to do was to go into Neil's new school and tell them that he wouldn't be taking up his place. It hit her hard as he had been so looking forward to beginning second level school. She called to see her friends Elaine and Lucy finding both of their sons, Calum and Tommy, kicking football in Elaine's back garden.

'Why is Neil staying there?' Tommy asked when they came in.

'His father lives in China now.' She tried to explain.

'But he'll be back soon, won't he?' Calum asked.

'Yes.'

'What's it like out there?' Tommy asked. 'Do they play football?'

'They do.'

'Will he be home for Halloween?'

Claire didn't know what to say.

'Don't annoy Claire now, go on out and play football.' Elaine said.

The two ran out.

'Thank you,' Claire was grateful to Elaine.

'They miss Neil you know, they're such good friends.'
'And he misses them too.'

'How did things go for you?' her boss, Liz, asked the following morning.

'Not great.' She found it hard to hide the despair which dogged her since Alan had taken Neil.

'If there is anything I can do, never hesitate to ask,' Liz murmured.

'That's so generous of you.' Claire really did appreciate her kindness.

She threw herself into work, anxious to make up for the time she had taken off. Although it didn't make any difference to how she felt. Neil was in her mind constantly. Waking up in the morning. Going to bed at night. Longing to hold him close, kiss him and tell him she loved him. That above all. Her biggest dread was that as time passed he would forget her. She couldn't bear it if that happened and resolved to do everything in her power to prevent it.

An idea occurred to her, and during her lunch break she called into a newsagents near the store. There she searched along the racks of cards for a particular one. Something with an animal picture on the front. It took some time, but eventually she spotted one which had a monkey swinging from the branch of a tree. She smiled. Delighted. It was perfect. Neil loved animals.

'My dear Neil, I hope you are happy,' she wrote. *'It was lovely to talk to you on the phone and I'm hoping that you are enjoying your time in the country and riding Yeh Yeh's horse. Tell me all about him. I hope that you have a good time fishing and that you catch lots of fish that Nai Nai will be able to cook for dinner. They should be very tasty.*

I chose this card especially for you. It reminds me of that last day we spent together at the zoo before you left to go to China with your Dad. It was a really lovely day and I hope that we will be able to go and visit the animals soon again. I love you very much and I'm longing for you to come home to me. Mum. xxx

Her eyes filled with tears as she addressed it. She couldn't bear the emptiness in her heart, unable to hear Neil's voice calling her, asking for whatever. Shouting with excitement. Laughing out loud as he ran in the garden kicking his football into the goal set up against the wall. And remembering how they used to sit together on the big red velvet couch watching television.

That night she stood looking at the red couch, stroked the soft surface of the cushions, and left the room. She simply couldn't sit on that couch again until Neil came home. Without him, she had nothing.

'I'm sorry, but if I receive a call from China, I'll have to take it,' Claire explained to her boss.

Liz nodded.

'It would be urgent.'

'If that happens, take your call and pass your client on to one of the other girls,' Liz smiled.

'Thank you very much.' She was so grateful to this woman who really only knew her for a very short time.

But Alan never rang and her frustration increased. She could hardly concentrate on her work, although her job meant everything to her. She was utterly dependant on it. For her sanity and financial reasons as well. Her mortgage was high and she had to struggle to meet her repayments and was on an interest only arrangement now. It was a further weight on her shoulders. Dragging her down. Until she didn't know what she should do.

'How did you get on in China? And how are Neil and Alan?'

Claire's mother asked. 'How soon will they be back? Neil will miss school?'

She had dreaded this question. 'Alan wants him to stay on in Beijing for a while.'

'Why?' Peggy was astonished.

'What are you saying?' her father barked.

'He wants him to learn the language properly.' She took a deep breath and hoped that her excuse sounded credible.

'But he speaks it very well,' her mother's eyes had filled with tears.

'I know, but he has to learn how to write it and that's not easy.'

'Why does he need to do that, we don't speak it here or write it either.' Her father seemed equally upset.

'I know, but the language is very important to Chinese people,' she tried to explain.

'Maybe he'll forget how to speak English?' Peggy asked.

'Then we won't be able to speak to him at all,' her father, Mick, pointed out.

'That won't happen. I'm sure he'll be back before then. Alan and his parents all understand English and they'll speak both languages with him.'

'What about school?'

Claire was nonplussed. This was something she hadn't even considered. 'I know there are international schools over there and Alan will send him to one of those.' She wished now that she had even thought of asking him about that when he had called her but she had been so anxious to talk with Neil, it hadn't even occurred to her.

'We're going to miss him.' Peggy dabbed her eyes with a tissue.

'Can't you persuade Alan to bring Neil home soon?' Mick asked.

'It's difficult, I don't want to be disagreeable.' She made an excuse, something which would be accepted by her parents. But the truth was that she was so angry she wanted to kill him for what he had done.

'But is he entitled to keep Neil for so long. Is that part of your divorce agreement?'

'Not exactly,' she hesitated.

'Why not go to your solicitor?' her father asked.

'I might,' she murmured, feeling that she wasn't able to control this conversation. She certainly couldn't tell her parents that Alan had threatened to keep Neil permanently. They would be very upset if they heard that.

'I think you're being very generous,' her mother said. 'If you feel anything like I do then it must be hard on you.' She lowered her head.

'Do you want me to talk to Alan?' Mick offered. 'Ask him to change his mind and bring Neil back?'

'Thanks Dad, but that could be difficult.'

'I hope he'll be home soon.' Peggy snuffled.

'And your sister will be coming back next weekend and she'll be very disappointed if Neil is not here.'

Claire hadn't told Suzy that Neil was still in China. Usually they texted a couple of times a week so it was easy to chat without mentioning it. Suzy worked as a lecturer in English Literature at Edinburgh University and Claire felt guilty that she hadn't told her.

'I'm sure he will be home by then,' she said hesitantly.

Chapter Six

'You'll be starting school next week,' Alan said.

Neil stopped practicing the scale on the piano and looked up at his father, brown eyes wide with surprise. 'We're going home?' he smiled widely.

'No, you'll be going to a new school here.'

The boy's expression changed. 'I don't want to go to a new school, I'll have no friends there.'

'You'll soon make new ones.'

'But they won't be Tommy and Calum. They'll be Chinese and I won't be able to speak properly to them.'

'You have done very well with your Mandarin so far.'

'Not really.'

'It's an international school, and there will be lots of other students there who speak English.'

'I don't want to go.'

'You must.'

'Why can't I go home, Mum won't know where I am.'

'She knows.'

'How?'

'I talk to her.'

'But I don't. I want to talk to her too,' he grumbled, his expression sulky.

'She's very busy, and doesn't want us. She's glad that you're over here with me.'

'Why doesn't she want us?' he asked.

Alan shrugged. 'I don't know.'

'Mum told me she loved me when I was talking to her on the phone,' he protested, trying to stop the tears from bursting out of his eyes. It wasn't manly to cry. His father had told him that so many times. But he found it hard. He couldn't believe what Alan was saying to him.

'Yeh Yeh and Nai Nai love you as well.'

'I know they do, but what did I do to Mum?'

'You did nothing.'

'I must have done something. It's my fault she doesn't want me anymore.'

Alan sighed deeply. 'It has nothing to do with you, it's her fault.'

'What did she do?'

'Stop asking questions, will you, Neil,' he said, his voice sharp.

'I could call her and ask,' Neil said hopefully.

'She's away at the moment.'

'Where?'

'America.'

'She didn't tell me that.'

'She asked me to tell you.'

Neil looked down at the piano keys.

'We'll fly up to Shanghai tomorrow. Yeh Yeh and Nai Nai are staying at the country house for a few more days.'

Neil didn't reply, resting his chin in his hand. He was very lonely for his Mum and couldn't understand why she didn't want him anymore.

Neil lay in his bed. The woman who looked after him, Ayi, had just closed the door and he was glad that he couldn't see her any longer. He hated how she was always fussing over him. Taking his clothes from the wardrobe when he could do that for himself. At home he did everything and his Mum had told him many

26

times that he was her man, and she depended on him.

Now that he was in Beijing he couldn't do anything for her. He wasn't able to take out the bins. Put clothes in the washing machine, and when the cycle was finished, take them out and put them into the dryer. Who would set the table for the two of them, and carry her briefcase out to the car. And when they went shopping to the supermarket together, he wouldn't be there to push the trolley. Tears moistened his eyes.

Chapter Seven

Claire had to phone the bank. Always tedious as she had to choose various options, and was transferred from one person to another. Her frustration levels began to rise as they asked her to repeat her personal information again and again and she pressed her lips together tightly. Irritated. Hurry up. Get on with it. In her mind there were other words. But she couldn't utter those too loudly. They were under her breath. Struggling to burst out furiously. But she had to maintain a controlled attitude at all times. She couldn't let them know that they were getting to her.

Eventually, she managed to talk with *a person,* but he didn't have any understanding and she felt helpless. 'Give me the name of your supervisor?' she demanded.

'He is not available.'

'When will he be available?' she asked.

'I cannot tell you that.'

She continued the sentence in her head. I want someone who has a human face. Eyes. Nose. Mouth. A heart.

'Can you put me through to his extension and I could leave a voicemail?' She softened her tone. No point in being too aggressive, she decided. But wondered would these voices even notice the difference.

'No, that is not possible.'

'So, I must talk to you?'

'Yes, I can deal with your account.'

And he did. Competently. Without understanding.

Claire explained that she was aware of having missed seven repayments and that although she was only paying the interest on the mortgage, was still behind.

'If you cannot pay the balance due, we will begin the repossession procedure on the property.'

'I understand. But I should be in a position to increase my repayments.'

'It would need to be a considerable amount and soon.'

'It will be, I promise you.'

She had been ground down. Like coffee beans to powder. She grovelled now. Her earlier fire had fizzled out and she was baked to a black cinder.

While she had promised to increase her mortgage repayments, she was left with the knowledge that she didn't know how that was going to happen. Now she was threatened with losing her home and found it very difficult to contemplate what it would mean to her. While she knew there were many people who were in the same position, there was a particular reason why she couldn't lose her home and felt a terrible pang of loss in her heart.

That evening she called to Elaine and Lucy. They were close neighbours and mothers of Neil's friends Calum and Tommy. Now, she wondered if she should come clean and explain that Alan was keeping Neil in Beijing against her will. To constantly tell lies was proving more and more difficult and it wasn't something she could do easily.

'How are the lads getting on in school?' she asked. Neil had been looking forward to starting secondary school with his two friends.

'Great, they love it.'

'Is Neil still in China with Alan?' Elaine asked.

Claire nodded. A lump in her throat.

'What about Alan's job, how can he stay away that long. It's almost a couple of months now, isn't it?'

'He's on extended leave apparently.' Claire had to force herself to give the girls a little more information.

'You must miss Neil, I know I'd be heartbroken.'

'How's your job?' Elaine asked.

'Busy, we've a big sale on. You should come in. There's great value.'

'I might, although the budget may not stretch that far, even with the discount, your prices are very high.'

'I know it is upmarket. I can't afford to buy anything myself.'

'Why?'

'As it is, I'm having difficulty paying my mortgage. I could lose the house.'

'Can we help?'

'You're so generous, but I'll get through.'

'It would only be temporary, till you get yourself sorted.'

'If it was one of us, you'd insist on helping. I know you.'

'We want to do something, it's important to us, isn't it, Lucy?' Elaine insisted.

'I've been toying with an idea, but I hate the thoughts of it.'

'What is it?'

'Renting out a couple of rooms. There's such a demand these days.'

'It's an idea. How much rent would you get?'

'They seem to vary from six hundred to eight hundred per month.'

'That's not bad, if you had two rooms rented.'

'There's a special tax rate.'

'What is it?'

'Fourteen thousand euro a year, tax free, and as far as I know it has no bearing on other income.'

30

'There's no point looking for more then.'

'I must look into it.'

'Sounds like a good idea.'

'But what if I get some sort of strange person, you know what I'm like about my own stuff and all of that.'

'Rather than lose the house then maybe you should take a chance.'

'We'll vet them for you. There will be three of us on the judging panel.'

They laughed.

'And get them to sign a contract. That's vital.'

'I must do it quickly.'

'We'll have a look into it as well. And make enquiries if anyone we know is looking for a place. It would be great if you had a recommendation. Makes all the difference.'

'We'll let you know if we hear of anyone.'

Claire felt better after chatting with the girls, and not quite so vulnerable as she contemplated the possibility of living with a stranger. Tears flooded her eyes. She had to stay in her home. To be here for Neil when he came home.

She opened a drawer and took a colourful card from a bundle she had bought. Yes, that looked about right. A grey elephant on an orange background. He would like that. She picked up a pen and began to write.

My dear Neil, I hope you are well and happy in Beijing. Are you going to a new school now? I hope you like it and are enjoying your classes. I'm sure you have made lots of new friends. I would love you to tell me their names. And don't forget to write to me. I am waiting for you to come home. I love you, Mum. xxx

She prayed that he would write to her but no doubt Alan gave him no encouragement.

But she longed to hear his voice again and know that he hadn't forgotten her. That most of all. Before she sealed the envelope, she searched for a photograph of Neil, Tommy, Calum, and herself. It had been taken by Lucy outside school before the summer break. Now she wrote all of their names on the back, dated it and sent it off.

Chapter Eight

Claire pushed open the door slightly. Able to see some of the posters on Neil's bedroom wall. Photos of his favourite football heroes. She stepped in. More of her son's room was revealed. On another wall, she could see *Superman* flying through the night sky. *Batman* grinning evilly at her.

'Thanks Mum.'

She could hear Neil's voice. So excited every time she bought him a new poster.

She looked around.

Everything in the room was exactly the way it was when he had left and the way it would be when he returned. He was a neat boy by nature. Board games stacked one on top of the other. Books in alphabetical order on shelves. She twirled a globe which stood on a low table. Feeling the warmth of his hand as he sent it spinning, always deftly stopping at China.

'That's where half of our family are from.' He would point to Beijing. 'Come with us this time will you, Mum?' He had asked her before he left.

'I can't, I'm sorry. I'm busy with work.'

'You're always working.' His lower lip pushed out, sulky.

'I'll come next time,' she had promised, now full of regret she had not gone with him.

'Will you?' He was surprised.

'Yes, my love.' She had hugged him.

He jumped up and down waving his hands in the air. 'And we

can do things with Nai Nai and Yeh Yeh.'

'Yes, that will be lovely.' She had agreed. Thinking to herself that it was highly unlikely that either of her in-laws would want to have anything to do with her. They didn't approve of western women who worked for a living and that had knocked her confidence over the years and she had always found reasons why she couldn't go to visit them in Beijing.

Tears flooded her eyes now, and she lay on the bed, head on the pillow, eyes closed. She sometimes came in here at night and even though the bedlinen was fresh, she could still get a sense of Neil's aroma as if he was lying beside her. Occasionally she actually stayed all night in his bed. Drifting in and out of sleep. Dreaming of her child who was so far away from her.

She longed to go to Beijing again. Even to stand outside the house where Neil lived with Alan. That last time she should have been more resilient, stood up to Alan and insist that he allow her to see Neil. But ...and there was always a *but*, his threatening attitude took her far down a route where the end result would be to lose Neil altogether to this Chinese family. And she couldn't bear the thought of that. She had to hold on to the little she had of him. Hold tight.

She checked her bank account on line. Her salary hadn't been lodged yet and as she had no overdraft permission, she had to keep a careful eye on the balance. That was the most worrying part of it.

She looked at the emails she had received from people who wanted to rent her rooms and printed them out. Staring at the names in confusion, unsure what she should do. Then Lucy called.

'Are you still looking for a tenant?' she asked.

'At this moment, I'm staring at the list and don't have a clue what I'm going to do.'

'Well, my mother knows a man who is looking for a room for

his son who is going to college and hasn't got anywhere yet apparently. He's staying with a relation at the moment but there really isn't room in the house.'

'A student?' Claire stuttered.

'Yeah.'

'I'd rather not have a student.'

'Why not?'

'I was hoping for someone more mature.'

'Keep you feeling young.'

'I suppose if he's recommended,' she conceded.

'It's everything,' Lucy said firmly.

'Maybe.' She was unsure.

'He's coming up next weekend with his father to try and get a place.'

'I could meet him, I suppose,' Claire said, although she was still doubtful. 'Can you get the father's phone number and I'll call him?'

'Sure, I'll ask Mum.'

She wondered would she like the young man? Would he like her? Was he studious and spent all of his time in his room? Or was he one of those who was out with his friends every night? Falling in the door at all hours when he had too much to drink. Did she want to contend with that sort of behaviour, she asked herself, knowing she would have no patience at all. But she rang anyway, determined not to leave any more time for procrastination. This was something she had to do immediately. Or fail in the attempt.

'Hallo?' The voice was soft.

'Mr. Aherne?'

'Yes?'

'Lucy's Mum gave me your number. I'm Claire Brennan.'

'Hi Claire, good to hear from you.'

He seemed quite pleased to hear from her.

'I believe you're looking for a room for your son in this area?'

'Yes, that's right.' He was effusive. His accent pleasant on the ear.

Claire felt reassured.

'I'm very anxious to get somewhere for Donal, he's in his first year and it's been difficult trying to find a place. Queues of people outside every apartment. We're getting desperate at this stage as there is no space available at my sister's house.'

Claire could sense the anxiety in his voice. 'I understand,' she murmured.

'I'd appreciate if you could let us see the room, that's if it's still available?'

'You can call at the weekend.'

'Thank you,' he said.

Claire could sense relief there.

'Would Sunday suit?' she asked.

'Yes, that would be fine.'

'Around lunchtime?'

They arrived on the dot of one o'clock. She was impressed. It showed how anxious they were. As it was her day off, she had spent the morning cleaning. Conscious that they would be giving her home the once over.

Donal was a tall young man as was his father. Dark haired. Both well built. The son particularly so.

'Thanks for giving us the opportunity to see the room, I'm sure there are many people anxious to rent it. This is a beautiful house,' Jim smiled at her as he shook her hand.

Claire didn't explain that they were the first people to see it, still wondering was she making the right decision to bring anyone into her home.

She led the way upstairs, and could feel herself quiver inside.

36

That vibration displayed the fear that she was starting out on this venture a complete innocent, having no clue as to how it would transpire. She imagined all of the people standing outside her house, waiting there in the hope of being that one who would be lucky enough to appeal to her. Should she employ an agent who would narrow down the lines into manageable numbers, somewhat like a competition. The long list. The short list. The final small group reducing to whoever was chosen to live in her house.

If she did employ an agent then he or she would take a commission no doubt, but in her mind she questioned anyone's ability to make such a decision on her behalf. No, she would do it herself.

She opened the door into the first back bedroom and led the way in. All her bedrooms had been decorated in neutral shades. Mostly in tones of cream. 'I'll let you have a look yourselves.' She left them there and went back downstairs. Standing in the kitchen staring out the window into the garden. When she and Alan had bought the house, they had employed a garden designer so that it would be maintenance free, and it looked very attractive. She was suddenly very possessive of her home and hated sharing it with a stranger.

She heard the sound of descending footsteps on the stairs and hurried out into the hall.

'You've a beautiful home,' Jim said. 'I think Donal would be glad to rent the room from you.'

'It would be great.' He nodded.

'What rent are you asking for it?'

They went on to discuss the financial side of things, and they still seemed to be interested.

'There are quite a number of people coming to see it,' she murmured, 'And I have to meet all of them before I can come to a decision.'

'Of course,' Jim said immediately. 'Maybe you might phone us then?'

'I will,' she agreed.

Claire rang Lucy. 'They seem quite nice people,' she said.

'I don't know them at all.'

'Maybe I'll give it to him, at least he has been recommended.'

'I think you should.'

'Although I'll need a second person.'

'If he takes the room then why not ask if he knows someone?'

'That's an idea. I'll phone later.'

She made up her mind and called Jim. He seemed to be pleased and told her that the young man would call the following day to confirm the details.

'Thanks for giving me the room,' Donal smiled.

'Come on in,' she said. 'I should have suggested you bring some of your stuff over.'

'I have some of it in the backpack.'

'It seems heavy,' she laughed.

'Books.'

She made a cup of coffee and they sat chatting in the kitchen.

'I have to arrange payment and we'll need your bank account details,' he said.

'I'll give you that.' She handed him a sheet of paper she had prepared earlier.

'My father will transfer the deposit into your account and the first month as well.'

'Thank you.'

Finished the details, she asked him what he was studying.

'Maths.'

'That's difficult.'

'I like it,' he shrugged.

'When will you be moving in?' she asked.

'I thought perhaps tomorrow? I feel that I'm taking up space in my aunt's house.'

'That will be fine.' Claire was glad that at last she had one of the rooms let. 'Although you'll need a desk for studying, I'll get one.'

'I have one in my aunt's house, Dad will bring it over if that's all right with you?'

'That's fine. I was wondering whether you have any friends who might need a room too. I have a second one, although it's slightly smaller than yours, but the price is the same.'

'There is a girl in my year who is very anxious to find somewhere.'

'Maybe you'd mention it to her?'

'Thank you. There is something I'd like to say. As I'm living here myself, I expect you to live as I do. I'll give you a key but I don't want you to bring friends around at all hours of the day and night. And there is no smoking or drinking, or drugs.' She felt like an old grouch laying down the law, and wondered whether she should even do that. But it didn't seem to matter to him.

The following day he came around with some more of his things and the girl he mentioned was with him. Sophie was very attractive with long blonde hair. 'I'm already staying in a B & B and it's expensive, so if you could rent a room to me I'd be thrilled,' she explained.

Claire immediately warmed to her personality, and took her upstairs.

'It's a beautiful room,' she gasped when Claire brought her in. 'I love it. I'm surprised you're letting it out.'

'This is the first time.' Claire held back on explanations.

'I'll really look after it for you,' she said earnestly. 'It's even nicer than my own room at home.'

'Did Donal tell you about my rules?' Claire asked diffidently.

'Yes, he did. But that's no problem for me.'

'Sorry, I feel a bit guilty mentioning such a thing, but it is important as I'm living here myself.'

'Of course, I understand that.'

'All right then, we have a deal.' Claire made up her mind immediately this time. She liked Sophie.

Within a couple of days, Claire had received rent and deposit from both of them, and contracts were signed. Her bank account looked healthy for the first time in months and she had enough to pay her mortgage repayment in full. It was wonderful to think that every month she would receive the rent and hoped that this would go a long way towards keeping her account in credit. She was on the up now and prayed she would soon have enough money saved to fly to Beijing and see Neil. Although she had no holidays left, she could always take time off at her own expense if Liz agreed. In the meantime, she decided that she would work overtime whenever she got the chance. Staying late in the evening and coming in early. Liz was always in work by seven and now Claire joined her in the early mornings.

She went into the staff changing rooms. Liz insisted they all wore one of the designer labels they sold at the store during the day and strangely it helped Claire. It was like putting on a costume so that she could play a part in a play. Now she was a completely different person. She checked her make-up in the mirror. Touched up her blusher and lipstick, and ran a comb through her shoulder length blonde hair.

'You look great,' Liz came in behind her.

'Thanks.'

'You really have grasped what I'm about here,' Liz said. 'I'm so glad you took the job with us.'

'I am too.'

'It's a long time since I've had someone working with me who understands what I'm about.'

Claire listened.

'This business is my heart and soul since the very beginning. I have a feeling that you put all of yourself into what you do as well, your sales figures are excellent, and I want to capture that.'

Claire looked at her, surprised. No employer she had ever worked for had said anything like that to her before.

'I do mean it,' Liz impressed.

'How do you know me in this way?'

'Takes one to know one,' Liz said, and smiled.

Claire was unable to believe that a complete stranger could appreciate her deepest self.

'Liz?' One of the other girls called and knocked on the door.

She went out on to the shop floor, followed by Claire. Liz welcomed one of their regular clients, and turned to bring Claire into the conversation as well. She was like that. Many of their clients were good friends of Liz who remembered names as soon as she saw people enter the store, and her staff were trained to do the same. She had a personal touch which was unfailing where business was concerned. Liz knew exactly what women wanted, especially if they had to attend an event and required something really dramatic. Her haute couture range took up the third floor. A mid-range of classic dresses, suits and coats were on the second floor, and was her *bread and butter* in terms of business. Her first floor displayed a range of accessories. Shoes. Handbags. Small luggage. Scarves. Hats. Ground floor had a catwalk if someone wanted to see a particular outfit, and all the staff had to be prepared to model the items if required. Each floor had its own fitting rooms.

And while Claire hadn't been so happy in the job at the fashion store up to now, unexpectedly getting to know Liz better had changed her mind and now she wanted to stay.

Chapter Nine

Claire had to go to Neil's new secondary school to explain to the Principal that Neil would be late in starting term. She felt nervous. 'I'm sorry, but I'm not sure when his father is bringing him back,' she explained, trying not to reveal too much, and let the woman know how emotional she felt.

'We can't hold a place for him, but as soon as you know when he is due home do let us know and we will try to fit him in.'

'I appreciate that, I'm sorry for causing you any inconvenience.' She left quickly then, regretting that she had called to the school so early in the morning. Now the pupils were arriving. The sound of their voices echoing. Chattering. Laughing out loud as they rushed through the corridors to their classrooms. The thumping of their feet on the floors. On the stairs. The banging of doors. Frantically she looked for Neil. For boys of his age. Hoping to see him but knowing it was impossible. And that evening she had the difficult task of calling to his music teacher and had to explain to her as well which wasn't easy.

Loneliness still stalked. She didn't know how to deal with it. Her choices were critical. Should she let the bank repossess her home, give up her job and go to find her son? But then, if she had no home, where would Neil go if he ever came back to find her. She imagined him throwing his arms around her. And knowing her. That most of all.

Claire longed to be in Beijing. At least she could walk the same streets that Alan and Neil walked. Breathe the same air. See the same sights. Hear the same voices. And most of all to have that chance to see them. But she had very little money. Every penny she had went to clearing the arrears on her mortgage.

The last time she remembered the power in Alan's voice. Telling her what he had decided to do. And whether he would allow her to see Neil again. Rage swept through her. She wouldn't accept it next time. It was blackmail.

In the meantime, she continued to send Neil cards but heard nothing in return. She was certain that Alan never gave them to him. When they arrived in the post, she imagined Alan's long fingers gripping them stealthily. Like a pickpocket in a crowded market. She wanted to shout out loud. Bastard. So that he could hear her voice. And know her feelings. Frustration surged like floodwater threatening to annihilate. The distance between them was enormous. Too far. She fought against the invisible barriers which stretched above and beyond her. Was life meant to be this cruel? The loss of her boy was like he had died. He had disappeared. Fluttered away like a bird borne on the wind.

Claire was home unusually early one evening and as Donal and Sophie were upstairs studying, she invited them to share dinner with her. She felt lonely, missing Neil around the house, and she was glad to have their company.

'You don't do much cooking here, where do you have your dinner?' she asked, although had been relieved that they weren't around the kitchen too much.

'We eat our lunch in the canteen, and just have a sandwich in the evening,' explained Sophie.

'Is that enough for you?' Claire asked.

'I'm not a very good cook,' she laughed.

'You haven't used the pots much,' Claire smiled.

'Except the one I burned,' Donal said sheepishly.

'I noticed that you'd obviously scrubbed it,' she said with a grin.

'Sorry.'

'Don't worry.'

As she served up, she thought how strange it was to be cooking for three. Even though Sophie and Donal were in the house for the last month, she still missed Neil, the one person in the world who meant anything to her. But this evening she enjoyed cooking pasta with a carbonara sauce, made up a mixed salad, and heated garlic bread.

'Wow, that looks delicious,' Sophie said when she saw the food on the table.

'Is there anything you don't like?' she asked.

'No, we eat everything,' Donal grinned.

She ladled the pasta into the bowl of sauce, and sprinkled parmesan cheese over that.

They sat down, and had just begun to eat when the doorbell rang.

Claire looked up.

'Do you want me to answer it?' Donal asked.

'Sure, if you don't mind.'

He went down the hall.

Claire could hear the door open and the sound of voices, and then the door closed again.

She stood up, her fingers splayed taut on the table and stared towards the door, a crazy hammering in her heart. Could it be Alan and Neil? She pushed back her chair and moved swiftly towards the kitchen door. Longing to see her darling son again.

Chapter Ten

'Will Mum be coming to see us soon?' Neil asked.

'No,' Alan said abruptly.

'Why?'

'I told you she doesn't want to see us anymore.'

Neil was silenced. He couldn't understand how such a thing had happened. Was it his fault? He tried to remember if he had annoyed his mother before he left on holiday but couldn't think of anything he had done. That morning she had kissed him and waved goodbye at the door when his Dad had picked him up to take him to the airport. Maybe she might have thought that he had seemed to be too happy that he was going to Beijing with his father. But he enjoyed his holidays with Yeh Yeh and Nai Nai. They always spoiled him. Maybe his Mum didn't like that. But they still made him practice piano for a few hours each day. He wasn't let off that. And every evening there were Mandarin lessons too from Yeh Yeh.

'How was school?' his Dad asked.

'OK,' he responded. Although he missed his friends, Tommy and Calum. And all the plans he had made with them about going on to secondary school.

'Do you like the teachers?'

'They're all right.'

Neil wasn't sure whether he liked the college or not. He felt out of place knowing none of the other students and wished he was home.

The classrooms were filled with noisy students, all talking and laughing at the tops of their voices. Speaking different languages too. In those first few weeks, he hadn't talked to them very much and kept to himself. But a few days ago, a boy dropped a book beside him in class, and Neil picked it up and handed it to him.

'Thanks,' the other boy smiled at him, and their eyes met. After class, they automatically walked together into the cafe and he was introduced to Robert's group of friends. Accepted by them, he felt more at ease, and gradually began to fit in. He was studying the same number of subjects as he had done at home, but his music teacher was much harder on him. Always reporting back to his father if Neil didn't achieve the high standards he set. He had played football at home in Ireland but wasn't allowed to play here. Physical exercises were done in the morning before classes started. The rest of his time was spent on schoolwork, and studying Mandarin. He had to work hard. It was expected by everyone. No one let him off even for a short time. Riding the horses and fishing with Yeh Yeh didn't happen now. Once Neil had started school, his life had changed. It was all work.

He missed his mother, and couldn't understand why she didn't want him anymore. His father refused to allow him to have his own mobile phone here, so he couldn't ring his Mum. All he wanted to do was to ask why. Sometimes he thought of buying a phone for himself, but his father didn't give him very much money. Just enough for his lunch each day. He had tried to persuade him to let him have a bigger allowance but Alan didn't agree with that.

'You don't need any more,' he had said.

'But the other students have much more than me.'

'No.'

'And some of them even have credit cards.'

Alan stared at him quizzically.

'You're not getting one,' he rapped. 'And if I hear that you've borrowed money or the use of a credit card, there will be a very harsh punishment.'

'But ...' Neil protested.

'Do not argue with me.'

Neil was silenced. He knew better than to disagree with his father. His Mum had been much more generous. Whatever he wanted she bought for him, although there often had to be a trade, and he had his chores to do. Bring out the bins. Hoover. Set the table for dinner and even sometimes help with the cooking. Suddenly, he longed to be home again. Here he didn't have anything at all to do. Even his clothes were laid out for him by Ayi. His room cleaned. Food prepared by servants. All he had to do was study and practice. Every day. Until he was so tired, he fell asleep the minute he put his head down. But he would have given anything to see his Mum and wondered what he had done which upset her so much she didn't want to see him again.

Although it wasn't that cold in Beijing now, he remembered autumn at home. After piano practice and dinner, his Mum and himself would sit on the big red velvet couch and watch television or a DVD for a short while before he went to bed. Later she would come into his bedroom. Tell him she loved him and kiss him goodnight. Now he missed those nights terribly. 'What have I done?' he whispered to himself, hoping she could hear him wherever she was.

Chapter Eleven

Claire followed Donal out into the hall, a desperate sense of disappointment in her heart as she stared at the man who stood talking with him.

'Jim, how are you?' She had to gather herself and try to behave in a hospitable manner. She had been so full of hope just for those few seconds and now the anti-climax almost crushed her.

He came towards her, hand outstretched. His grip was warm.

'Come in, have you driven up?' she asked, leading the way into the kitchen.

'I had business in Dublin today,' he explained.

'We're just having something to eat, will you join us?'

He looked at her with a smile. 'Thank you.'

'There's plenty.'

'Dad, this is Sophie,' Donal introduced her.

Claire quickly reheated the pasta and sauce and plated up.

To her surprise she enjoyed the evening. Getting to know Jim and Donal and Sophie better. As they chatted, she found out quite a lot about their families. But that left big gaps in her own history, particularly when Jim asked if she had any children? She didn't know what to say at first, but then decided to come clean. In that moment, she couldn't imagine what lie she might conjure up. She pointed to a photograph of Neil.

'That's my son.'

'Good looking boy,' Jim said, with a smile.

She could feel tears welling up in her eyes.

'Anyone for more pasta?' she asked, standing up abruptly.

None of them wanted any, so she made coffee. There was no more mention of Neil.

'When are you hoping to go to China?' Lucy asked.

'As soon as I can get the money together.'

'How about time off?'

'It will be at my own expense.'

'Neil will be delighted to see you,' murmured Elaine.

'If Alan allows it,' she grimaced.

'Be confident.'

'I think Alan is a …' Lucy burst out but then stopped herself speaking for a moment. 'Why is he doing this?' There was strong emphasis in her words.

'I don't know.' Claire was downcast.

'But you must know. When did he first mention that he wanted to take Neil to China?'

'He never said it.' Claire was short.

'But why is he keeping Neil? Your custody arrangements were quite fair.'

'The Chinese people are different, it's all about their family. Their sons. Alan wants to possess Neil.'

'Is he involved with another woman?'

Claire sighed. 'I don't know.'

'That could be it.'

'Maybe.' Claire wasn't sure about that, although she had considered the possibility.

'It was a complete surprise?' Lucy continued her questioning.

'Yes.' She found herself becoming irritated, and didn't want to be like that with her friends. But it was difficult to be otherwise. She couldn't understand herself.

'Are we being too inquisitive?' Elaine seemed suddenly

sympathetic.

'No, you're not. I'm sorry I sound a bit touchy. Although that always happens when I talk about Alan,' she admitted.

Lucy put her hand around Claire's shoulders.

'Sorry,' Elaine murmured.

Claire stood up. 'Fancy some smoked salmon and brown bread?'

'Sounds good,' they smiled.

'Give me a minute.'

They were meeting tonight in her house and it was good to have her home to herself and her friends. It was always such a relief when she knew that Donal and Sophie had gone home for the weekend.

She busied herself preparing the food and coffee in the kitchen, and slowly her irritable mood moderated slightly. She cut chunky slices of bread on the wooden board, and as she smoothed yellow butter, she was aware that her hands actually shook. She stopped what she was doing and squeezed them into fists. But it didn't make much difference. What was happening to her? She stopped what she was doing as tears clouded her eyes. The slices of bread merged together in a hazy formless lump of brown. She reached for a tissue and wiped the moisture in her eyes until she managed to see again.

'How's it going?' Lucy appeared in the doorway.

'Fine thanks.' She turned away and placed the slices on a serving dish.

'Can I do anything for you?'

'You could bring in the dishes for me, thanks,' she managed to say without breaking down.

'Right you are.'

Claire carefully poured milk into a jug, and then put the sugar bowl, mugs and the coffee pot on a tray, and followed her.

'This is lovely,' Elaine exclaimed.

'Coffee?' Claire poured.

'Thank you.'

'I love to come over here, it's so peaceful.' Elaine lay back on the armchair, and kicked off her high heels which fell crookedly like discarded toys.

They suddenly looked at each other, a look of guilt on their faces.

'Sorry, we shouldn't have been going on about how quiet the house is, it's tough on you without Neil.'

She nodded.

'You're great to go out to China again. I think I'd be scared stiff,' Elaine admitted.

'I've no choice.'

'But how are you going to find him?' Lucy asked.

'I have a secret dream to see him walk out the door of their house when I'm there.'

'Alan will hardly allow that.'

'I know. He'll probably have security men watching,' Claire said bitterly.

The girls looked at her, astonished.

'He's capable of anything.'

'How did you ever marry him?'

'Fell in love.'

'We've all done that.'

'Here we are, three singles who have all been through the mill because we've fallen in love with the wrong men,' Lucy laughed. 'But how do you know whether you've made the right decision?' she asked.

'That's the hard question.'

'But have we learned anything because of the experience? Go on, tell me.'

'Well I have, there's no way I'm going to commit again.' Lucy was adamant.

'I'd give anything to share my life with a man,' Elaine said.

'Describe him,' laughed Lucy.

'You know, to have someone there in the evenings when you get home just to talk about what happened during the day.'

'Someone who can cook,' Lucy grinned.

'A chef.'

'A person who would share everything. Look after the kids, hoover, throw a wash in the machine, rush down to the shops to get a loaf of bread if we ran out. I'm not looking for much,' she laughed.

'Ask *Alexa*.'

'She'll give you the answers you're searching for.'

'It's the future.'

'Soon we'll all have robots who will do everything around the house. We won't have to do anything at all ourselves.'

'Maybe we won't even need a partner.'

'But a robot is no good in bed. Cold and very uncomfortable,' Lucy giggled.

'And we need soft, pliable and sexy.'

'Very sexy.'

'It's all about trust,' murmured Claire slowly.

They looked at each other.

'Yeah, it is,' Elaine agreed.

'I trusted Dave and wasn't suspicious about anything. Although maybe I should have been.' Lucy twisted her lips. 'You can never tell, people have hidden sides.'

'Dark,' added Elaine.

'Secret.' Lucy nodded.

Those words exactly described how Claire felt about Alan, although she didn't mention that.

'Does Alan take good care of Neil?' asked Elaine.

'I'm sure he does,' reassured Lucy.

'I hope so,' Claire whispered.

'Of course, his grandparents are there too.'

'He's very fond of them.'

'I'd go with you if I could,' Elaine said. 'You need someone, to keep you company.' She picked up her handbag. 'This is from us, Claire, just to help.' She opened it and handed her a white envelope. 'As we can't go with you.'

Claire stared her in astonishment, and then opened it.

'Girls, you shouldn't have.' She took out a card which had a number of folded fifty euro notes inside. 'It's too much.' Tears brimmed in her eyes.

'It's a few euro, but it will help towards your expenses,' Lucy explained.

'You're just too good.' She reached across from where she sat opposite and put her arms around the girls.

'We wanted to help, and that's all we can do.'

'Thank you, I'm so grateful.' Tears drifted down her cheeks. 'I've been saving like mad, I just need to go out there again.'

She had an immediate image of the crowded streets of Beijing. Bicycles, scooters, cars and trucks, fighting for space. Throngs of people. And above all the cacophony of voices trying to be heard above the level of other noise. She wanted so much to be there and the generosity of her friends would be a big help.

She remembered the day Neil was born. The hours she spent giving birth until at last he arrived into the world, and she held him close to her body, a soft wet baby whose little hands waved around, fists clenched, giving those mewling new born cries until at last he quietened and reached for her breast. How beautiful he was. Tears had flowed down her cheeks as Alan kissed her.

Both of them were so emotional. Loving this precious little being so much. Now after all the years she had spent looking after Neil she had lost him. Lost her precious boy. He had been taken away by the man she once loved and she couldn't find him.

Her life was dark. She was caught in a tunnel.

Searching for a light in the distance which would lead her to Neil. But all she could hear was the sound of her own heart beating. A dull echo which was always there.

But she was worried. What did Neil think about her now? What had Alan told him? Had he explained to him why they were both still in Beijing? And had he ever given him the cards she sent? If he hadn't, then surely Neil would wonder why she made no contact. Question after question tumbled through her mind. There were no answers. She couldn't logically find any, and was frustrated. But the worst question. Quite the worst. Wouldn't leave her. Did her child think she had abandoned him?

Chapter Twelve

Claire walked through the exit doors of the airport at Beijing. It was very crowded and she stood there, staring around her. People joined the queue for taxis in an orderly fashion and eventually she was next in line. The driver got out and put her bag in the boot. She climbed in and handed him a slip of paper with the hotel name she had reserved printed on it. He nodded, and immediately accelerated at speed and cut his way into the lanes of traffic. Weaving in and out in company with the rest of the taxis until they joined the motorway.

Holiday Inn was the same hotel she had stayed in that last time, and there was a familiarity about the place as she checked in and went up to her room. She was tired but decided to go out immediately and get a taxi to Alan's home. It was evening now and the taxi pulled up outside the gated complex. She stared inside, longing to see her son somewhere around, maybe kicking a football up against a wall or playing with friends. But there wasn't a person in sight. It was deserted. She paid the man and walked through the pedestrian gate. Hurrying fast as she made her way towards the house. It looked exactly the same. Nothing had changed. She rang the intercom. Her heart pounding.

A woman answered. Even though Claire had tried to learn a few words of Mandarin, the language the woman spoke now was impossible to understand.

'I'm looking for Alan Wang Li,' she said.

There was silence.

'Is he there? Do you speak English?'

It was the same as it had been on the last occasion, and she was frustrated. She rang the bell again. There was no answer. She stood there. Her phone in her hand waiting for Alan to call. But he didn't.

Back at the hotel, she lay on the bed and although she waited for the phone to ring, she drifted off to sleep. She didn't know what time it was when she woke up, but immediately she grabbed her phone and checked if there had been any calls. But to her disappointment there were none. Her heart was tortured. What did this mean? If Alan didn't make any contact with her then what chance had she of seeing Neil? And now Alan would know she was in Beijing, no doubt the woman who had answered the intercom told him immediately as she had last time.

She ate breakfast, and as she was crossing the foyer heading for the lift, someone called her name. Excited, she turned around immediately, certain that it had to be Alan. But she couldn't see him, or Neil either. All the faces were strange and she didn't recognise any of them. As she stood there, she realised that she must have heard someone speak a name which sounded like her own. Her heart dropped and she turned back to the lift.

'Claire?' A man came down the stairs at a pace.

She didn't recognise him at first, but then she smiled. It was the father of the young student who was staying with her, Jim Aherne.

He looked at her in amazement.

She wasn't sure what to say.

'I saw you from the floor above and couldn't believe my eyes,' he said.

'What are you doing here?' she asked curiously.

'Business. We design engineering components for clients all over the world, and they're made here. I come over a few times a year and meet the suppliers.'

Claire felt awkward.

'Would you like a coffee?' he asked.

'No thank you, I've just finished breakfast.'

'What are you going to do for the day?'

'I have no plans,' she hedged.

'Sorry, I should have asked, are you here with friends?'

'No, just myself.'

'Taking a break?'

She nodded.

'Do you know Beijing well?'

'No, I was here once before but I didn't see very much.'

'It's lovely to see you, I …' he hesitated for a few seconds. 'Tell you what, if you would like to do some sightseeing, I'd be delighted to be your guide. Here's my card, give me a call.' He handed it to her. 'I'm here for another couple of days.'

'Thanks,' she smiled.

She walked towards the lift and pressed the button. She was surprised to see Jim here. More than surprised. She hadn't expected to see anyone she knew here in this metropolis of so many millions. The only person she wanted to see was Neil.

She went into her room and sat there staring into space. All the time holding her phone in her hand and waiting for it to ring. Then a question crossed her mind. What was the point of staying here? The housekeeping staff would arrive shortly and she would have to move out if she wanted her room cleaned. And if Alan called she would pick up the call anywhere. Maybe she might take up Jim's invitation. She hadn't seen anything of Beijing, so why not? But now she didn't want to make a call, just in case she missed one from Alan. She rang Reception and asked them to call Jim in his room, hoping that he would still be there.

'Hallo?'

'Jim?'

'Yes.'

'It's Claire, I thought maybe I might take you up on your offer of sightseeing. As I said, I haven't seen much of Beijing, and I know it's a fascinating city.'

'That would be lovely.'

He seemed pleased, she thought.

'What time would suit you?' she asked, wanting to give him the option of making it very short.

'I'm free all day. I've already had an early morning meeting here at the hotel, and I'm awaiting an update so I can proceed to the next stage. Why don't you come down to the foyer now and I'll meet you there.'

She smiled to herself. 'See you.'

'Well, this is a surprise,' he said when he arrived.

'It is to me as well,' she had to admit, laughing. Unable to believe that she had agreed to meet a man whom she hardly knew.

'Where would you like to go?' he asked as they stepped out on to the pavement.

'I don't know, there's so much to see.'

'This is an amazing district,' he explained. 'There are wonderful art galleries and so much more to see. You could spend all of your time here.'

'Sounds fantastic. But in spite of how little I've seen of Beijing it stills blows me away, and is so different to our way of life. All those sounds and smells and sights are thrilling, and they make me long to see more,' she spoke quickly, surprising herself with the intensity of her response.

'Perhaps the Forbidden City?' he suggested.

'It's amazing I believe.' Immediately she was enthralled by the idea.

But was reminded that all those years she had refused to go to

China with Alan and Neil because she felt so inadequate, there was still that dream in her heart to visit the country on her own with her son. But a sense of guilt now dominated. Her first time here should be with Neil. To share his heritage and passion for this place as he had described it to her when he returned from previous holidays. She wanted to see it from a young boy's viewpoint.

'Look here, Mum. Look there. See that.' He would direct her excitedly as they wandered the huge palace complex of the Forbidden City in the footsteps of the emperors. She had a weird feeling that she didn't want to visit this place without Neil. All the time waiting for her phone to ring. Touching it occasionally as it sat in her pocket. Praying that she wouldn't miss Alan's call. 'Thank you, Jim, but I've heard there are long queues there unless you book in advance.'

He nodded.

'Maybe we could just stroll in the city?' she asked softly, reluctant to explain how she felt. Certain that he wouldn't understand.

'I like that idea myself. Why don't we take a rickshaw to go around?'

'Sounds good.'

'Come on,' he laughed. 'We'll ask the driver to take us through the hutongs, the old part of Beijing.'

As they careered down the narrow laneways, she hung on to the rickshaw, all the time staring out into the crowded streets, searching for one familiar face.

'The best restaurants and bars are around here, maybe we'll have a bite of lunch after a while.'

They stopped off first for a cool drink, and walked through the streets. In a traditional restaurant they enjoyed a spicy hotpot, and ate some delicious flatbreads.

'I love the food, it's amazing.'

'There are so many different dishes from all the provinces of China. Try some of these noodles?' he offered.

'No thank you, I've had enough.'

'The portions are large.'

'You can say that again,' she laughed.

'This is China.'

'It's a wonderful place,' she sighed.

'What brought you here?' he asked, his grey eyes warm.

'I just wanted to have a break. There was a competition on the radio and it gave me the idea.'

'Did you win?'

She laughed. 'I didn't even enter.'

'How long are you here?'

'Just a few days.'

'Would you like to have dinner with me this evening?' he asked. 'I'd like to express my appreciation for taking my son and Sophie into your home, and ...' he smiled. 'For looking after them.'

She looked at him, unsure. They had just had lunch and she really couldn't take the day any further.

'Come on, we'll go somewhere really good.' He noticed her reluctance and hesitated. 'Have you a date with someone else?'

'Oh no.'

'Then let's not spend the evening alone.'

'Maybe.'

'Two strangers in a foreign city,' he said with a grin.

He was getting to her.

Chapter Thirteen

'I miss home,' Neil said. Anxious to let his father know how he felt. 'And my room.'

'You have a nice room here.'

'It's not the same. Could I have some posters for the walls? It's so bare.' He could feel tears moisten his eyes.

'I told you, put nothing on the walls.'

Neil thought that his room was like an hotel.

'This is your home now.'

'For how long?' It wasn't his home, he lived in Blackrock with his Mum.

'I am not sure.'

He felt scared. 'I don't like it here.'

'You've been here many times.'

'But only for holidays.'

'This is for longer.'

'But why?' he asked in that slow way that he had. He knew he was whining. That was what his Dad called it. Whining. Alan always made it sound like it was something awful. Something which he hated.

'It's just the way things are.'

'But are you not going back to your job at the hospital at home?'

'No, I'm working with Yeh Yeh now. He needs me to help him.'

'But what about your patients.'

'They'll be fine.'

Neil froze. That feeling of not knowing what was going to

happen whirled around him. He hated it. Now he couldn't find any words. His mouth was dry. Nothing would come out. He wanted to argue with his Dad, and explain, but his eyes seemed to grip Neil's who was mesmerized by his gaze. He shrank away from him. One foot stepping back, the other following.

'It's time for piano practice,' Alan said. 'Your teacher tells me you need to work harder.'

Neil didn't like his teacher. He was a small thin wizened old man. Master Xin. He always carried a chopstick. When Neil made the slightest error, it was raised and quickly struck across his knuckles. It was just a light smack, but it caught him out. Made him feel he was inadequate and hopeless and that he would never reach the standard everyone expected.

'I'm trying hard,' he grumbled.

'You'll never be a concert pianist if you don't make an effort. It requires much dedication. At home there were too many other things getting in the way. Football. Cinema. Spending time with your friends. Your mother encouraged that and it's why you are not as good as you should be. Now you can make up the time which you have lost. We'll be hoping to get you into a prestigious music college when you have graduated here. But they won't accept you unless you have exceptional talent. And you must succeed, do you realise that?'

Neil nodded.

'We want you to be very famous,' his grandfather said, coming into the room. Neil felt caught out as he realised that Yeh Yeh had overheard their conversation. He felt threatened. As if their hopes lay on his shoulders and weighed him down.

'Are you listening?' There was a waspish sound in his grandfather's voice.

'Yes.'

'Look at me,' Yeh Yeh demanded.

He raised his eyes.

62

'You know the Chinese people always strive to achieve the very highest level in everything we do. It is part of our nature, your nature.'

'I'm only half Chinese,' he muttered.

'Don't speak like that to your grandfather,' Alan intervened.

'You have enough of our genes. They are the strongest,' added Yeh Yeh.

'But what about Mum's genes?'

'They don't matter. You are Chinese. Look there. See.' The old man pointed to the long mirror on the wall, and pushed him in front of it. 'Alan, stand beside Neil. Now you can see how much you look like your father.'

His Dad moved closer to him. Neil's heart thumped. He did look like his father and did that mean Mum wasn't his mother at all?

'Yeh Yeh is right,' said Alan.

Neil was afraid to argue and compressed his lips, reluctant to anger his father who could make life very hard if he did. He had got so used to being with his mother when his father had left home, now to be around Alan all the time without his Mum made him long even more to be with her. But as his father had explained that she didn't want him anymore he wondered now was his grandfather right. Was Claire his real Mum?

'It is time for your lesson,' his father said abruptly.

Neil went into the room where the Steinway piano stood and opened it. The black and white keys waited. He was drawn to them. His grandfather had bought him the beautiful piano when he had arrived this year. But he would have preferred to play the one they had at home. That was where he enjoyed his music. From the age of four he had begun his lessons, encouraged by Claire. Although he worked his way through the various grades, the marks he achieved were never good enough for his father Now Alan expected even more from him.

The Master sat on the stool beside him. Nodded his bald head in time with the tempo, and tapped with his chopstick on the wooden frame of the piano. Neil concentrated, his eyes on the musical notes, the melody of the concerto ringing in his ears. Suddenly, he missed a note and immediately the Master struck. It always gave him a fright, but he forced himself to continue on and concentrate even harder. He couldn't afford to make any more mistakes. He finished the piece.

'Again,' the Master muttered in Mandarin.

Neil returned to the beginning carefully. Getting through that difficult run of notes without any mistakes, keeping tempo, and making sure he managed to achieve the right levels of loudness and softness. To his relief, he finished. But the Master had him repeat it again and again until it was absolutely perfect. The lessons were due to last for two hours but it was almost three hours before it was finished. Neil stood and they bowed to each other. The lesson was over. But he had to look forward to another tomorrow, and the next day, and the next.

Chapter Fourteen

Claire was so unused to having men make propositions to her she hesitated about accepting Jim's invitation. But yet there was something about him that appealed to her and she was torn in two. But the words stuck in her throat, what to do?

'Come on,' Jim persuaded. 'What's so wrong about dinner?'

'All right, thank you,' she agreed. Giving in to her earlier misgivings.

'I know a good restaurant.'

'I'll see you later, I've stuff to do this afternoon,' she hedged. Aware that he was probably wondering what she was doing and who she was with. She decided it wasn't any of his business and he wouldn't be interested in listening to her tales of woe.

'Eight o'clock?'

In the afternoon she took a taxi to Alan's parents' house. Now she didn't have any confidence that she would meet Alan but was prepared to make another effort. She waited outside the house. Impatient. Staring at the beautiful garden and hoping someone would appear. Praying that it would be Neil.

The intercom crackled.

'Can I see Alan Wang Li?' she asked, raising her voice a little. But wanting to shout out loud and wake them all up. But there was only silence. She pressed the bell again, more than once. Infuriated.

She saw a woman watching her through a window, but then

she disappeared. Claire was disappointed. But then she couldn't believe her eyes as the electronic gates clicked and slowly began to open. Trembling she walked up the steps and the woman, whom she assumed to be a maid, opened the glass door and she walked in. She pressed her hands together nervously and followed her through a spacious white tiled hallway. At the back, were double doors and she opened them and ushered her through. The room overlooked a garden which stretched away into the distance, a luxurious mass of greenery and tall trees half hidden in a mist.

A woman sat on a couch watching her. She was probably in her sixties, Claire thought. Thin. Dressed in a beautifully cut designer suit, purple on black. It was Alan's mother. Claire joined her hands together and bowed, anxious to show respect. The woman stood up and did the same.

Claire wondered what she should call her. Women kept their maiden names when they married, and she didn't even know what that was.

'We have not been formally introduced. I am Lien,' the woman said simply.

'I am Claire,' she replied. 'And I am very pleased to meet you, Lien.'

The woman indicated that she should sit on a low chair in front of her.

The door opened. A girl dressed in traditional Chinese costume in a rich scarlet carried a tray on which there was a delicate china teapot with small cups decorated in an artistic floral design.

She set it down on the table between the two women. Picked up the teapot and poured tea into Claire's cup. Then she poured for Lien.

Claire picked up the delicate china cup and sipped.

Lien sipped.

It was only now Claire realised she should have brought a gift to her mother in law. It would have been expected. She knew there were many customs in China, and was afraid she would contravene the etiquette of social mores.

'It is very nice to meet you at last,' Claire said.

'And I you,' Lien nodded.

'I am lonely without my boy, my heart is broken inside.'

'I understand.'

'But you have my son, why don't you give him back to me?' Tears spurted in her eyes.

'The matter is not under my control.'

'What do you mean?' she demanded. But then softened her voice, realising that if she were to antagonise the woman then it wouldn't do her case any good. She reminded herself that it was the first time she had met either of Neil's grandparents.

'I want you to understand how I feel. If someone took your only son from you when you were young, would you not feel bereaved of him?'

'I have lost a child.' She bent her head.

'I am sorry.'

There was a moment of silence between them.

Claire heard a knock on the door but was afraid to look around, her heart beating fast. The maid reappeared and spoke to Lien. She raised her head and looked towards the door. Claire was surprised to watch her expression change to one of extreme apprehension.

Quickly she stood up and bowed to Claire who did the same.

Then she indicated that she should follow the maid who brought her to a back door.

She opened it and led the way down a flight of stairs. Claire's heart began to race as she thought that she was being taken to see Neil. She was shaking as she walked with the woman through the garden where she opened a door and pushed her out into a narrow back lane.

Claire turned around. 'Where is Neil?' she asked.

But the door was banged in her face and a high solid metal gate had slid across blocking any further view of it. She was desperately disappointed. They had thrown her out of the house into this laneway. It was deserted and there were no doors or windows to be seen. The wall was a dark grey concrete, so different to the front of the house. She followed the laneway but it wound around in a confusing direction and eventually she found herself outside the complex altogether but couldn't understand how she got there. She was baffled. To have met her mother in law personally meant a lot. This could be her chance to see Neil again. But she was disappointed that their meeting had been curtailed so fast and determined that she would go back to see her again tomorrow. It would be her only chance to persuade this woman that she must help her to be reunited with her son.

Chapter Fifteen

'*Gan bey*,' Jim raised his glass of wine and clinked hers.

'*Sláinte,*' she smiled.

'Did you enjoy the meal?'

'Yes, very much. The various dishes are amazing. And it's nice to share a selection.'

'Coffee?' he asked.

She nodded.

He ordered.

She stared out through the windows of the restaurant across the twinkling lights of Beijing, the streets still crowded with lines of moving traffic.

'It's an amazing city, isn't it,' Jim commented.

'Mysterious,' she murmured.

'Anything could be going on, life is so varied here.'

'I've seen that. Such wealth on the one hand and poverty on the other.'

'Yes, it's a conundrum.'

'I suppose it's like a lot of cities. While I don't see as much obvious poverty at home, there are a lot of homeless people living on the streets. But I worry about the families who only have rooms in hotels. They have to leave in the morning and wander around for the day before they can go back. It's cruel and unfeeling treatment.'

'I was very aware of that when we were trying to find accommodation for Donal.'

'I don't know what students do. Have all of his friends found somewhere to stay?'

'I think so, but it costs them a lot of money, or I should say, the family. Mum and Dad have to fork out. I would certainly have had to pay whatever it was so that Donal got his chance to go to college. His mother would have come back to haunt me if I didn't.'

'It must be sad to have lost your wife.'

'Cancer,' he said, grimly.

'Very hard on you, and Donal too.' She remembered that the young man had said he had no brothers or sisters.

'Now it's just the two of us.'

'It's lonely, I'm sure,' she murmured. She thought about her own loss of Neil and wondered which was the hardest. Still, Jim had no hope of seeing his wife again, but she was positive that she would see Neil. She refused to think otherwise. And since meeting Lien today, she felt even more confident in spite of the fact that she was forced to leave so abruptly.

'Did you enjoy yourself this afternoon?' he asked.

'I just wandered around,' Claire said vaguely.

'It's good to get a feel of the place. Although if you like, I can take you further tomorrow?' he offered.

'I don't want to take up all of your time.'

'You wouldn't be.'

'Jim …' she hesitated.

His grey eyes met hers.

'Sorry to say this, but I'm here because I needed a break away from everything. Even spending time with other people,' she said hesitantly, feeling embarrassed.

'I understand, I suppose I wanted to extend the invitation just in case you wanted company.'

'Thank you, I appreciate that.'

'Jim?' Someone thumped him on his shoulder and he looked

up. 'Tony?' he smiled.

'How's it going?' the large blocky man grinned.

'Good thanks, this is Claire Brennan,' he introduced her. 'Tony O'Keeffe.'

'Lovely to meet you, Claire, would you like to have a drink with Peter and myself, we're just up there.' He waved to another table. 'Come and join us.'

'Would you like to?' Jim asked her.

'Yes, why not?' She stood up.

Tony ushered them to their table.

Peter stood up and shook his hand. 'Good to see you, Jim, it's been a while.'

Jim introduced her again.

'We're quite a party now,' Tony laughed. 'Glass of wine?'

'Thanks Tony, Claire?' Jim looked at her.

'I wouldn't mind another.'

Tony waved to the waiter and ordered a bottle of wine.

The waiter brought fresh glasses and poured.

'Well, Claire, what's the story? Are you on holiday?' Tony asked.

'Just for a few days.'

'Are you with a group?'

'No,' she smiled.

'Travelling around on your own?' he sounded surprised.

She nodded.

'Bit dangerous eh?'

'I haven't found it so.'

'Where have you been so far?'

'Just around the city.'

'Visit the Forbidden City, it's the highlight,' Tony said.

'I probably will.'

'And you must go to the largest structure in the world, a thirty-two-metre glass platform which will give you the most amazing views of the valley. Unless you have vertigo,' he laughed. 'Although I hope you haven't.'

'How're things in the diplomatic world of Beijing?' Jim asked.

'Not much different to normal.'

'You work at the Irish Embassy?' Claire asked.

'Yeah, and Peter here as well.'

'What position do you hold?'

'Third secretary,' he grimaced.

'You're obviously kept very busy,' Claire smiled.

'You can say that again,' he sighed. 'Issue passports. Attend functions. Translate documents. Help people who are in difficulties, you name it we sort it.'

'You can do that?' she whispered.

'Yeah, we represent Irish citizens out here as we do in the diplomatic service all over the world.'

Jim noticed how she tapped her fingers on the soft surface of the white tablecloth.

'Have you a problem?' Tony asked.

She stared at him. Her eyes wide, blue, glistening.

'No, it's not me,' she lied.

'Thanks be to God you haven't a problem. I've had enough of people and their difficulties.'

'Do you have any success in searching for missing people in China?' she asked.

He shook his head. 'China is a very big country and it would be almost impossible.'

'I know someone who needs help.'

'One of your friends?'

She nodded.

'Here's my card.' He handed it to her. 'You may as well tell them to give me a call anyway, although I'm not sure what I'll be able to do. Now would you like another drink?'

'I'm happy with my wine.' She raised her glass. 'Thank you

72

very much.'

'Me too,' Jim added.

Peter accepted a top-up.

'I'm having a whiskey. I don't know how you can keep sipping plonk all night. Order a whiskey, knock it back, feel it hit your throat, then you'll know you've had a drink, a real drink,' Tony chortled.

Jim laughed. 'It doesn't mean that much to me. I can take it or leave it.'

'Sounds boring.'

He shrugged.

The waiter brought the whiskey. And Tony did knock it back without a moment's hesitation. Jim looked at Claire. He felt awkward, knowing Tony could get fairly intoxicated very quickly, and aggressive as well.

'You're a very beautiful woman.' Tony leered at Claire, leaning closer to her.

'You've had too much to drink, Tony,' she laughed at him.

'Yes, I agree,' Jim added.

'Are you suggesting I'm impaired?' Tony had an edge of annoyance in his voice.

'No, not exactly,' she smiled.

'Claire, here we men enjoy a few jars. We need something to get us through the days. The long tedious days. Understand me?'

She nodded.

'And when I meet a beautiful woman I want to see her again. Is there some chance that we might get together when Jim here has departed?' he grinned.

'I won't be here for long.'

'When are you heading back?'

'In a few days.'

'We'll have time to do some sightseeing.'

'It's a fascinating city. Have you been here before?' Peter asked.

'Just once.

'I'll take you around,' Tony suggested.

'I could be meeting friends,' she said vaguely.

'The friends who need help?'

'Perhaps, I'll give them your card.'

'Where do they live?'

'I'm not sure, I have a note of it back at the hotel.'

'It's easy to get around Beijing, the metro is quite good,' Peter said. 'And taxis.'

'I usually take a cab.'

'You want to watch those drivers, they can charge you way over the odds if they think they can get away with it.'

'So far I haven't thought taxi rides were that expensive.'

'You didn't mention you knew people here?' Jim asked.

'I may not even meet them. They're just acquaintances.'

'We could do something tomorrow.' Tony was very enthusiastic.

'I don't know.'

'God, you're evasive.' He pulled a face. 'Where did you get this woman from, Jim?'

'Come on, Tony, you're putting Claire on the spot.'

'Sorry, Claire, I suppose I am. Take no notice of me.'

'I think I'll head back to the hotel. It's getting late.' She picked up her handbag and stood up.

'Me too,' Peter said. 'My wife is out for the evening so I'll have to let the babysitter go home.'

Claire took out her credit card. 'I should pay my share of our meal,' she said to Jim, and waved at a waiter who was passing. He stopped. 'Can you bring the bill please?'

'No, let me get it, I invited you,' Jim intervened.

'Please?' she smiled.

'I would prefer to pay,' he said.

'You're a stubborn woman as well,' Tony grinned. 'But beautiful.'

'Tony, keep your opinions to yourself,' Jim said.

'I'm just complimenting Claire,' he grinned at her.

Jim took out his own credit card.

'You do your thing, we'll get ours,' Tony said, and he and Peter paid for whatever they had. 'Fancy going on to a club to party?' he asked.

'No thank you, I'm tired,' Claire wasn't in the mood.

'As I said, I've to let the babysitter go. Good to meet you, Claire, look forward to seeing you again.' He shook her hand and then he asked the waiter for their coats.

'I'll walk you back, where are you staying?' Tony asked Claire.

'Holiday Inn, same as me,' Jim said.

'Oh, sharing?'

'No Tony, not sharing.' Jim raised his eyes and looked at Claire, who giggled.

'I'll walk the two of you back then. Since no one wants to enjoy themselves.'

'It's the opposite way for you.'

'I need the exercise.'

Jim said nothing more and the three of them walked back to the hotel and stood at the entrance.

'Fancy a night cap, guys?' Tony asked.

'You two go ahead if you wish, I'm for bed.' Claire pushed the circular glass door open. 'Goodnight and thanks for the evening, it was very enjoyable.'

'Will I see you tomorrow, Claire?' Tony stopped the whirl of the door.

'I'll call, I have your number.' She patted her handbag.

'We could have lunch.'

'Maybe,' she smiled and they went into the lobby of the hotel.

Chapter Sixteen

Claire stood at the window which overlooked the city. In all that visual confusion she wondered where Neil could be. Was he in that house with Lien? Was she keeping him from her? A prisoner? A wave of fury swept through her and she wanted to go over there immediately and demand that Lien allow her to take her son home.

On this visit to Beijing, Claire had decided to be more proactive and had looked up international schools online and now had a list of them in the area. She was certain that Alan wouldn't send Neil to a regular Chinese school as his level of Mandarin was not good enough and might hinder his progress. While she had a list of the schools she couldn't go in and ask them if Neil was a pupil there, knowing well that they wouldn't give her any information. No, she had decided to watch the children going in from some vantage point in the distance hoping that there might be a café nearby where she could sit inconspicuously and hopefully see Neil going up the steps and into school.

She thought about Tony and Peter who worked at the Embassy. She had almost been tempted to explain why she was in Beijing and ask for their advice when she was introduced to them by Jim. But had been reminded of Alan's threats and hesitated. Knowing that students of Neil's age started school very early in the morning, after a light breakfast she asked the porter to order a taxi for her, and got him to explain to the driver where she wanted to go.

The first college was a series of high-rise buildings surrounded by beautifully manicured lawns, and to her relief she found a café near the entrance. She ordered tea and sat there wishing she had a pair of binoculars so that she could get a closer view of the students who were going into the school. A short time later, she put money in the saucer beside the bill which the waiter had placed on the table and left. She walked across the road and found herself at the entrance gates among a group of late-comers. But as she gazed around, to her disappointment there was no sign of Neil. She continued on, climbed the steps and went into the main hallway, looking around for an office.

'Can I help you?' A woman wearing a dark uniform appeared, a pleasant smile on her face.

'I was wondering ...' she blurted, and hesitated. She wasn't prepared for this and every time she heard footsteps on the corridors she wanted to turn around and call Neil's name. 'Do you have a prospectus for the college, I'm thinking of enrolling my son here. I'm from Ireland and my husband is taking up a job but we're not sure whether we will be based in Shanghai, or Beijing,' Claire explained, just in case the woman mentioned they already had an Irish boy in the school.

'Come into my office.' The official led the way to a door and went in ahead of her.

'I'm looking at various colleges,' Claire murmured.

'And there are quite a few in Beijing, although most are not as prestigious as we are,' she said, handing her a brightly coloured brochure.

'Thank you.'

'Now would you like to give me some details? Perhaps the name of your son to start?'

'As I'm still at the early stages of making a decision, I will have a look at the prospectus and come back to you.' She stood up, anxious now to get on to the next college.

Another taxi brought her there, but there was no chance to see if Neil was attending it as the classes had already begun. She would have to wait until they were taking a break which would be at lunch time probably. And then she wasn't sure of the exact time either. She got out of the taxi and decided to go into a large shopping centre which she noticed nearby. It was enormous. Floor after floor. Shops selling all the well-known designer brands. Clothes. Shoes. Accessories. Everything for the home. Whole floors devoted to computers, beauty, travel. It was mesmeric. Claire wandered in and out of the stores and took a few photos of brands which she thought might appeal to Liz. Although she was constantly looking out for Neil. Perhaps he wasn't at school today. Maybe his grandmother might have brought him here to shop. She stopped off at a floor which sold sports gear and imagined what Neil would like. But everything was extremely expensive and as she had brought presents for him with her, and had no opportunity to give them to him, there was no point in buying any more when she didn't know whether she would see him or not.

Before twelve she went back to the college and was directed by the porter to the office. Again, she talked to the person there about the prospectus. Listening all the time for the clatter of footsteps which would tell her that the children were free for lunch. But the place was silent, and she began to wonder if there was some reason why. 'Are the students here today?' she asked, looking around.

The man shook his head. 'It is our school holiday. A commemoration of our opening. But it means that I can show you around. Come with me.' He began to walk across the wide spacious foyer.

'No thank you, that won't be necessary,' she said, following him, thinking that this idea of going around the schools was a complete waste of time. She explained to him that she was in a

78

hurry, thanked him and promised to return.

She went to another college after that but could not see Neil among the boys milling about in the grounds much to her disappointment. Outside, she sat on a bench, and wondered what she should do. Meeting the two guys from the Embassy had presented her with an opportunity if she wanted to grab it. She thought about it for a moment. Then took her phone from her pocket and pressed call.

'Tony O'Keeffe.'

'Hi, it's Claire here.'

'Good to hear from you, how's it going?' he responded heartily.

'I'm fine and I thought I'd take you up on your invite,' she said hesitantly, not sure whether she should be calling him at all. But the fact that he worked in the Embassy gave her that tiny inkling of hope.

'Sounds good, what time suits you?'

'I'm free now.'

'Perfect. Maybe we'll go to one of my favourite restaurants. It's the *Red Dragon*.'

'Give me the address.'

'Can you write it down?'

'Yes, just a minute.' She took a notebook and pen from her handbag.

'It's nice to see you, Claire, thanks for coming.' Tony rose to meet her.

She sat down.

'What would you like to drink?'

'Water will do.'

'Sure?'

'Yes, I don't drink this early in the day,' she said with a smile. 'Have to keep a clear head.'

'I'll have a beer if you don't mind.'

'Not at all.'

She hoped he wouldn't drink too much, she preferred a sober Tony far better than the man she had met the night before.

The restaurant was busy, the sound of chattering voices surrounded them but they managed to order lunch and were served quickly. She felt more relaxed in Tony's company today, particularly when he chatted about his life in Beijing.

'Have you a family?' he asked.

'I'm divorced. I have one son.'

'How old is he?'

'Thirteen.'

'On the cusp of manhood,' he grinned. 'Does he get up to much devilment?'

A wave of loss swept through her. Neil was the sweetest, most gentle of boys, and had always been that way. How dare Tony suggest that he might be troublesome? Irritated, she almost asked the question, but just managed to stay controlled as she glanced around, thick eyelashes fluttering, always looking out for a tall thin boy with dark hair just into his teenage years.

'Have you noticed someone over there that you know?' Tony's eyes followed her glance across the room.

'Eh no,' she was embarrassed that he had caught her looking for Neil.

As they sipped tea after they had finished their meal, he returned to her query of the night before about his work at the Embassy. 'You were saying you know someone who might need help,' he said.

'I don't really want to break a confidence. I'm not sure what they want to do.'

'Well, tell them I can look into it if they want. We offer a service to Irish nationals abroad no matter what the circumstances.'

'I'll mention that.' She was in two minds. And didn't know what to do.

A voice in her head shouted out loud. I want my boy. Give me back my boy. It was just as simple as that. Her boy Neil. 'Actually, I should tell you the truth,' she said.

He raised his eyebrows.

She went on to tell him about Alan and Neil. 'I'm sorry, I made up these fictitious friends.'

'Not at all. I can understand your position about not wanting your ex to know what you're doing.'

'I can't go down the legal route. I might never see my son again.'

'We're here if you need us,' he said, comforting.

'Thank you,' she smiled.

'Now would you like to do some sightseeing? I can take you around, maybe visit various places. What do you think?' Tony asked.

'I don't really have the time now, I'm going over to the house to see my mother in law. I'm hoping she'll help. Today I was going around some colleges.'

'Any luck?'

'No.'

'Do you remember Peter?' he asked. 'You met him last night.'

'I do, he's very nice.'

'He has a son who attends one of the international colleges.'

'Has he?' she was astonished.

'Robert is his name. Do you want me to ask Peter to mention Neil to him, maybe he knows him if they go to the same college.'

'Would you?'

'I will. Just by the way. I won't make a big thing out of it. If he knows an Irish boy named Neil, would I ask Peter's wife, Alison, to call you?'

'Thanks so much,' She handed him her business card.

'My pleasure.'

She looked at her phone. 'I really should be on my way.'

'What a pity.' He leaned closer to her.

Her immediate reaction was to move back in her chair. 'Surely you have to work?'

'I'm my own boss, and I'm a bit bored with lost passports and trade documents.'

She smiled at him. 'Thanks for lunch.'

He took her arm as they left the restaurant.

She couldn't free herself from his grip until she managed to step out into the street and settled her handbag on her shoulder, forcing him to release her.

'We'll get a cab back to the hotel,' he said, and waved to one driving past in the line of traffic. The taxi pulled in immediately.

'Thanks again,' Claire said, held out her hand and he grasped it tightly. Immediately, she felt claustrophobic. Yet she needed something from him. Whatever that might be. For Neil's sake.

She remembered that promise she had made her son when she had divorced Alan. *I will never leave you, Neil. I will always love you.* There was no end to her love.

Chapter Seventeen

The limousine was parked outside the garage at their house. Neil picked up his bag and walked down the steps. The chauffeur, Kim, came around and opened the door for him. He climbed into the back and sat down. The man got in, started the engine and reversed down the driveway. Neil hated being driven everywhere. He hated the control everyone had over him. The household was run like a machine. Every part of it clicked into place precisely. All the servants did their jobs efficiently.

He wished that it was his Mum who was driving him to school. He would always push a CD into the player. His choice of music blared. Too loud she always said. But let him have his way and listen to heavy metal. His mind caught in the beat. Swirling with the rhythm. Their eyes would meet in a quick glance as she pulled up at the traffic lights. And they would smile at each other and have a laugh. And he would feel so happy and content, knowing that this was all he wanted.

Now, as this man drove him to the college, a place where he knew no-one very well except a boy named Robert, there was no contentment. It was so very different. They arrived and Kim pulled up outside and came around to open the door. But Neil was already out and had banged it closed. He needed some independence and was delighted he had beaten him to it for once. He was in through the swing doors quickly and caught up with Robert whom he saw walking ahead of him to the hall where they would practice PE before class.

'Got your assignments done?' Robert asked, as they swung into the classroom later and sat at their seats.

'Just about. In between practice.'

'At least my parents don't push me to do piano or anything else.'

'My grandfather and father are pathetic,' Neil grimaced.

'I'm lucky, although my Dad wants me to do well in my exams, but I'd like to be a footballer.'

'I haven't much chance of that here, but I used to play at home,' Neil admitted.

'Why don't you come along and play on my team?'

'My father wouldn't allow it.'

'Come after school, he won't know.'

'I have to study and practice piano as well,' Neil groaned.

'I don't bother with study sessions. The Chinese students work too hard.'

'I'm only half Chinese. My father is from here, my mother is Irish.' Fear darted through him as he remembered his grandfather's remarks about him being more Chinese than Irish.

'You're Irish?'

'Yeah.' He wasn't going to say Chinese at all no matter what he looked like.

'We're Irish too.'

'From where?'

'Dublin. But we've lived in lots of other places around the world, we've only been in China for three years.'

'I thought you were American,' Neil admitted.

'We were living in New York, and Chicago before that.'

The teacher came in. The day had begun. At break they had milk shakes in the café. And continued their conversation about their families.

'My mother is from Dublin,' Neil explained. 'But she's in America now.'

'Where?'

'I don't know.'

'What's she doing there?'

Neil shook his head, dejected.

'How is that? Don't you see her?'

'No.'

'Does she call?'

'No.'

Neil sat there, sipping the vanilla shake through a paper straw. He didn't want to talk any more, just wanted his Mum.

Chapter Eighteen

Claire waited outside the house.

'Can I speak with Lien please?' she asked in Chinese, having practiced the phrase.

There was silence.

'Lien please?'

Claire was impatient. In her own mind she was saying she really should learn to speak more of the Chinese language. Now she looked up at the house and prayed someone would come out to her like that last time. She really wanted to talk to her mother in law again. But nothing happened. She pressed her hands together and prayed.

A figure appeared. Someone was there. Her heart beat with excitement as the electric gates opened with a click. Claire walked briskly up the steps to where the maid stood waiting for her.

'Thank you,' she whispered.

The maid closed the door behind her, and then led the way through the hallway and into the same room where she had met Lien on that last occasion.

This time, her mother in law was dressed in stunning gold brocade, her oriental features set proudly, eyes glowing deep brown. So like Neil's, Claire thought instantly, struck by the family resemblance.

She joined her hands together and bowed.

Feeling very nervous.

'I apologise that I have not made an appointment to see you,' she said and handed her a box of sweets. 'This is a gift for you and I have brought presents from Ireland for Neil.' She pushed the bag closer to the woman.

Lien bent her head.

'My thanks to you.' she murmured. 'It is most kind.'

'Please tell Neil that I brought them.' She knew that the art of giving gifts in Chinese culture was fraught with pitfalls. But wanted to encourage this woman to like her. To understand her. While they had only met recently, Claire wanted to appeal to her feminist side. A thin hand waved her towards a chair opposite. She sat down. An ornate table was like a line of division between them.

The door opened and as before the maid came in carrying a tea tray. This time the tea had a rich red shade with a perfumed fragrance.

'It is *Da Hong Pao* tea,' Lien murmured.

'It has a beautiful aroma,' Claire said.

'A mixture of the woodlands and the sweetness of fruit,' she continued.

Claire drank her tea in silence. Thinking perhaps it was more appropriate to wait until they had finished before speaking again.

Slowly, they took sip after sip until they put down their cups.

'Thank you for seeing me again,' Claire said.

'You are my daughter.'

'Thank you,' she whispered. So grateful to this woman for giving her that recognition.

'Your child is my child.'

Claire's heart began to beat erratically.

'Lien, can you understand how I feel about my child?'

'I can. As I said to you, I was prevented from having more than one child. In the days of the *One Child Policy* here in China, I became pregnant with a second child.'

She stopped for a few seconds.

Claire listened intently.

'I had to have an abortion.' Lien's lip trembled and for the first time her face showed emotion. Tears welled up in her eyes and drifted down her cheeks. 'I have never forgotten. It is always in my mind.'

Claire took a deep breath, tears of loss in her own eyes.

'And more so, I was sterilised.'

Claire was so shocked she couldn't say anything. She stared astonished at the other woman. Tears streamed down her face also. She wiped them away although Lien let the tears dry naturally on her own face. They both sat there silent in grief. One woman sharing another's emotion.

'It was the normal for women at that time. No-one could object. It was the law.'

'I can't imagine such a thing.' Claire was appalled.

'It was sanctioned by the government. There were too many children and not enough money to support them all.'

'That must have been very hard on women.'

'I knew many others who also had to endure such mutilation.'

Claire cringed at the word she used to describe what had happened. 'Then you can understand how the loss of my son affects me?'

'Yes, I can.'

'Won't you ask Alan to send Neil back to me?' she begged.

'My son and his father want to keep him here with us. He is half Chinese and they want him to grow up in our own traditional way.'

'Alan has not asked me for permission to keep him here, I only gave permission for a holiday as I had done previously.'

'But sons are very important to Chinese families.'

'I know that, but it is against Irish law.' She was aware that she sounded impatient and decided to pull back.

'I cannot go against my husband or my son.'

'Why should they have complete control?'

'In our family, men make all decisions.'

'That's so wrong.'

'It is surely the same in Ireland?'

'No, not usually.' Although Claire wondered if she had also allowed Alan to keep her under control when they were married. Perhaps she did. She was shocked at the idea. But it probably was the reason she divorced him. Now she realised that he was still manipulating her from a distance. Like a puppet.

'Dear Lien, couldn't you let me see my boy?' She reminded herself that she may have to compromise to some extent. 'I only have two more days here in Beijing and I would give anything to hold him close to my heart.' Her voice trembled.

'I cannot.'

'Could you give me Alan's telephone number please?' she asked hopefully.

'No.'

'Please, Lien, I will always be grateful to you.' She leaned closer to the woman, but the table was still a barrier between them.

'It is not possible.' Her face stiffened.

'I just want to see him for a short time. Even an hour. To talk. To get to know him again. It is a long time since I have seen him. So many weeks, days, hours, minutes, it is never ending.'

The woman gazed at her with an impassive expression on her face.

'Do you think Alan would agree with that?'

'I am unsure.'

'Ask for me.'

'I will try.'

'Thank you so much, Lien, for doing this for me.' She picked up her phone, and pulled a business card from the wallet.

She handed it to her. 'That is my number.' Claire felt that she had bonded with Lien and their shared tears made hope attainable.

The woman stared at the card.

'I will be leaving the day after tomorrow, please call me.'

Chapter Nineteen

Neil and Robert shrugged into their coats in the locker room after their last class of the day and walked towards the doors. A woman with blonde hair hurried towards them, smiling widely. Neil immediately stopped in his tracks. Shocked.

'Mum?' he cried out loud and ran towards her. A crazy thought in his head that it was her. She had on her blue jeans and a black coat.

'There's my Mum,' Robert said.

But Neil didn't hear him as he ran closer to the woman, his heart beating fast. Then he stopped running and his tongue caught in his throat as he realised that this person wasn't his mother after all. He had been so sure. He stumbled and almost fell on the floor. It was only then he realised that the woman was smiling at Robert.

'Mum, this is Neil and I told you his Mum is Irish too.'

'Hallo Neil,' the woman smiled at him.

'Hallo,' he whispered, feeling his face redden.

'How was school for you two boys?' she asked.

'All right,' he said.

'Have you much homework to do?' she smiled.

'Not too much,' Robert grinned at Neil. 'But Neil has to stay back to study.'

'That's a pity. But wait a minute, would you like to come around on Saturday week to Robert's birthday party?'

'Mum, I was telling Neil all about it.'

'Where does your Mum come from?' she asked.

'Dublin.'

'We're from Dublin too. We'll have to meet. Maybe your Mum and Dad might come to the party as well?'

Tears flooded Neil's eyes.

Robert's mother looked down at him.

'I must go to class,' he said, embarrassed.

'See you tomorrow,' Robert said.

'Bye.'

As Neil stared at his study books, he found it hard to concentrate on his work. He couldn't put the image of his own Mum out of his mind after seeing Robert's mother.

When he arrived home, he went in search of his father and found him with his grandfather in the study. He was so anxious that he spoke in English. 'Dad, can I talk to you?'

'What about?' He didn't look up.

'I've been invited to a birthday party by Robert.'

'Not now, I'm busy.'

He bit his lip, anxious to say what he had in his mind, although he realised that he shouldn't have interrupted him. It was always a mistake to do that.

'Go and have something to eat. Your Master will be here in half an hour.'

'I want to talk to you.' He raised his voice.

'No.' Now he looked at Neil, his eyes angry.

'Do not argue with your father, it is very bad manners,' his grandfather added.

Neil pursed his lips, cowed. He could never say what he wanted to say. He always had to wait until it was the right time to speak and his father chose to give him his attention. Sometimes it could take days. He sat at the kitchen table eating a bowl of noodles, still annoyed that he couldn't talk to his father.

There were so many rules which prevented him from doing what he wanted. It was awful living here. He couldn't even choose what food he liked to eat. Even his Ayi didn't speak much except to give him orders. She stood over him now and encouraged him to finish. He didn't really want to. He wasn't hungry. But he knew she would stay there until he had eaten every morsel. He had to stuff it into his mouth. So quickly he almost felt sick.

'You must wash and brush teeth before lesson,' Ayi commanded.

He did as he was told, and without any other choice he went into the music room. The Master had already arrived and they bowed to each other politely.

Neil sat on the stool and opened the music for the piece he had worked on the previous evening. It was Beethoven's Piano Concerto No. 5 in E flat. The Master tapped the first bar with his chopstick, and Neil placed his fingers on the keys and began, although there were parts of the concerto which still needed attention, and he knew his teacher wouldn't be happy if he didn't get it absolutely right.

He played on. Loving the surge of the music, as it rose and fell, *forte* and *pianissimo*. He got it right at the beginning, but then made a very small mistake and instantly Master Xin tapped his knuckles sharply. His intake of breath was loud but that was all he did as he continued on managing to keep perfect timing. He gritted his teeth, hating that he had given his teacher the opportunity to punish him. But it made him even more determined and he succeeded in completing the section without any further errors.

'Once again,' the Master ordered.

He went back to the beginning. This time he managed to get through it without any mistakes. And when his teacher had left at the end of the lesson, he continued to practice, dissatisfied with his own performance.

His father came into the room and stared at him as he pounded the keys, fingers flying. Neil was so engrossed he didn't even notice, working off some of the earlier stress within him.

Then Alan walked across to the piano. 'Quite good.' He patted him on the shoulder.

'Thanks, Dad.'

'Did you finish your homework at college?' Alan asked.

He nodded.

'What were you talking about earlier when you so rudely interrupted my business with your grandfather?'

Neil didn't feel he could mention it now. 'Doesn't matter.'

'You seemed anxious enough about it when you came home.'

'It's OK.' He folded away his sheets of music and stood up.

'Go on, tell me what it is. Yeh Yeh isn't here now.'

'I've been invited to a party.' His voice was low.

'Whose party?' His father sounded surprised.

'Robert,' he muttered.

'And who is this Robert?'

'A boy in school.'

'When is the party?'

'Saturday week.'

His father was asking so many questions, Neil suddenly felt confident that he might actually allow him to go.

'Did he send you an invitation?'

'It will come tomorrow.'

'When you receive it, you will give him your regrets.'

'Why can't I go?'

'I don't want you to go,' his father snapped.

'Mum always let me go to parties.'

'What your Mum did is irrelevant now.'

'But there will be a magician, and games, and Robert said it will be fun.'

'You're not going.'

'Dad, it will just be for the afternoon, it won't take long,' he begged.

'No, and that's final. You are too busy with your piano and Mandarin lessons at the weekends. There is no time for frivolous parties.'

Neil felt crushed. He had never argued with his father like this before.

'Please?' his voice trembled.

'Don't mention the matter to me again.'

Neil closed the piano lid. An urge to bang it hard came over him, but he resisted, knowing it would only cause more problems, and then his father would never change his mind.

The next day Robert did bring in the invitations and handed them to all of his classmates. Everyone was keen to go but Neil said nothing, too embarrassed to explain that he wasn't allowed. It was only as he was on his own with Robert that he apologised.

'What if you show your Dad the invitation?' he asked.

'I will do that when I go home.' He took it out of his inside pocket and stared at it. It was printed on white card with red writing, and his name was written neatly with a black pen. He knew Robert had done that himself.

'Thank you for inviting me,' Neil said, feeling awkward and very disappointed.

'My Mum was wondering what your mother's name is?'

'Claire Brennan.'

'Mum said she'd like to meet her.'

Neil nodded, twisting his hands behind his back to avoid showing how much he longed to see his Mum.

'My Mum's name is Alison,' said Robert.

They went into the front hall of the college.

'See you tomorrow,' Neil said.

'There's Mum.' Robert waved to the woman who waited at the

door talking to some of the other mothers and students.

'Hallo boys. Did you give out your invitations, Robert?'

'Yes, but Neil can't come.'

'Why not?' She looked at him.

'I've to study.'

'His father won't let him come,' Robert said.

'Why don't I call him?' she asked.

'No thank you, he's made up his mind,' murmured Neil.

'That's a pity. But tell him there's an adult party as well, so he could come to that.'

'I'll ask,' Neil said, but he knew that his Dad would never agree.

Chapter Twenty

Claire wandered through the silk market. This was very different to the modern shopping centre with numerous shops selling masses of colourful silk products. So many wonderfully vibrant scarves were displayed, drifting throws, metres of shining fabric which tantalised her. But Claire couldn't afford to splurge on something for herself, or even her mother or sister or friends as she might have done in the past. And now forced herself past the shops, ignoring the shouts of the owners who encouraged her to come into their store and have tea with them. She smiled to herself, being quite a good haggler, but wasn't going to take on any of these people even for the fun of it. She might never get away. So she ignored their shouts and went on. It was a nuisance in a way as she wouldn't have minded browsing and having a closer look.

She checked her phone to see if there were any missed calls and then as if by magic it rang. 'Yes?' She replied, wondering who it was.

'You come to see Lien at three o'clock today,' a voice said in English.

'Thank you.'

Her heart raced. She couldn't believe it. Immediately she looked for the number but it was private, and she was very disappointed. But she saw that it was just before two now and she barely had an hour to get there. Then it struck her that she should buy a gift for Lien on this occasion also and Neil too.

One stall sold miniature silk roses in decorated pots. Claire looked up her phone and found that a deep pink rose can convey gratitude and appreciation, so she bought one for Lien.

At another stall she bought some sweets for Neil, praying that he would be there. After making her purchases, she turned in the crowded aisle to make her way back to where the entrance was. But that wasn't easy. She went up and down different aisles but couldn't judge where the entrance or exit was. Unable to ask for directions in Chinese, she began to panic, trying to push through the people who walked ahead. Some coming towards her, others away. Their dark eyes staring at her blankly above their masks. She grew more frantic as time passed. Then she turned down an aisle which wasn't quite as crowded and saw a flower seller. She couldn't tell whether it was the same young girl who had served her earlier but decided to ask her for directions. Then it struck her that she should google the words *exit please*, and stood near the stall and searched. The words came up - *qing tuichu* – and she showed her phone to the girl who immediately smiled and indicated the direction she should go. Claire felt so grateful she wanted to hug her. She tried to say the words for *thank you* which were *xie xie* in Chinese and hoped that she would understand her. It seemed that she did as she smiled broadly and nodded. Claire turned to the right and followed her instructions. To her relief, she finally caught a glimpse of the dull sky outside, and hurried out, reassured when she arrived on the street. At last the terror of being lost in that place finally left her and she hailed a taxi to take her to the house.

Claire's hands shook as she thought that she might see Neil any moment now. Tears moistened her eyes but she brushed them away, reluctant to let Lien see her emotion. She stared up at the glass doors of the house and could see the figure of the maid inside. The gate opened. She went through and up the steps.

In the hall she looked around but could see no evidence of Neil being there. The maid stood back while she went into the room.

This time Lien sat near the window in front of a small circular lacquered table, which had a beautiful design in mother of pearl on its surface. She was dressed exquisitely in turquoise silk today. Claire joined her hands and bowed to the woman. Then she handed her the bag which contained the pink rose and the box of sweets for Neil and bowed again.

'I am very grateful to you,' Lien said.

'It is not much,' Claire murmured. 'But the sweets are for Neil, could you tell him I brought them?'

'I value your esteemed gifts highly.'

'Thank you for inviting me to your home again,' Claire said.

'It is my pleasure. Please sit down and have tea with me.'

Where is Neil? She wanted to shout out loud at Lien. Disturb her perfect poise. Where is my son? She was tired of the endless serving of tea and the ceremony around that.

At that moment, the maid entered and served a pale green coloured tea. It began again.

She became more impatient. Each slow sip represented another second that Neil was away from her and she had difficulty hiding her feelings.

The maid came to remove the tray.

When she closed the door, Claire took a deep breath. 'Lien, do you have news about my son?'

Lien shook her head. 'No, I am sorry.'

'Did you ask Alan if he would agree to let me see Neil?'

'Yes, but his answer was negative.'

'And your husband, Neil's grandfather?'

'The same.'

'What am I to do?' Tears filled her eyes.

'I do not know. It is very upsetting for me to be in this position,' Lien said.

'And even worse for me.' Claire was angry. 'To be controlled by two men.'

'I will try again.'

'But I am returning to Ireland tomorrow. There is no time.'

'You will have to come back again.'

'I must see him today, please Lien, please?' she entreated.

'I will ask for you.' Lien stood up. 'But I cannot promise.'

The door opened and the maid waited for Claire to leave.

She stood there, feeling helpless. 'There must be something I can do, tell me?'

'I will think about it for you. But you must leave now, I cannot let it be known you have been here to see me.'

'I'm grateful to you.' Claire had to say it, although she really didn't feel that way. She bowed then, her hands joined, as did Lien. Then the maid ushered her down that stairs and out the narrow door which led into the laneway as had happened before. She didn't get so much of a fright this time when the metal door slid closed behind her but she immediately burst into tears to find herself outside in this world again. There was a terrible finality about the bang of the door, and she couldn't control her feelings. She had been so excited earlier about meeting Lien, certain when she asked her to visit, she had something positive to tell her about Neil. Now she was crushed and wondered would she ever see her boy again.

Confused she walked in the direction of the front of the house. But that lane ended in a cul de sac and she had to turn back and hurry in the other direction. Confused, she panicked but the lane twisted and turned, and she was reminded of being lost in the market earlier today. Her eyes were still clouded over with tears and she couldn't really see where she was going. As she ran past the steel door, she put out her hand and touched it. It was cold, and hard, and now she felt like banging on it with her fists until Lien came out. But she knew that wouldn't happen.

As she stood there, all she wanted was to find her way out of here and couldn't remember how she did that the last time. She couldn't remember anything today. She dried her eyes with a tissue, and stood there, trying to get her mind straight. Eventually she found the front of the house and decided to wait until Neil came home, or Alan returned. The evening was closing in now and she was confident that she wouldn't be noticed by anyone. There was a grove of trees at the side of the house and she stood among them, praying that Neil would come home soon, he couldn't still be at school. She pushed her hands into the pockets of her jacket. It was extremely cold. She kept her phone in her hand, eyes darting here and there. Time passed. It grew dark. She shivered and pulled up her collar. Suddenly the gleam of headlights shone through the wrought-iron gates and a large car waited outside as they slowly opened. She felt caught in the lights like a rabbit as she stood there and had to move back further into the grove of trees. The car drove across the front of the house and disappeared around the side.

Her pulse raced as she realised that it could be Alan's car. But it was going so fast it was impossible to identify anyone inside and she wouldn't have been surprised if the windows were blacked out as well. The lights shone on the walls beyond the back of the house and were then switched off and she was left in the dark again. Claire shivered, wondering now was there any point in waiting. She followed the deeper shadows among the trees, made her way towards the pedestrian gate, slipped through, and took a taxi back to the hotel. In her room, she made some green tea to steady her nerves.

She lay on the bed with the pillows tucked behind her and sipped it, deep in thought. She only had a few hours left in which to find Neil. And now that Lien had more or less indicated that she had no success in persuading Alan to let her see Neil, her hopes of holding him close had disintegrated. She didn't bother eating dinner, just ordered a sandwich.

All night she lay wide awake. Telling herself she had to be sharp. Prepared. For whatever. But nothing happened and she rose about six o'clock, showered, changed, and packed the few items she had brought with her. Then she made tea, went to Reception, and asked the porter to order a taxi to take her to the airport. All of this she did on automatic. A dull ache inside her.

On the aircraft, she lay her head back and closed her eyes. Sleep caught up with her but it wasn't restful and she awoke and dozed on and off. The steward served lunch, and she ate the rather tasteless dish just because she felt hungry. Neil was on her mind all the time, and she was desperately disappointed that she had no opportunity to see him. Now she didn't know when that would happen and was heartbroken.

Chapter Twenty-one

Alan didn't allow Neil go to the party. Anyway, he didn't want to meet Robert's mother again, as she reminded him too much of his own Mum. He resented that his Dad treated him like a child when he was already a teenager. He knew that his Mum would have agreed immediately and it upset him that he couldn't ask her. Even the other night he had asked Alan if he could write a letter.

'She is living in America and I don't even have an address.'

'What about home?'

'It's rented.'

'You mean there are other people living in it?' Neil was upset at the thought. And imagined another child sleeping in his bed, and sitting on the big red velvet couch in the evenings watching television with his mother.

'She wouldn't leave the house empty.'

'That's awful. What will I do if I go home?' He was very sad.

'You won't be going home.'

'Why not?'

'Because we'll be staying in China. You like it here now, don't you?'

'I don't. I miss my friends. I told you that. Tommy and Calum.'

'What about your friends at school here?'

'I like Robert.'

'He is a friend, isn't he?'

'Yes, but not like my friends at home. Do you think we could invite them out here for a holiday and they could stay with us here?'

Alan laughed. 'It's very expensive to travel to China from Ireland, they couldn't afford it.'

'Maybe we could send them the money?'

'Don't be ridiculous, Neil, you can put that out of your head.'

Neil said nothing. He could see he was getting nowhere with his father. He never did. Alan turned his back and walked away from him as usual with nothing resolved. Neil stared down at his books on the desk. He had to finish the grammar exercise, and then practice the symbols for the different words. He actually liked that. He picked up the special pen that he used and drew the words. Everyone spoke Mandarin in the house and he had become much more fluent. But in school he spoke English which he preferred. It made him feel like he was at home with his Mum. He thought about their house. Walking up the drive. Calling out that he was home, and Mum coming out of the kitchen or wherever she was and hugging him. He missed that so much. Her hugs. No one hugged him here.

He stared out the window. Longing to run outside, pick up a football and practise kicks against the wall. Bang bang bang. It was what he enjoyed most in the garden at home in Dublin. But there was no grass here. There was just concrete and gravel and trees. He didn't have a football here. It was so frustrating. His foot itched, and he kicked the air. Again and again. Then he took some sheets of used copy paper, rolled them in a ball and kicked them around his room instead. And he enjoyed the feeling it gave him. Took him home to his own back garden where he played with his friends. He was excited. Rolled some more sheets of paper around the ball and aimed at an imaginary goal which was the width of his wardrobe. Bang again. He kept kicking the ball.

'What is that noise?' A voice shouted from outside. It was Ayi.

She was like his *jailer*, he thought. He groaned, ran to pick up the ball and pushed it into a drawer. There was a knock on the door. He opened it and stared at her.

'What are you doing?'

'Nothing.'

'What was that noise?'

'I dropped some of my books on to the floor.' His face flushed. She stepped into the room.

He picked up his bag from the floor. 'I've put them back in now,' he muttered. Resenting the fact that she had interrupted his game.

'You are doing your homework?'

He nodded and sat at his desk again.

'Dinner will be ready in ten minutes.'

'I will be down then,' he said, picked up his pen, and bent his head over the copybook.

She left the room silently.

When the door closed, he threw down the pen. 'Stupid woman,' he said to himself. Hating how she insisted on keeping him to her timetable. Minute by minute. Why did he even need someone called Ayi who looked after him like he was a child of only six or seven. He was going to talk to his father. Tell him to send her away. He didn't need her.

He took his chance when dinner was over.

'Dad?'

'Yes?'

'I don't want Ayi around, I'm too big for her.'

'But she looks after you.'

'I'm not a baby.'

'I didn't suggest you were a baby. But she takes all your clothes for washing, ironing, dry cleaning, and anything else.'

'I can do all that myself.'

'I seem to remember your Mum did everything for you.'

'I want Mum. I don't want Ayi around,' he grumbled.

'And your Mum doesn't want you. I keep telling you that.'

His tone cut through Neil. He couldn't understand how his Mum didn't want him.

'Anyway, I can't sack Ayi without good reason.'

'Give her something else to do,' Neil suggested.

'There is nothing. She is busy with you.'

'She is always watching me.'

'And is only looking out for you just in case something happens.'

'What's going to happen to me? I'm thirteen now,' he burst out angrily.

Alan waved him away. 'Enough. It's almost time for your music lesson. Your Master will be here soon. Go and prepare yourself.'

He wasn't going to talk to him any longer. Neil always knew when he spoke to him in that way. It was a signal. An order. Don't annoy me anymore. Head down, Neil left the room. He hated this house. So plain. So unfamiliar. When he used to come here for his holidays he hadn't minded so much. But knowing that he wasn't going home made a big difference. Now it had turned into a prison. Although his father called it home and wanted him to call it home. But he couldn't. Not inside his head anyway. Or his heart. That place where he felt everything. His home was in Ireland. And he wanted to be there with his Mum. She was so lovely and warm. A sharp pain swept through him as he thought about her. Wondering where she was. And why she didn't love him anymore. That hurt most and reminded him that maybe she wasn't his real Mum at all. Almost in tears, he hurried upstairs to his room.

His lesson would begin soon and he had to wash up beforehand. Scrub his hands and fingernails and make sure that there were no ink stains since he had been writing earlier.

Master Xin would be displeased with him and no doubt he would complain to his father. He thought about the piece he had had to prepare for today's lesson and hoped that he would play well. There was no time to practise any further now, but when he had dried his hands, he placed his fingers on the bed and with the tempo ringing in his ears, he began the piece, and played it through a couple of times until there was a knock on the door and Ayi appeared to tell him it was time.

He didn't say anything, and with a sigh he just stood up and followed her downstairs. It was something he had to do every day. There was no choice in this place he was supposed to call *home*.

'Dad, how do you celebrate Halloween?' asked Neil. 'Do children dress up?'

'There is a Ghost Festival which is similar.'

'What is that?'

'We celebrate the night when the ghosts of the past appear.'

'Will we see fireworks?' he asked.

'No.'

'I have a spooky wizard outfit at home.'

'We don't wear outfits here,' Alan sighed. His expression grim.

Neil could see it, but he still continued. 'Some of the boys in school are having scary parties. Robert invited me to his house.' He was full of excitement, maybe this time it might be different.

'You're not going,' his father said bluntly.

'You never let me go anywhere. I'm going to tell Mum.' He was angry, and really didn't care what his father thought.

'You can't tell her.'

'I can if I want. I can send her a message.' Neil felt angry again.

'I told you she's not in Ireland, and I don't know her address. Give over, Neil, you're driving me crazy. Get on with your work.'

Neil closed his mouth but after a moment, he spoke again. 'Is

Mum lost? Did she disappear when she went to America? And is anyone looking for her? Have you asked the police to search?'

'No, she's not lost.'

'Then why don't we see her anymore?'

'I keep telling you, she doesn't want to. Now I've had enough. Forget about her.'

'I can't.' Tears moistened his eyes and he turned from his father so that he wouldn't see.

'Get on with your work. How are your characters?'

He showed his Dad the work sheet. He examined it.

'Not bad. Go and show it to Grandfather.'

He took it into the other room where the old man sat reading.

'Yeh Yeh, Dad said to show you my characters.' He held out the sheet.

The man looked at it. 'Do you understand their meaning?'

'Some of them.'

'That is good.'

'But there are so many of them.' Neil had to admit that. He didn't think he would ever learn them all.

'There are many thousands, but you will succeed.'

'I hope so.'

'You are a good student, Neil. You have what we call *qín láo.*'

'Thank you Yeh Yeh. Does that mean *hardworking?*' he asked.

'Why yes, it does.' He pointed to the characters. 'Write in Mandarin.' He handed him his pen.

Carefully he drew the characters, which took him quite a length of time. Yeh Yeh nodded approvingly.

For once he felt good. His grandfather didn't often compliment him on his Mandarin. But he had worked hard recently and it eased the tension of his earlier conversation with his father.

That night he dreamed of being home in Ireland. Seeing his own room again. Lying in his own bed. Helping his Mum around the house. Playing with his friends. They were often in his dreams as well. But there were nightmares too. They were frightening. And he was always running towards his Mum, but she was far away. He called out but she didn't hear him. He fell on the ground but couldn't get up again and all the time her figure was growing smaller and smaller in the distance until she disappeared altogether and he woke up, terrified.

Chapter Twenty-two

Claire found it hard to drag herself into work the day after she arrived home in Dublin.

'How did you get on in Beijing?' Liz enquired.

'It was fine, thanks. And I really appreciate that you gave me the time. I had a look at some of the fashion while I was there, and took some photos. The stores carry all the bigger names, and some I didn't even know.'

'I must visit one of these days, although the air quality in Beijing is very bad.'

'Most people wear masks.'

'I'd hate the thought of that.' She crumpled her face in distaste.

'I don't like wearing one either, but a lot of people suffer from respiratory problems as a result of not doing so.'

'It's been hectic since you left.'

'Good sales?'

'All the usual clients in to grab the bargains.'

'That's good.'

'There's something I've been thinking. You've a good eye for fashion and as you know I'll be heading over to the *Paris Fashion Week* to see some of the new designs for next year. Would you like to join me? I would love your input.'

'Of course, thank you for asking me.'

'I'll be choosing our range for the next Spring/Summer season.'

'I'm very honoured that you would choose me to go. There are other girls working here much longer than myself.'

'You have something they don't have, and I want you to share it with me. Between us we will choose a wonderful range for next season,' Liz smiled enthusiastically.

'Thank you so much.' Claire couldn't believe this was happening.

'Unfortunately, I'm giving you very short notice as it's next Tuesday week. In the hope that you would be able to come, I've already arranged accreditations for both of us, so I'll just need your ID.'

'I'll bring in my passport in the morning. But as I have a couple of people staying at my house I'll have to check.'

'Could you let me know in the morning?'

'Yes, I can.'

'I'll get on to the travel agency to book your flight and I've already asked them to reserve rooms for us at the hotel where I usually stay.' Liz made notes in the diary.

'Thank you so much for giving me this opportunity.' Claire was so grateful.

'It's going to be a wonderful few days in Paris and I'll enjoy having you along,' Liz said with a smile. 'It's a tough gig in some ways, but with such a buzz it's like fashion heaven.'

Claire wondered what had just happened. How come Liz had chosen her to go to Paris. It seemed incredible. But there were problems. How would Donal and Sophie get on in her absence. She was only just back from Beijing and was now giving them another opportunity to have a free house and hoped they would behave themselves. She shuddered.

She considered ringing Jim. Asking his opinion. He knew his own son. She lifted the phone. Pressed his number in her Contacts list. It rang out. She was suddenly excited, looking forward to talking to him.

'Jim?'

'Claire, how are you?'

'I'm fine.'

'How did you get on in Beijing that last couple of days?' he asked, his voice warm.

'Not much happened. I just checked out some fashion outlets.'

'Did you do some sightseeing?'

'No.'

'Pity.'

'There's something I wanted to ask you.'

'Sure.'

'It's about Donal.'

'Is there a problem?' His voice was guarded.

'No, it's nothing like that,' she immediately reassured. 'I have to go away on business for a few days, and as I'm only just back from China I'm slightly worried about leaving Donal and Sophie here on their own again.' She felt guilty saying it, wondering would he resent her inference.

'I understand perfectly,' he laughed.

She was relieved.

'What do you think?'

'With young people it's always risky.'

'I'm not sure what to do. This is an opportunity for me in my job, I'd love to avail of it.'

'You have to, if it's worth that much to you.'

'Would you have a word with him or is that asking too much?' she suggested.

'When are you going?'

'Tuesday week, and I'll be back at the weekend.'

'I'll make it my business to drop in at some point. I should be up in Dublin.'

'That makes me feel a bit better.' She was relieved.

'I'm sure if you talk to them anyway, they'll understand. They're not completely irresponsible.'

That evening, she did chat to Donal and Sophie together, feeling a bit like a teacher. But the two of them didn't seem to think there was any problem.

'We have our own keys, sure we'll just come and go as usual,' Donal said.

'I know I said all this before I went to China, but there are to be no drinking parties just because you have an empty house,' she smiled as she said it.

They looked at each other.

'We understand,' Donal said.

'If I can't depend on you then it will make all the difference to me and I have to say that if anything happens then your contracts will be cancelled and you'll have to go.'

'We'll look after the house, don't worry,' Sophie assured. 'Just let us know if anything particular is happening, or anyone is calling.'

'Or if you want us to do anything,' Donal added.

'Thank you.' She felt a lot better about leaving them on their own and went in to work the following morning and told Liz that she would love to go to Paris.

'I'm delighted,' Liz hugged her.

The thought of the trip gave her a boost, even though she was still desperately lonely for Neil, unsure when she might get a chance to go to Beijing again.

Jim phoned her before she left for Paris, confirming that he would call around to see how Donal and Sophie were getting on, and she was very grateful to him.

'Enjoy Paris,' he said.

'It's a long time since I've been there,' she admitted, feeling a sense of nostalgia for the old days when Alan and herself had first met.

'I think we all have romantic memories of Paris.'

Chapter Twenty-three

On Saturday after work, Liz invited Claire to choose clothes for the week ahead from the store.

'I like to wear pieces from the designers we sell. We'll be meeting them there and they always like to see their own designs actually being worn by ordinary women instead of only on the fabulous models who swan up and down the runway.'

'I've never been at a couture fashion show, it's going to be amazing I'm sure,' Claire admitted.

'Apart from the designers we carry, I'm always interested in seeing new ranges, perhaps the ones you saw in China. We always need a fresh look.'

'I have to admit that some of them were a bit fantastical and might not suit our clientele in Dublin.'

'As you know, most of our clients like a classic look for day wear, although the younger ones certainly like something unusual when they're going to a particular event. Just to make a statement and maybe catch the headlines.'

'I'd say the style is magnificent, French women are so chic and even in their everyday lives they look beautiful.'

'Style is everything, and we're going to look just as chic as they are.'

Claire booked into the beauty salon before she left. While it was something she hadn't done in a long time, it was necessary and she enjoyed it. She had a facial, manicure, pedicure, and her hair re-styled.

It was a big dent in her budget. Although she felt it was the least she could do to look as good as possible for this very special event. The clothes were from their own designer range and both Liz and herself should look really elegant.

Hotel du Louvre was fabulous, and she couldn't believe that Liz had booked into such a luxurious hotel. The weather was pleasant, the autumn sun shone and that made all the difference.

'I'm off to bed early, Claire, I hope you don't mind?' Liz asked after dinner.

'Not at all, I've no intention of going on the town,' Claire smiled.

'It's hard going. There are runway shows each hour approximately, although I don't intend to go to all of them. We'll just choose the ones we stock ourselves first, and then see what else is out there which might be to our advantage. But we'll be kept busy. And then I have invitations to receptions by some of the fashion houses, so we have to find the time to go to those as well.'

'I had a look at the schedule you gave me and there is so much I can't imagine getting around it all.'

'Most of the shows are at the Carousel du Louvre, which is below the Louvre Museum, although a few are in other venues.'

'I particularly like Stella McCartney and Vivienne Westwood.' Claire was excited.

'And Victoria Beckham too.'

'I wonder what tones and textures will be popular for next year,' Claire asked, finishing her cup of coffee.

'I didn't like some of last year's collections, a lot of checks and leathers, it would have to be an improvement on those,' Liz smiled. 'Now, what will you wear tomorrow. We want to make an entrance when we arrive.'

'I thought I'd wear the black Armani with the white trim.'

'Perfect.'

To get to the Louvre, they took the hotel limousine which Liz had arranged even though it was just a short distance. 'Right, this is it,' Liz smiled as she swung her legs out of the door and stood up on purple stilettos which were at least six inches in height, and exactly matched her Givenchy coat and dress.

They went into the foyer, presented their accreditations and were ushered through to the reception. There were quite a few people already gathered. White jacketed waiters moved from group to group with trays of champagne flutes, and others stopped to offer coffee and hors d'oeuvres.

'I think I'll have coffee, it's a bit early for champagne,' quipped Liz.

'Same for me,' Claire was anxious to keep a clear head during the day.

'Liz?' a handsome silver-haired man appeared beside them. '*Ma Chérie*?' He kissed her.

'*Enchanté Pierre,*' she said, and then turned to Claire. 'I'd like to introduce my colleague, Claire Brennan.'

He took her hand. 'How lovely to meet you,' he said in perfect English.

'Likewise, Pierre,' she murmured, smiling. She felt a bit out of her depth because her knowledge of French was limited and she didn't even have the confidence to try using a few words.

'*Maintenant* …' he began and then stopped speaking for a few seconds. '*Désolé*, I forget myself …' he smiled at her. 'But there are many people I have to see, *tout a l'heure.*' He drifted off into the crowd.

'Interesting man,' commented Claire.

'Very,' laughed Liz. 'Important and influential in the fashion business.'

They moved through the people, and Liz was in conversation with many of them. And Claire was more than surprised to hear that she could speak French, Italian and German.

'You're so fluent in languages,' Claire said as they helped themselves to hors d'oeuvres.

'I have a smattering.'

'More than that.'

'I always feel it's good to be able to speak with people in their own language, but most revert to English if there is anyone else there. Like Pierre did when he realised that you didn't speak French.'

'I have a little, but he wouldn't have been very impressed with my childish efforts.'

'Do you speak Mandarin with your family when you visit them in China?'

'No, they all speak English.'

'That's a pity, although I'm sure you have picked up some of the language, you go over fairly often,' Liz seemed very interested.

'I don't see much of them, although I did meet my mother in law for the first time on the last visit.'

'The first time?' she looked puzzled.

'It's a long story, I'll tell you about it later.' Claire had been thinking that she should tell Liz what was happening in her life, particularly if she needed time off unexpectedly. But she had to wait for the right moment to mention it. Even though she was caught up with this trip to Paris, Neil was always there in the back of her mind.

'*Isabelle, come vá?*' Liz smiled at the beautiful dark-haired woman who walked towards them.

'*Molto bene, e tú?*' she kissed Liz.

'This is my colleague, Claire Brennan, and it's her first time at Paris Fashion Week.'

'You will enjoy, Claire, it is a wonderful show, your head will be spinning.' Isabelle kissed her as well.

'I am looking forward to seeing your designs,' Claire said.

'They are always exquisite.'

'Grazie.'

'I see you are showing your collection this afternoon?' Liz asked.

'Yes, I am so nervous, you wouldn't believe.' She raised her eyes to heaven and fluttered her hands dramatically.

'It will be very successful I'm sure,' Liz smiled confidently.

Claire had chosen to wear one of Isabelle's evening dresses at dinner and she felt very honoured to meet this particular designer personally.

'Let's go into the salon.' Liz put down her coffee cup, and they walked through. 'It's time.'

They had a good position in the second row and were delighted to be so close to the runway. There was a loud buzz of chat which slowly diminished as a man in a black tuxedo appeared.

'*Le maitre de cérémonie,*' murmured Liz.

A thrill fluttered through Claire.

He began to speak in French. She was able to understand most of what he was saying, as she knew the content, but then he switched to English, and she relaxed back in her chair.

The first models appeared on the runway, the gowns they wore floated as they moved with that smooth slinky walk. The designs were very delicate this year. The fabrics floated like gossamer and revealed shimmering bodies as the models passed by.

It was the beginning of an amazing day. They attended two designer shows in the morning, Ulyana Sergeenko, and Iris Van Herpen. After a delicious lunch, they attended Dior, followed by Isabelle's show whose designs for this season were really classy. She used black in many of the suits and gowns and Liz was really enthused. 'I can think of new clients who will love her designs for next year, although there are a few of our regulars who are real devotees already who will scream out loud,' she said excitedly.

'I know who you mean,' Claire laughed.

They went back to the hotel to rest and took the limousine to the Palais Royale for dinner with Isabelle's Fashion House. Claire felt good wearing the silver full length gown designed by Isabelle and when they arrived she was very pleased to see her wearing it.

'*Bellissima, mi fa piacere*,' she said, and embraced Claire when she saw her. Then threw her arms around Liz. '*Vieni, siediti vicini a me.*'

Both Claire and Liz felt it was a compliment to sit at the table beside Isabelle. It was a very pleasant evening although Claire didn't say very much as mostly the guests were speaking in a mixture of English and Italian, but she could follow the conversation which was invariably about fashion. Afterwards, a few of the other people there decided to go on to a club but Liz and Claire declined. She needed to soak up as much about the fashion business and be on top of her game over the following few days so really late nights wouldn't help, and neither would too much alcohol, the inevitable result of a night in a Parisian club.

Early the following morning, Claire and Liz cross-checked their notes on lines and designs they had seen so far.

'I must say you've certainly tuned into the business quickly, and that particular line was one I hadn't really considered. I'm really looking forward to hearing what you think today.' Liz seemed really pleased.

They kept to their schedule and went to the salon at the Louvre to see the shows of Julien Sournié, Estelle Martine, and Givenchy which were all fascinating. Once again there was a reception in the evening, and they met even more interesting people in the fashion world. For a change, Claire was on a high.

The following day they went to shows which specialised in

shoes and handbags.

'This is my forte. You know what I'm like,' Claire laughed.

'Mine too,' Liz grinned as they swanned through the foyer.

As she followed, Claire suddenly felt guilty. Why was she feeling happy? The question resonated. Her heart sank as she realised that she shouldn't feel this happy. Or maybe it wasn't being happy. This sudden rush of feeling was inexplicable. Since Neil had been taken from her, there was a dull mass inside her. Sometimes it caught her breath. Sometimes it made her feel physically sick. Sometimes she felt like choking on it. And suddenly, today, it wasn't there. She looked at Liz, and their eyes met. This woman had changed her life. And Claire couldn't even tell her how that had happened. She had given her something very special. Even if it was only for this moment, one moment, she was grateful.

Claire looked at the schedule. 'Bruno Magli.'

Music blared. It was some tune from the sixties. She couldn't remember the group, but the rhythm whipped up something in her. She looked up with anticipation as the first model came out, wearing a pair of red suede shoes with amazing glass heels. Then the next model appeared dressed in blue leather and thigh-high silver boots with matching trim. She whistled silently, wishing she had the courage to wear a pair of fantastic boots like those.

'What do you think,' Liz whispered.

'Amazing.'

'Do you think we should order?'

'In every colour,' Claire smiled. 'And in the full range of sizes.'

Liz giggled. 'Right.'

Next, it was Stefi Talman among others. And later they attended the bag designers. Seeing the most beautifully crafted handbags from an Italian company, Boldrini Selleria.

'The delivery is quite slow,' warned Liz.

'But they're beautiful.'

'I love Wandler, those geometric shapes are so different and very unusual.'

'The leather looks so soft, and the colours have such richness.'

'There's quite a mix of trends. We could order smaller designs as well as the larger totes.'

'Gives us more opportunity to sell a handbag to suit the style the client is wearing.'

'There is such a range available, although it's a risk investment.'

'We'll have the best range in Dublin.'

'The word will go around.'

'Should we invite all the clients to a reception and give them an idea of the various clothes we've decided to order. It will blow their minds, particularly the accessories and the range of shoes and boots.'

'Let's organise that as soon as we get back.'

'Great idea.'

They went to the final event and said goodbye to all the people they had met over the few days, and headed back to the hotel. Before she went to sleep, Claire took a colourful card with a bright rainbow across the top from her briefcase and using it as a desk she lay back on the pillows and thought about what she would say to Neil.

My dear Neil, I hope you are well, and enjoying school. I'm sure your teachers are all very nice to you and that your studies are not too hard. What subjects do you like best in the new school? Tell me what they are. Are you still playing the piano? I miss the sound of your music in the house. I would love to hear you play. What is your favourite piece of music now, tell me what it is and I'll listen to it and imagine that it is you playing the piano at home.

I am very busy in the store, but when I see you we will definitely make plenty of time to have lots of fun. When you come home, we will have a big celebration. I am sending you a new scarf and gloves which I hope will keep you warm in the winter. I am looking forward to hearing from you. Maybe your Dad might let you call me or send a text on your phone to me. I'm sure he has bought you a new one by now, as you forgot to take yours when you left.

I send you much love and kisses and wish I could see you soon. Mum. xxx

Claire and Liz were home the following afternoon. She had really enjoyed the few days in Paris much to her surprise, but that element of guilt which had stolen over her yesterday weighed heavily. A feeling that she shouldn't even be happy. She had allowed her husband to take her son away. How weak she was. Why didn't she stand up to him? Employ solicitors. Go to the Irish Embassy. Ask them to speak to Alan on her behalf. She hated herself for not having the strength.

Chapter Twenty-Four

Jim called to Claire's house during that week she had been away. Donal was surprised to see him. 'I just wanted to see the two of you, hope you're hard at work,' he laughed.

'Doing a bit, Dad,' Donal replied with a broad grin.

'How is Sophie?'

'She's studying at the library. She prefers it, while I'm happy enough here.' He closed the door behind his father. 'I was just about to have a coffee, would you like one?' Donal walked up the hall.

'Thanks.' Jim followed his son into the kitchen.

Donal made the coffee.

'Are you happy with the course?' Jim asked. Aware that a number of first year students often became bored within a few weeks.

'Yeah, I'm enjoying it.'

'Glad to hear it.' They continued chatting until Jim finished and stood up to rinse the cup at the sink.

'You're working in Dublin this week?' asked Donal.

He nodded.

'You could have stayed here. There are two beds in my room. I can shove all the stuff off the one I don't use,' he laughed. 'Won't take that long.'

'No thanks, I'm booked into the Clayton. I have to stay somewhere, and I certainly can't stay here. What if Claire arrived back? We'd be in right trouble then.'

'She wouldn't mind,' Donal said. 'She's very easy-going.'

'Perhaps,' Jim smiled.

'Anyway, I'll have to get back to the books.' Donal walked down the hall with his father.

'You'll be in Ennis at the weekend?'

'Going to the match.'

'Have you got tickets?'

'Yeah.'

'Any chance of a spare one?' Jim asked.

'I'll ask around, I'm sure to get one.'

'How are you fixed for money?' Jim asked.

'I can always do with a few euro,' Donal grinned.

As Jim drove back to the hotel, he thought about Claire. She had been on his mind since he had first met her. Seeing her in Beijing had accentuated his interest even more, although she had not responded in any way to him. In fact, on the night he had invited her to dinner she had been guarded in her conversation, and he had to watch Tony make a distinct play for her. Although, Jim was glad that she didn't seem particularly interested in him. although he knew she had lunch with him. Tony was a well-known womaniser, and Jim had met various girlfriends over the years. Most of them had been among the ex-pat community and hadn't lasted very long.

To his surprise, Claire actually called him the evening she returned from Paris.

'Jim?'

'Claire? How did the trip go?' He wondered why she had called.

'It was amazing, although we didn't see much of Paris, it was all business, shows, receptions, dinners. Paris Fashion Week is in a world of its own.'

'I'm glad you enjoyed it.'

'I did, which surprised me,' she had to admit.

'I'm not into designer gear,' he laughed. 'I get out of my formal suits just as soon as I can. The sort of business I do dictates that I wear suits. It's really nice to talk to you, it seems ages. I called up to Donal the other night, just wanted to keep an eye on what was going on. But he had the head down in the books, and Sophie studies in the library every evening apparently.'

'That's right. I hope they both do well, they deserve it.'

'I was going to call you tomorrow,' he admitted.

'Beat you to it.'

He could hear the humour in her voice.

'Would you like to have dinner with me some night next week?'

'I must check my diary.'

He could hear that hesitancy in her voice again, and immediately felt disappointed.

'Give me a call if you have time.'

'What night would suit you?'

'How about Tuesday?'

'Yes, I'm sure I'm free.'

A sense of euphoria swept through him. 'I'm looking forward to seeing you. I'll pick you up about seven-thirty?'

He pressed the off button and yelled out loud. That was amazing, it was like telepathy. Was she thinking about him as much as he was thinking about her?

Chapter Twenty-five

On Tuesday evening, Claire decided to wear a plain black dress, black suede stilettos, and her black coat trimmed with faux fur. Her only jewellery was a silver necklace and matching earrings. Downstairs, she glanced at herself in the full-length mirror in the hall and thought that she didn't look so bad considering she hadn't been sleeping at all well since she returned from Paris. Her mind was so full of Neil, she tossed and turned trying to get to sleep, but it proved almost impossible and it was only in the small hours that she eventually drifted off, and even then, he was always there in her dreams. She wandered into the kitchen to check everything was turned off, and that the back door was locked and as she passed his photo on the counter, she stroked it gently. A pang of loss swept through her and she had to try hard to prevent herself from crying. Just then the doorbell rang, and she blinked rapidly as she hurried down the hall and opened the door.

'Hi, you're looking wonderful,' Jim said.

'Thank you.' She invited him in. 'I'm just about ready,' she said, thinking that he looked attractive this evening, wearing a grey jacket, slacks, and open necked white shirt.

'No hurry, I booked a table for eight o'clock.'

'Would you like something before we go, cup of coffee or a drink?'

'No thanks, I won't be drinking anyway as I'm driving.'

'Where are we going?'

'It's a small restaurant off South William Street.'

La Maison was a cosy place and was packed with patrons this evening. Claire hadn't been here before and liked the atmosphere. They were taken to their table and the waiter handed them the menus.

'What would you like to drink?' Jim asked.

'Water thanks, it's mid-week and I have to work tomorrow.'

'We'll both have to stay sober,' he laughed. 'Now let's order.'

The waiter came with some hors d'oeuvres and they picked at them as they waited for their food to arrive.

'This is very different to the last time we had dinner in Beijing,' Jim smiled.

'It was very enjoyable and nice to meet your friends, Tony and Peter.'

'And some coincidence for us to meet at the hotel, one million to one I'd say.'

'Yes, it was.'

The waiter arrived with their starters.

'This looks delicious.' Claire picked up her knife and fork.

'I've only been here with clients a couple of times.'

The main course she chose was a prawn dish, simple and tasty. Jim ate hake.

'I don't eat meat these days, gave it up a year or two ago.'

'I'm much the same.'

They continued to eat, both enjoying their meals. They talked of Beijing, and he explained about his business. She was so anxious to ask him about that fascinating city, anything else she might have said seemed pretentious and meaningless. She looked around the restaurant. Watched the people chatting, their faces animated with interest in each other.

The waiter returned with the dessert menu.

Jim smiled. 'Do you have a sweet tooth?'

'I like to read the menu but very seldom choose anything.'

'Let's share something.'

She glanced down the list and smiled. 'How about *chocolat a la crème*?'

'Perfect.'

The dessert came on one plate, with two spoons.

She was more relaxed. A stream of conversation about her work, her friends, her family, and before she even knew it was going to happen she was talking about Neil.

'Yes, you showed me his photo.' His grey eyes brightened.

She lowered her head to hide the tears and dabbed her face with the white cotton napkin.

He put out his hand and covered hers.

'What is wrong?' he asked softly. 'Where is he?'

'Beijing.'

Understanding flashed across his features.

His hand pressed hers gently. 'You should have told me.'

'I was afraid.'

'Why?'

'I don't know. You see, that's the problem, I don't know.' She covered her face.

'Don't cry, Claire.'

'I must leave,' she whispered. 'I feel embarrassed.'

'There's no need to feel that way.' Jim let go of her hand and signalled to the waiter for the bill.

He paid quickly with his credit card and the waiter then brought their coats. He helped Claire on with hers, and they walked out.

'Would you like to go somewhere else?' Jim asked, putting his arm around her.

'No thanks.'

'Let's go to the car then.'

They walked back in silence to where he had parked the car and sat in.

'I always find this underground carpark fascinating,' he said.

'It takes me back to when it was used as a bonded warehouse. I imagine that years ago all these archways were full of barrels of brandy and whiskey. See how they seem to go on forever?' He looked into the distance.

She could see what he meant, and even though the divisions were full of parked cars, there was still something mysterious about it.

He put his hand on hers for a moment but made no move to start the car. 'I'm sorry if I said something to upset you.'

'No, it wasn't your fault. It's just very raw,' she murmured. Unsure of what to say to him.

'I understand. But you saw your son when you were over that last time? How did he seem then?'

'I didn't see him.'

He looked puzzled.

'I may as well tell you the truth,' she decided.

He waited.

She took a deep breath and explained. Unexpectedly, it seemed to help. To keep telling lies to everyone up to now was stressful.

'But that's illegal?' he exploded.

'In Ireland, but in China things are very different. They haven't signed up to the international agreement on child abduction.'

'I wonder would the Embassy help?'

'I've told Tony about Neil when I was in Beijing but I can't ask him to do anything. I'm so afraid that Alan will find out.'

'I understand.'

'How long will it take you to get home?' she asked.

'I should be home in a couple of hours.'

'It's a long journey at this time of night.'

'There'll be no traffic on the road so it will be easy.'

'Thanks for driving up especially,' she said. 'I appreciate that.'

'It's my pleasure,' he smiled.

'And thank you for the lovely dinner.'

'I'm glad you enjoyed it.'

She pressed down the handle and pushed open the door. Conscious that her dress had slid up and was very revealing. 'I'm sorry I lost control earlier, I hope it didn't spoil the evening for you.'

'Not at all, don't even think about that. I'm just sorry about the situation with Neil. I hope you will have some contact with him soon.'

'Thanks.' She stood up.

He climbed out the other side of the car and came around to her. Drew her close to him and kissed her softly.

'This was very special,' he murmured. His fingers stroked her cheek.

Her heart throbbed. She could feel its rhythm resound within her.

'Can I see you again?' His eyes searched hers.

'Yes,' she whispered, as if to pledge her whole life to him for ever.

'I'll call you to arrange another evening.' He kissed her again. His lips warm.

To her astonishment deep inside she wanted more of him. But something held her back. And she obeyed in spite of herself.

'Drive carefully,' she said.

'I'll be thinking of you.' He drew her close again for a moment. 'If I can be of any help with my contacts in Beijing please let me know.'

She walked up to the front door, and looked to where he stood, and waved. He did the same, climbed into the car, flashed the lights once, and drove away into the distance of the night.

Jim drove steadily along the motorway. He couldn't believe what had happened. It certainly hadn't been part of any plan he might have had. He admitted to himself that he had been attracted to Claire from their first meeting, and when he met her in Beijing it had cemented those feelings. But this evening he had been so glad to meet her again. As she became very emotional about her son Neil, it seemed to affect him. He was now seeing a different Claire. Someone who cared so deeply about Neil she couldn't hold back her feelings and all he wanted to do was to put his arms around her and hold her close.

His emotions were running so high, he felt like a teenager who had just met a girl in school and planned to ask her to the disco. But did she return his feelings? That was the big question. He had not felt so deeply about anyone since his wife had died. What was Claire thinking at this very moment? She had to be either regretting meeting him or looking forward to seeing him again. But how was he going to know which it was?

He was puzzled. But then remembered she had said she would meet him again. Since he had first met Claire, and she had stolen her way into his heart, he had found himself in a very unexpected place. A man in his forties. A widower with a grown son. And he was in love.

What would Donal think of him having a relationship with a woman other than his mother. That was the most difficult part of it. But guilt was there too and that would have to be faced as well.

Chapter Twenty-six

What had just happened had shaken Claire. And now her mind was possessed by Jim's eyes and his smile. His kisses had been so intimate she wondered did it mean he felt something for her. When she met him in Beijing she certainly hadn't anticipated that there might be a relationship between them. There was only one thing on her mind and that was to hold Neil in her arms once again.

But she had to admit that she was attracted to Jim. Delight raced through her at the prospect of seeing him again. This was the first time that any man had shown interest in her since long before she was married. Still, perhaps his invite to see her again was just casual? His kisses didn't necessarily mean anything. Don't think about it, she reminded herself and tried to sleep, finally managing to drift off. She needed her rest as she had to catch an early flight to London with Liz to visit a fashion show the following day.

'I'm getting used to this lifestyle,' Claire said, laughing as they checked in to a five-star hotel. She had to hide her own feelings while she was with Liz. She was her employer after all. A long grim face was not something which she would expect from an employee. They were in the fashion business. Out there in a glamorous world of beautiful people. The whole thing had a Hollywood feel about it. So she smiled and chatted enthusiastically as if it was the only thing that mattered to her.

'Enjoy it while you can,' Liz said as they took the lift up to the second floor.

The porter escorted them to their rooms, and they were followed by another who carried their bags.

'Let's change and head on over to the museum where the show is being held. We've been invited to a reception there before it opens. How long do you need?' Liz asked.

'Shower, re-do my face, change. Just half an hour?'

'I'll order a car then, meet you in the foyer.'

Claire went into her room. A beautifully appointed suite which she could never have afforded to stay in herself. She put down her bags and stared around. Just then, her phone rang. As ever excitement charged through her as she thought that it might be Alan and she grabbed it.

'Claire, how are you?'

It was Jim, and immediately she was disappointed. It was always like that every time her phone rang. She just wanted it to be Alan. Or even more than Alan, her darling Neil.

'Thanks for last night, I did enjoy it.' She was grateful.

'So did I, although I was sorry to see you so upset.'

'It happens,' she said in an effort to brush it off as if it didn't matter which was always difficult to do.

'Are you busy today?' he asked.

'I'm in London.'

'For pleasure or work?'

'Work.'

'Hope it goes well.'

'We'll be at a fashion show today and fly back tomorrow. Liz needs to see what particular designers are trending for next year. It's mostly evening wear.'

'Sounds glamorous. Enjoy.'

'I'm sorry, but I can't talk for long, I've about twenty minutes to get ready.'

'Not to worry. I'll keep in touch, maybe we can get together soon,' he said. 'Good to talk to you. Take care.'

Liz came down in the lift just a couple of minutes after Claire and together they walked through the doors. A man, dressed in top hat and tails, walked down the steps ahead of them and held open the door of a shining black Mercedes.

'I thought it was a taxi?' she gasped.

'Compliments of the hotel,' Liz said with a grin. 'Regular treat.'

'That cream suit you're wearing is exquisite,' Claire said, admiring the chic lines.

'Thank you, although I'm not feeling great today,' she grimaced.

'What do you mean?' Claire was concerned.

'I'll explain later,' Liz patted her hand.

It was only when she made that remark Claire thought Liz looked very tired and hoped there was nothing amiss. The fashion house had booked a whole floor of the modern art museum for their show, and as they were served champagne and finger food they walked around and looked at the various paintings which adorned the walls. But they didn't get much chance to admire them as people immediately saw Liz and came over to make her acquaintance. Quite a number of them were people they had met in Paris so there was a lot of chat about that show. As people began to drift into the room where the runway had been set up, Liz suddenly put her hand on Claire's arm and gripped. She looked at her and was shocked to see that she had become very pale.

'Are you feeling all right?' she asked.

She nodded but didn't say anything, although her tight grip on Claire's arm didn't ease. They continued on, and she was very glad when they reached the chairs and Liz was able to sit.

'Can I get you anything?'

'Water, if you wouldn't mind.'

Claire went over to the bar and came back with a glass of water for Liz.

'Thank you.' She sipped it, and slowly the colour seeped back into her cheeks.

The show began and Liz seemed to improve, following the models as they minced down the runway wearing the most extravagant evening gowns.

'The beading is exquisite,' Claire said, as one model passed wearing a black silk creation with diamante beads in a swirling design.

Liz nodded, but didn't say anything else.

Claire was worried about her and hoped that the show wouldn't continue for too long. Although it took time for the models to appear, walk down the runway and display the clothes. There was a loud ripple of applause at the end and one of the designers came over and took Liz's hand.

'Would you like to join us for dinner, Liz, there are just a small group of us?'

'I'm sorry, but I'm quite tired this evening, if you wouldn't mind?' Liz apologised.

'Of course not, but we'll miss your company and Claire as well of course,' she smiled at her.

'Thank you.'

Their car was waiting outside and they were taken back to the hotel.

'I think you should go to bed, Liz,' Claire suggested.

'Yes, I will,' she sighed.

'Are you in pain?'

She nodded.

'Have you ever had it before?' Claire asked.

'I haven't been well lately,' Liz admitted.

'Come into the bedroom, just lie down for a while.'

She agreed to do that, lay on the pillows and closed her eyes.

Claire covered her with the quilt. 'Are you warm enough?'

'Yes thanks.'

'I'll order tea and toast, maybe that would help?' Claire sat by the bed.

She nodded.

'Should I ask a doctor to call to see you?'

'No, I've to go to hospital in Dublin next week for tests.'

'I'm worried about you.'

'I'll be all right, and we're going home tomorrow, thanks be to God.'

Room Service was very quick, and to Claire's relief, Liz actually drank some tea and ate the toast.

'What do you take for the pain?' Claire asked when Liz had changed into her night wear and climbed into bed again.

'I've some tablets in my handbag.'

'I'll get them for you.'

Liz drifted off to sleep and Claire stretched out on the chaise longue in her bedroom. She was very worried about Liz and wasn't going to go to her own suite in case she had a turn during the night. She would have preferred to get a doctor but obviously Liz didn't want that, so she decided to keep an eye on her.

Claire only dozed off occasionally and every time she checked on her, Liz was heavily asleep. Obviously, the tablets had helped. She slept on in the morning as well, and Claire didn't wake her until she had ordered breakfast.

'How are you feeling?'

'I'm all right now,' Liz smiled.

'You look better, I'm so relieved.'

136

'Thanks for looking after me through the night.'

'I did nothing.' She put the tray on her lap.

'You were here all night, I did wake at one point and saw you lying on the chaise longue.'

'Eat up. It will keep you going. Do you feel strong enough to travel back?' Claire asked.

'Can't wait to get home,' she sighed.

'We'll take our time. I've organised the car to take us to the airport, and, I hope you don't mind but I've booked a wheelchair to go through. You know it's much quicker.'

'At this stage I don't care, thank you.' Liz patted her arm and smiled.

They arrived at the airport in good time and caught the flight without any delay.

'Thank you so much for being there for me, Claire.'

'I was glad to be with you. But I wonder should you ask your own doctor to call just to check you out?'

'No, I'll be seeing my consultant tomorrow.'

Chapter Twenty-seven

On the Friday leading up to the Halloween celebration, the boys and girls in Neil's class were allowed to wear a Halloween outfit into college and have a party at lunch time. Neil felt excluded from it as he didn't have an outfit to wear and spent the previous few days worrying about what he was going to do. But finally, he took courage.

'Dad?'

'Yes?'

'Can I ask you something?'

'Of course, you can.' He seemed to be in good humour this evening and Neil felt confident.

'On Friday we are having a Halloween party and we can wear our outfits into school.'

'Halloween?' he barked.

Neil nodded.

'Why do you keep mentioning Halloween. I told you that you couldn't go to the party.'

'But this is different, Dad.'

'What's different about it, Halloween is Halloween and we don't celebrate it here.'

'I thought you said you had a ghost party, and the teacher told us about that.'

'It's entirely different.'

'The teacher said it was a pagan festival and lots of countries will celebrate.'

Alan had a look of frustration on his face. 'That's nonsense.'

'But the teacher …' Neil began again.

'Stop, that's enough. You're not going into school wearing anything other than your uniform.'

'We could make something,' Nai Nai murmured.

'What do you mean, Mother?' Alan barked.

'I have some fabric in the sewing room. Neil can tell us what he wants, and I can make an outfit.'

'Really Mother.' Alan was cross.

'He will stand out among the other children if all of them are wearing outfits,' she pointed out.

'They should all be wearing their school uniform.'

'Alan, please, our boy could be ostracized, surely you don't want that?'

Neil listened. Unable to believe that Nai Nai was standing up for him. She had never done that before.

Alan stared at his mother, silenced for a moment. 'Let me think on it,' he said sharply, and stood up from the table.

Neil looked at Nai Nai. 'Thank you,' he whispered.

'What type of outfit would you like?' she asked.

His eyes lit up. 'At home, I had a wizard outfit with a pointy hat and a black cloak with gold stars and moons on it. And I had a wand.' He described it in detail.

'I'm sure I will be able to make such an outfit for you, I have some fabric.'

'Can you?' He had a wide smile on his face.

'I am very good at sewing.'

'But Dad might not agree,' he said, suddenly gloomy once again.

'I will talk to him.'

'Thank you so much Nai Nai. My Mum always let me wear a Halloween outfit.'

'You will have one this time as well.' She stood up and kissed him.

He was very grateful to Nai Nai and hoped that his Dad would agree with her plan to make him an outfit and let him wear it to school. That reminded him of Halloweens when he was at home. The fun he had with his Mum as they put up the scary signs in the windows. Vampires, witches and wizards, sparkling lights on the trees in the garden and around the front door. And he enjoyed eating the Halloween brack his mother always bought, meeting his friends all dressed up in their outfits and walking down the road to watch the fireworks which were going off in various places. And his Mum always allowed him to ask his friends around afterwards. But now he really missed his Mum and wondered when his father would take him home.

To his great excitement, the following evening, Nai Nai called him into her own room.

'Look at these pieces of fabric here, do you think they would suit?'

He nodded.

'I'll have to make a long cloak, and cut some shapes out of the other colours and sew them on.'

'It looks great.' He was really pleased.

'I will check the size,' She took a tape and measured the length from his shoulder to his heel. And took the other measurements as well. 'What size do you want the hat to be?'

He showed her by holding his hand above his head.

She then took up a pen and made a drawing of the outfit.

'That looks great, Nai Nai, I like it.' He hugged her.

'You will be as good as anyone else at the school festival, my grandson. It will be ready by tomorrow when you return from school.'

'Thank you, Nai Nai.' Neil was very grateful to his grandmother. And only wished that he could show the outfit to his Mum, and tell her how excited he was to be going into school on the following day dressed up for Halloween.

'Who's going to win the prize for the best outfit,' Robert grinned at Neil.

'You will, vampire,' Neil laughed.

'Come to the party tomorrow, will you?' Robert asked.

'Sorry I can't, we're going somewhere, Dad has plans,' Neil explained hesitantly.

'Pity, let's get some more food.' Robert thumped him on the back.

It was one of the best fun days Neil had since he had come here. And he loved every minute, even though he didn't win the first prize. When he arrived home that night, he put his wizard outfit hanging on the outside of the wardrobe and lay in bed looking at it, remembering other Halloweens.

Chapter Twenty-eight

'How are you, Liz?' Claire enquired.

'Not so good.'

'What do you mean exactly?'

'They're keeping me in hospital for more tests.'

'I hope you're all right.' Claire was worried.

'So do I. But it causes a difficulty with work. Would you be able to step into my position for a few days?'

'If you think I'm able?'

'Of course you are.'

Phones rang constantly and clients arrived needing personal attention and it was very busy right through the week. Claire was still there at eight o'clock on Friday and she was very glad that the sales figures were good since Liz had left her in charge all this week.

Finished at last, she was just about to leave the building when she received a call from Jim.

'I just drove past and saw all the lights on.'

'I'm just closing up.'

'Would you like to have a drink?' he asked. 'I'm sure you have had a hectic day.'

'Thanks, that would be nice.'

'I'll pick you up.'

'Just drive down the lane on the left of the building, turn right and I'll let you into our own carpark.'

Jim looked around admiringly when he came in.

'Liz runs a very luxurious fashion store.'

'Are you normally here alone at this time of night?'

'No, usually Liz is here too, but she's not well.'

'Nothing serious?'

'I hope not.' They walked out to the back, and she pressed in the code and all the shutters closed electronically.

'Where would you like to go?' he asked.

'Sometimes the staff go to *The Bank* for a coffee, it's quite a nice place and not too far away.'

'I know it.' They walked up the laneway towards the brightly lit street. 'You should be careful walking here, it's very dark.'

'I drive out usually, but now that I have a tall bodyguard with me, I'm not worried,' she laughed.

They went into the pub and managed to get a comfortable seat near the back. It was very busy. Lots of people chatting, the noise level high. The usual Friday night.

'What are we going to drink? We're both driving. Would you like a coffee?'

'That would be fine, thanks.'

He managed to get the attention of a passing waiter and ordered.

'It's lovely to relax, it's been madly busy. But I am worried about Liz.'

'I hope everything is ok.'

'So do I.'

'I'm delighted to see you. I had a meeting in town. It ran late,' Jim explained. 'And I fly out to Amsterdam in the morning, and then on to various other places next week. Have you heard anything from your son, Neil?'

'No,' she said abruptly.

'It's terrible. Your husband must be very insensitive.'

'Ex.'

'To prevent a child from seeing his mother is really hard on both you and Neil.'

The waiter arrived with their coffee.

'Did he enjoy being with his grandparents on previous occasions?'

'He did, so I don't feel it's a prison or anything like that. They're very wealthy and when I went to Beijing that first time Alan let me talk to him on the phone, and he told me he was having a great time. Fishing and riding with his grandfather at their country place.' Claire sipped her coffee. The heat of the place was getting to her and she felt tired.

'More coffee?' he asked.

'No thank you, I think I should go home. Tomorrow will be another very busy day,' she said.

'I can see it on your face.' He was sympathetic. 'Let's go, you need your rest.'

She stood up, and he helped her on with her coat, a pale pink three-quarter length, which she wore with a black felt hat.

They walked back to the store, his arm around her. The town was busy with Friday night revellers, but all she wanted to do was to go home.

'It was lovely seeing you again, Claire.'

'Sorry, I'm not good company tonight. I'm always exhausted by the end of the week.'

'You'll always be good company to me,' he smiled.

She looked into his eyes and could see that he meant it.

'Maybe you might give me a call when you feel better?' he asked.

She nodded. Not sure when that would be and feeling guilty that she had curtailed their evening.

'Thank you.' He kissed her on the cheek. A light brush of his lips.

'I'll reverse out first and wait until you lock up.' He climbed

144

into his car.

She did the same and followed. With the remote control she closed the gates, and then inserted the code for the alarm system. He drove away towards the north side of the city, and she turned in the opposite direction.

The situation with Neil, and Liz being ill, all weighed heavily on her, and she was sorry to have been so dreary with Jim. What must he have thought of her? When he took her out to dinner recently she had broken down. Tonight she wasn't much better. She imagined that it was probably the last time he would meet her. He had actually put the ball in her court anyway. And she didn't know what to do with it.

Claire was kept very busy welcoming clients and taking them around the different departments. Quite a number of them needed help with their choices, and this was an aspect of her job which she enjoyed. Always interested in giving her opinion as to what suited a particular person. Reluctant to say that this dress was too fussy for the event. Or that jacket was too long for the person's figure. Her mood lifted.

In the afternoon, her phone rang. She looked around and noting that everyone in the store had a sales person with them, she hurried into the office, excited to see that it was a Chinese number.

'Hi Claire,' a woman with an Irish accent said. 'This is Alison, Peter's wife.'

'It's lovely to hear from you.'

'Tony was telling us that your son, Neil, may be going to one of the schools in Beijing. My son Robert goes to the International College and has a friend called Neil Wang Li.'

'Neil,' Claire whispered his name.

'I presume Neil is the same age as Robert, thirteen?'

'Yes, I wondered what he looks like?'

'He's a lovely boy. Tall and quite thin. He has black hair, and brown eyes. Do you think he sounds like your boy?'

'Yes.' Tears filled her eyes and she couldn't speak for a moment. 'Does he get on well with your Robert?' she blurted, wiping her eyes with a tissue.

'They're quite friendly. But he's not allowed to come over to our house, Robert had his birthday party a while back but Neil couldn't come unfortunately. He seems to spend all of his time studying.'

'Does he play piano?' Claire asked.

'Yes, I believe he does.'

'And it's the International College?' Claire asked. She couldn't believe she was hearing this, it was amazing. 'Do the boys talk on the phone?'

'Neil doesn't have a phone. Robert and Paul can't understand that at all.'

'Paul?'

'Robert's younger brother, he's nine.'

'Even speaking to you, Alison, has eased my mind. It would be wonderful if it happens to be my Neil. Thank you so much for calling me, I do appreciate it, take care.' Claire cut off the call, her mind in a crazy place. She felt shocked. It was almost as if she had seen Neil but then had lost him again. For those few minutes as Alison had talked about the friend of Robert, she was there with her. Seeing this boy whom she had described, and recognising him, she had wanted to scream his name out loud. But that had been in one moment of madness. Now she had no opportunity to gather her thoughts, which were frittered away into a million pieces of memory and refused to be caught by her shaking fingers.

Chapter Twenty-nine

Claire was a worrier by nature and had been in worry mode since Neil had left. Now added to that she could imagine Liz going through all the tests, some of which might be very invasive. And as it could take some time to receive the results, Claire was on that same journey with her.

She checked in with Liz. 'How did you get on today?' she asked.

'Well, unfortunately I'll be staying here. I must have a triple by-pass.'

'That's awful.'

'Heart blockage.'

'I'm so sorry,' Claire was shocked.

'The doctor said I could have a heart attack at any time, so I'm probably lucky to be still here.'

'When will you have the surgery?'

'In a couple of days.'

'I hope you'll be all right.'

'They tell me it's a very successful operation. But it does make an awful mess of my life,' Liz admitted.

'I can look after the business while you're in hospital if you can trust me, so don't worry about that.'

'It's my biggest concern.'

'Relax, I'll look after things for you.'

'Thanks so much, Claire, I do appreciate it. I have every confidence in you.'

'And I'm sure you'll be back on your feet in no time and feeling really good.'

'I hope so.'

'Can I bring you in anything? You didn't think this was going to happen so I'm sure you'll need extra night wear and other bits and pieces.'

'Would you?'

'Of course, but do you mind a stranger going around your apartment?'

'I don't consider you to be a stranger, Claire, so never think that.' She could hear a laugh in Liz's voice.

'Thank you.'

'Could you pop into me here and I'll give you a key and tell you where everything is.'

'I will of course. I'll be over later.'

Claire went in to see Liz in hospital every day, and she was glad that she made good progress until finally she was discharged into a nursing home for convalescence. 'How are you going to manage on your own when you get home, Liz?' Claire was concerned for her. 'Have you any family who could look after you?'

'No, I'm an only child. No sisters or brothers, and no cousins either. My father and mother were neighbours and most of their families were killed in the Second World War when a bomb dropped on their homes in London.'

'That's tragic.' Claire was shocked.

'It's life.' Liz was resigned.

'But you do have lots of friends?'

'And they've been in and out to see me, they're great.'

'What if I came over and stayed with you. Then I could set you up for the day, do the cooking and be there at night as well.'

'That would be far too much to ask. I'll manage by myself. But

148

thank you so much, I do appreciate your generosity.'

'But you can't look after yourself, anything could happen. Look, let's try and see how it goes. If it doesn't work out, then we'll look at alternatives,' Claire persuaded.

As she was spending time with Liz, Claire was more than surprised to find that her own home was kept spotlessly clean by Donal and Sophie, so much so it seemed that it hadn't changed at all when she dropped in and out every day.

'How are you two getting on?' she asked, when she arrived one evening and found them cleaning the kitchen.

'We're fine,' they grinned at her.

'Thanks for looking after the house.'

'We try.' They looked at each other.

'You're doing a good job, but don't let housework stop your studies.'

They laughed.

Donal's phone rang. 'Excuse me, it's Dad,' he stood up and listened. 'He has just flown in from London and wants to check on me,' he grinned.

A whirl of excitement shivered through Claire. Was Jim only interested in seeing Donal, or did he want to talk to her as well? She asked herself. Although, he couldn't have been very impressed with her the last time they met.

'He doesn't trust us to keep the house clean, sure he doesn't, Sophie?'

'And he wants to have no trouble with our landlady,' she giggled.

'Well, I think you're doing very well,' she smiled at them. 'I'll just go upstairs and change.'

She hurried up. Because she was staying with Liz, she just went into work wearing casual clothes and changed into haute couture when she arrived at the store and did the same when she left. But now, she was caught, and she didn't want to look at her worst.

She drew over the sliding mirrored doors of the wardrobe. She needed to choose something better than what she was wearing but didn't want to make it too obvious that she had made a special effort because he was calling, particularly in front of Donal and Sophie. She chose red jeans, red and navy sweater, and matching jacket. She combed her hair, refreshed her lipstick and sprayed perfume.

When she went down, Donal and Sophie had gone back to their rooms, and she put on the kettle and made herself a cup of coffee. She would be having dinner with Liz later and really only wanted to collect the post and have a quick look around. She wouldn't have minded checking the bathrooms, but couldn't really do that while the two young people were actually there. She decided to come home tomorrow at lunch time, and leave out fresh bedlinen and towels as well. Donal and Sophie usually kept their bedrooms in good order and she didn't have to worry.

There was a ring on the doorbell and she went to answer it feeling a little apprehensive.

'Claire?' Jim's grey eyes were warm, and his smile set her pulse racing.

He walked closer, and took her hand. He held it in both of his for a few seconds. 'It's lovely to see you,' he said.

'Thanks.' Now she tried to loosen her hand from his, but he still held on.

'Any news from Beijing?'

'No.'

He let go of her hand.

'I'm going out,' she said awkwardly.

She thought there was a disappointed look in his eyes. Or perhaps that was in her imagination. She ushered him in and explained about looking after Liz. He was immediately sympathetic.

'That must put a lot of pressure on you.'

'I'm very fond of Liz so I don't mind. She has no one to look after her. And she has been very generous to me particularly when I've needed time off to go to Beijing.'

'How is she?'

'Actually, she is doing quite well considering, but I like to keep an eye on her.'

'She's lucky to have you.'

Her body language dismissed that.

'I'll just have a quick word with Donal,' he said.

'Go on up.'

'If you don't mind?'

'Not at all.'

He went upstairs.

Claire put on her navy coat, and picked up her handbag from the kitchen table.

After a short time, Jim came down and they walked out the door together, and she closed it.

He stood with her in the porch, the light on.

'Our lives are very erratic,' he said slowly.

'Yes,' she had to admit that. And could feel emotion sweep through her. What did he mean?

She looked into his eyes. And could see the grey with flecks of gold in their depths. Caught in his gaze, she found herself longing for him to touch her. She moved just a little nearer. His arms reached. His face close to hers. Warm, with the slightest stubble. The breath swept out of her in a long sigh as she leaned into him.

'Claire,' he whispered. His lips stroked. Velvet soft. His tongue entwined with hers, moist, warm. She was in a dream place.

But suddenly she dragged herself back to reality. 'I must go.'

'I'm sorry, I've delayed you.' Jim cupped her face in his hand. He walked her to the car. She opened the door. Not sure what she should say to him.

'How are you feeling these days?' he asked.

'Not too bad. There's a lot happening.'

'I can imagine. If you want a break, just give me a call and we can get together.'

She wanted to say yes, but still she hesitated. 'I'll see …'

Chapter Thirty

'It looks as if our Neil isn't coming back to us,' Claire's mother, said.

'We miss him and hearing all his stories about school,' Michael added. 'It's been months since we've seen him.'

'He'll have grown so tall we won't know him.' Peggy began to clear the table.

'And he will have forgotten us,' her father, Michael, murmured.

'He won't,' responded Claire. Anxious to persuade them that it would never happen.

'I hope not,' Peggy murmured.

'Rusty misses him too,' her Dad added. 'I think I'll take him out for a walk before it gets dark.'

'Let's wrap up,' Claire advised. 'Leave the dishes Mam and we'll go for a walk as well. Do us all good.'

They walked to the park, the dog rushing ahead of them on the lead. 'Well, he's enjoying himself anyway,' Michael laughed and followed the dog.

'Having Rusty is the only thing that keeps Dad going these days,' Peggy said.

They watched him walk across a grassy area into the trees ahead of them.

'If we could only give him hope that Neil would be home soon, it would make all the difference. I worry about him.'

'I have to be hopeful, for Neil's sake,' Claire said.

'Do you think we'll really see him again?' Peggy took her handkerchief from her pocket and dabbed her eyes.

Claire pushed her arm through her mother's and hugged close. 'Of course, we will.' Every time she called to her Mam and Dad, she had to bolster them up, as they always brought the subject of Neil up in one way or another. 'I am determined to see him again.'

'I'm saying a Novena. Our Lady always answers me, I've great faith in her.'

'Thanks Mam, I love you.' Even though her parents looked for reassurance from her, she felt she was the one who was always comforted by their love and concern for her and Neil.

Her Dad came back. 'This fellow has run me off my feet.'

'Give him to me, I could do with a bit of exercise.' Claire took the lead and began to run, Rusty loping beside her.

'Come on boy,' she called, and speeded up. She hadn't any time to run recently. Even a half an hour each day would keep her fit. She waved to the parents and raced ahead. Her hair flying in the breeze. Feet in trainers pounding the gravel path. She was reminded of the days when Neil and herself would run with Rusty. Holding Neil's hand when he was young and the dog was only a puppy. She would have given anything to feel his warm hand in hers. Anything.

The dog slowed down. He was twelve years old now and wasn't as energetic as he used to be. She stopped and gave him a rub, then turned and walked back to her Mam and Dad. Feeling better already, she smiled at them.

'I'd like to be able to run like that,' her mother said.

'Don't you go to your exercise class?'

'I do, and I love it, although I wish I could persuade your father to do something to keep fit.'

'My knees aren't the best,' he laughed.

'I've already suggested you should come to our class.'

'Wouldn't I look well in with a crowd of old ones,' he grinned.

'The cheek of him, Claire, did you ever?'

She laughed. They weren't old really. Her mother was seventy-one, and her father was seventy-three. And they were fairly sprightly, her mother particularly so. She knew what they were going through with the loss of Neil, having looked after him since he was a baby. A tiny thing who when he looked up at them from his cot, they were as important to him as she and Alan were. Now she wondered if he missed his Gran and Grandad. Or had Alan persuaded him that his life was now in China and to forget about everyone in Ireland.

'Do you think there's a chance we'll see him at Christmas?' Peggy asked.

'I've booked a flight to Beijing next weekend, I haven't much time as it's so busy at this time of the year.'

'And everyone rushes in for the sales which begin even before Christmas these days.'

'Like you used to do yourself,' Claire laughed. 'I remember the crush at the shoe counters in Arnotts and me hanging on to your coat as you searched for bargains. I was terrified I'd lose you among the crowds of women.'

'You poor thing. I have to say I loved the sales and always wanted to find a few pairs of shoes at a good price.'

'Which usually happened.'

'The bargains meant we could have new clothes and shoes every year. I used to save up my money. I had three jars at the top of the kitchen press, remember? One for birthday presents, one for Christmas and one for the sales.'

'It was a terrible temptation for us. I remember Suzy and I pulled the table over so that we could climb up, but we were just too short, and anyway if we heard you coming that plan was immediately abandoned,' Claire giggled. 'And it happened more than once.'

'I knew all about it but turned a blind eye unless you smashed the jars,' her mother laughed too.

Claire remembered her childhood as they walked back to the house. All the things which were so important to her. The rainbow colour of the days. Always bright and sunny. Playing with Suzy and their friends in the fields behind their home. Although the green sward had been swallowed up by a development of houses and apartments in recent years. Sucked up into concrete blocks. Like a milk shake through a straw. Claire stared out through the kitchen window.

'How are your lodgers?' Peggy asked.

'They're fine actually.'

'You seem to be happy now about having them living in your house,' her mother said.

'I'm lucky to have them. And they're nice young people. Quiet, clean, and it's made such a difference to being able to pay my mortgage.'

'You could have lost your home otherwise.'

'Anyway, I don't see that much of them, they're usually out or in their rooms studying.'

'Don't they come downstairs to eat?'

'They only have coffee and toast in the morning but I'm usually gone by then. They have lunch in the college and they're not around much in the evening, and anyway they're gone at the weekends, and will only be with me for the college terms. So it's fine.'

'And then you'll be able to pay off some of the arrears of your mortgage.'

'That's all I want.'

Peggy stood up. 'Would you like some scones? I promised I'd make some for your Dad.'

'Let me help,' Claire offered.

'It won't take long, you sit down and relax.'

156

'Thanks, Mam.'

Peggy weighed out the flour and other ingredients. Then she sieved them into the big yellow bowl, added margarine, egg and buttermilk, deftly cut the dough into rounds, brushed with egg and put them in the oven.

Claire watched her mother. Longing to put her arms around her and hold tight like she had done when she was young. Tears sprang into her eyes and she looked out the window reluctant to let Peggy see her emotion.

'I've bought Neil's Christmas presents, pyjamas, a dressing gown, and as few other bits. Should I send them?' Peggy asked.

'I'll take them with me.'

'That would be great.'

'I'll be bringing books and computer games. I can't take too much obviously,' added Claire.

'He'll be delighted I'm sure,' Peggy smiled, clicked on the kettle and took out mugs and plates from the press. A delicious aroma drifted from the oven and she took out the scones. Sliced them in two, buttered and spread her own home-made strawberry jam.

'Thanks Mam, these are delicious.'

'I'll give you a few to take home.'

'Thank you.'

'Suzy is coming home for Christmas,' her mother said with a smile.

'I was talking to her the other day, I'm looking forward to seeing her.'

'It will be lovely to be all together although ...'

Claire understood what she meant. It would be even nicer if Neil was home too.

Peggy didn't mention him again, and Claire appreciated her sensitivity. There was little to be said.

Her phone rang. It was Lucy.

'Just catching up,' she said. 'Would you like to meet for a drink?'

Claire hesitated. 'Sorry, I can't, not this evening.'

'Come on,' Lucy coaxed.

'I'm with Mam and Dad at the moment and I'm not long here. Sorry.' She could hear herself sound really dull and boring. 'But thanks for phoning, I appreciate it.'

'Give me a call when you're leaving,' she said.

'I will.' She promised but didn't mean it.

'You're lucky to have such friends, it's important to keep in touch,' her mother commented.

'I know, Mam.'

'Cherish them.'

After Claire left some time later, she did call Lucy.

'Where are you?' she asked.

'I'm heading home.'

'We're waiting for you.'

'The place sounds packed,' she said, struggling to hear above the level of chattering voices in the background.

'It is, we're holding a seat for you, just about.'

'I don't think I'll come in this evening, sorry.' She felt guilty.

'Why not?'

'I've booked a flight to Beijing in a week's time so there's a lot to be done.'

Someone screamed with laughter.

'She can't come,' Lucy said to Elaine.

'Why not?' She came on the line. 'What's with you, kid?'

'I've too much to do,' she tried to explain.

'It's probably the last chance we'll have to get together before Christmas.'

'All right, see you there in about half an hour.' She gave in.

Chapter Thirty-one

Claire stared at the personally written *Thank You* card. 'How lovely,' she whispered and began to read the words Liz had written noting that she had lodged a large sum of money to Claire's account, and also that she had increased her salary substantially. 'You're so generous, thank you.' She hugged her.

'It's nothing compared to what you've given me,' Liz smiled warmly.

'But it's so much, you shouldn't have.' Tears brimmed. For someone to be so kind to her threw into stark contrast the attitude of Alan and his father.

'You'll be going to Beijing and I wanted to make it easier for you. I'll be running the store from home,' Liz laughed. 'And I'll call in later in the week just to chat to everyone.'

'Thanks for giving me the time off, it means a lot to me, I'm very grateful.'

Claire thought the day of her departure to Beijing would never arrive. Although she actually began to feel more Christmassy, and decided to bring down the trees and decorations from the attic. Usually the house was festooned with garlands, four sparkling Christmas trees downstairs, and twinkling lights adorned the trees in the garden. It had always been such an exciting time. Neil particularly enjoyed dressing the trees and arranging the decorations and they made it a big day of celebration.

She pulled down the attic stairs, climbed up and began to haul down the boxes.

'Claire, do you want a hand?' Donal asked as he appeared out of his room.

'I wouldn't mind,' she laughed.

'Clearing out the attic,' he asked with a wide grin.

He was a nice guy and spent most of his time studying these days. Her few words to Sophie and himself about their behaviour when they first arrived seemed to have worked. Indeed, she hardly saw them.

'I'm bringing down the various Christmas trees and decorations,' she explained. 'But I don't like asking you to do that, I'm sure you're busy.'

'I'd love to. I always did the tree at home, but this year, my Dad had it done by the time I got home last weekend.'

'If you like,' she wasn't quite sure what to say, but let him bring down the boxes.

'How many trees have you got? It seems like a lot of stuff.'

'I've four.'

He seemed astonished. 'One's enough for us,' he laughed.

'They just increased over the years. Fashions change.'

They each lifted a box.

'Which one is which?' he asked.

'They're marked.' She examined the sticker. 'This one is the sitting room.'

'I'll bring it in.'

'TV room.' Suddenly Claire was brighter. She hadn't been looking forward to this and now that Donal had offered to help she felt a lot better.

'And the hall.' He put it on the wooden floor.

'Dining room.'

'We'll need the ladder. Have you got one?' Donal asked.

'It's in the shed.'

'Where is the key?'

160

She gave it to him and he brought in the ladder.

The front door opened and Sophie appeared. 'How are you?' She stopped and stared.

'Decorating the Christmas trees,' Donal announced.

'Can I help?' she asked.

'Course you can,' Claire said, surprised.

'Great, just let me put away my stuff.' She bounded upstairs to her room.

Claire was amazed to see how Donal and Sophie got stuck in with such enthusiasm. There was much chatter and laughter, and she felt that this house hadn't known so much noise since Neil went away. But with that came emotion. Missing him so much on this first Christmas. Every beautiful bauble placed on the branches of the trees meant so much.

'You have so many ornaments, they are just gorgeous. I love this little fellow.' Sophie examined a sparkling snowman and held it up to the light. 'And this darling little angel is really beautiful.'

'I've been collecting for years.' Claire was sentimental, remembering how Neil had loved all those miniatures and had his favourites as well. Donal and Sophie stood back and looked at their handiwork. They seemed delighted.

'Fantastic.' Sophie clapped her hands.

'This house is like Santa's grotto,' Donal laughed. 'You should invite the local kids in. I'll play Santa Claus. I know someone who has a Santa suit.'

She laughed at the idea, but immediately thought that unless Neil was home then nothing like that would ever happen.

When Claire came back to Beijing, a biting wind whirled around her as she stepped out of the exit doors at the airport and walked towards the taxi rank. She was excited and prayed that she would see her darling boy soon.

She had become more confident on this her third visit, and knew where she wanted to go. It was dark now and the city lights were even brighter with glittering Christmas displays across the streets and on buildings and shops. She was surprised to see it, but was aware that the Chinese people celebrated Christmas but for them it wasn't a religious festival but purely commercial. As before, Claire felt a wave of excitement through her as she thought about Neil, and her eyes darted here and there hoping to catch a glimpse of him going somewhere with Alan or his grandparents. She stared into the windows of other cars but saw no one who looked familiar.

The room in the hotel was identical to the previous one in which she had stayed on the last occasion. But the view was different this time. Instead of being above the front door of the hotel, this room overlooked the back of the building, and a very narrow street which was crowded with people. She planned to go to the house on the following morning and prayed that Lien would allow her to see Neil. Being a Saturday, she hoped that he wouldn't be in school and there would be a greater chance of seeing him. She thought of how she would give Neil everything she had. Her heart. Her soul. Her very depth. She wanted to put her arms around his thin frame. Hold him close to her. Out loud, she tried to speak the words she wanted to say to him. But her voice trembled, and the words were caught in her throat until she was almost unable to breathe. She turned back into the room and sat on the bed. She was tired after the journey and wanted to sleep but couldn't, her mind going around in circles as she thought about Neil.

Unable to face going out into the busy streets on her own this late at night, she phoned room service and ordered a dish from the menu. She went to bed, but as usual couldn't sleep well, disturbed by the noise of traffic, police sirens, shouting and other unfamiliar sounds in the area.

She awoke fairly well rested, filled with enthusiasm. She chose to wear a pale grey suit, with a matching blouse, and over that a black padded jacket to keep herself warm against the cold wind. She ate breakfast in the hotel restaurant, and then put on a mask and asked the porter to hail her a taxi.

Claire reached the house hoping that Alan or Lien would invite her in. Something to give her hope, to put an end to the confusion within, to brighten the darkness of the tunnel down which she was being inexorably drawn. Maybe Neil would be there. Maybe he would hear her voice. Maybe he would want to see her and rush from somewhere. Her life was one big *maybe*.

Someone answered the intercom and she asked for Alan. Her heart beat rapidly and she held her breath until finally the gate clicked and swung open. Claire walked up the steps and the maid took her jacket, and led her into the same room where Lien sat waiting, as usual dressed elegantly in silk. The intricate embroidery was reminiscent of the Chinese designer Liz had mentioned, although Claire had no opportunity to visit her fashion studio on the last occasion. She put down her handbag, and other bags which held the presents for Neil from home. Then she bent her head and joined her hands. Lien did the same. Claire picked up a parcel wrapped in red paper, bowed and handed it to Lien. It was an Irish linen tray cloth which she hoped would be acceptable to her mother in law.

'Thank you, Claire.' Lien bowed. 'I am most appreciative, please sit.'

There was a knock on the door and Claire's heart began to race as she immediately thought that it might be Neil. But as usual it was another maid carrying a tea tray. They drank slowly. Silently. Lien explained which particular tea they were drinking today, and Claire had to try to appear interested and that was difficult. She was very bored with tea drinking, and all she wanted to do was to ask her about Neil.

'How long will you stay in Beijing?' Lien asked with a gentle smile.

'Just for a weekend. At this time of the year we are very busy at home.'

'I hope you don't find it too cold here.'

'I have a warm jacket.'

As she sipped the tea, Claire's mind went around in circles. She always had to be so careful when meeting Lien, aware that in Chinese society many things were unacceptable and could even be seen as downright insulting in certain circumstances. She finished her tea and put down the cup. The thin almost papery china was so delicate she had to take great care when she handled it, terrified that it would crack accidentally. The design on the tea set was quite exquisite. Each time she had come here and been offered tea, they had used a different set. Today was a design of trailing pink roses, with the inner surface being gold leaf.

'Are Neil and Alan here?' she asked.

'No.' Lien shook her head. 'Although they are both well,' she replied.

'And when will Neil be back.'

'He is at college.'

'On a Saturday?' Tears moistened her eyes.

'He is studying.'

'Can I wait for him,' she begged.

'His father and grandfather will not allow it. I have told you before.'

'But surely you can try and persuade them to at least let me see him or even talk to him?'

'I have no power in this house.'

'I can't imagine that,' Claire murmured.

'It is true.'

'Maybe I should go to the police?' She tried to prevent the rising level of irritation within.

She shook her head. 'No, that is not advisable.'

'Then what should I do?'

'I cannot help you.'

Claire stared at Lien. Speechless. She had such hope when she came in, but now that had become nothing. It was the same every time she came here. She was distraught and had to hold back her tears so as not to reveal her weakness to this woman.

'I am very sorry,' Lien said softly.

Almost as an afterthought, Claire lifted the bag she had brought with her. 'These are Christmas presents from my parents and myself for Neil. Would you give them to him please?' She put them down closer to Lien.

There was a sound outside. A look of fear passed across Lien's face. 'You must go, quickly,' she whispered.

Someone knocked on the door and pushed it open.

Claire looked around, surprised to see Alan staring at her.

She stood up.

'What are you doing here?' he yelled.

'I came to see my son.'

He spoke rapidly to his mother in Chinese. Even though Claire didn't understand the words she could sense the malice in his voice and felt sorry for Lien, and guilty too that she had been the apparent cause.

Lien didn't reply, but Claire could see her lips compress nervously and her hands clasp together.

'Get out, Claire,' Alan ordered. 'Now.' He spoke as if she was of no consequence even though she was the mother of his child. His voice was guttural and full of venom, and she knew exactly how he felt about her as well as his mother. She dreaded that he would ever speak to Neil in this way.

'I want to see my son,' she said abruptly.

'You can't see him.'

'Why not?'

'It would be too upsetting for him.'

'Just for a few minutes? Please?' she pleaded. Aware that she had always done the same thing with Alan since he had taken Neil. Begging like a homeless person in the street.

'You have to leave.' He moved closer, his hand outstretched in a provocative way.

She turned back to Lien.

'Thank you very much for the delicious tea, Lien, I enjoyed our chat very much,' she said it deliberately so that her mother in law would understand how grateful she was to her. Then she bowed. Lien did the same.

She picked up her handbag.

'Come on,' Alan growled impatiently. 'I don't want you around here any longer.'

At that moment, Claire thought she could hear the sound of a piano in the distance. Suddenly a dam opened and all the pent up darkness within her heart rushed and danced over rocks and tumbled downwards. She ran into the hall. 'Neil, it's Mum here,' she called.

'Shut-up,' Alan roared.

'Neil.' She raised her voice.

'Stop shouting.' Alan was enraged, and he grabbed her by the shoulder.

'Let go of me.' She struggled to free herself from his grip.

Lien spoke to Alan in Chinese. While she kept her voice low, there was a level of anger there which surprised Claire.

But he didn't take any notice, and this time grabbed hold of Claire's hair and hauled her towards the front door.

'How dare you,' Claire cried out. 'Help me Lien?'

Lien spoke again in Chinese.

'Get out of here,' he shouted.

Claire tried to resist him but he opened the front door and attempted to push her through on to the steps.

'You're a bully. I'm calling the police.' She tried to open her bag to get her phone.

'They won't take any notice of you.'

'This is assault.'

'Go home, Claire, I don't ever want to see you again and you won't get Neil back.' He pushed her again.

She tripped and almost fell down the steps.

The gates into the estate swung open and a dark limousine drove along the road at a fast pace, and then turned up the side of the house.

The maid appeared behind Alan holding Claire's jacket, and he flung it after her. It wrapped itself around her face, and for a few seconds she couldn't see anything until she managed to pull it off.

'I know the Irish Embassy staff here and I'll be talking to them,' she screamed.

He was expressionless as he stepped inside and slid across the glass front door.

She could hear it close. She managed to get her balance at last and limped down the steps. By then the automatic gate had slowly opened, and she went through. She stood outside, staring up at the windows. All the while a terrible longing within her to see Neil's face. Had he overheard the row between herself and his Dad. Such an angry exchange between a mother and a father was always upsetting for a child. She wanted to tell him that it wasn't his fault. She only wanted to love him. That was all. But the windows remained blank, and dark. And did not reveal the secrets of that house. Only the reflection of the misty grey sky above.

'Mum, Mum?'

She couldn't believe it was Neil.

She stared around, not sure where his voice was coming from. Then suddenly he appeared, running fast. She rushed towards him and he flung himself at her.

'Mum? Mum?' His arms encircled and he clung tight. 'Is it really you?' He looked up into her face.

'Of course it is, I love you, my Neil.' She burst into tears. Time stood still for her.

'Neil?' someone called.

She looked up to see a man in a dark uniform run quickly towards them. Immediately, she took Neil's hand and began to rush towards the gates.

'Let's go, Neil, we're going home.'

She could feel his hand clasp hers.

'Stop,' the man shouted.

The front door opened. Alan appeared and ran down the steps. She glanced around but her heart dropped as she could see that the distance between them was decreasing. Running like this with Neil was something she had only imagined. It was in her dreams. This attempt to escape. Now she was here her legs almost refused to carry her any further. Progress grew slower and slower.

'Claire?' Alan yelled.

She put more impetus into her strides. Thumping on the hard concrete. The effort jarred. This was her chance and she had to take it and get out of here with Neil as quick as she could.

'Stop.' Alan grabbed her hair from behind.

'Let me go,' she screamed.

The man in the uniform clutched Neil's jacket and dragged him from her.

'Mum?' Neil cried out loud and tried to get away from the man. Screaming for his mother. 'Let me go, Kim, let me go please?'

Alan's grip prevented Claire from continuing any further and slowly he forced her to come to a halt. He hauled her around to face him, raised his hand and swept it across her face. The resulting thump was so painful her head rebounded.

'Neil?' she shouted but could see that the man in the uniform was dragging him around the side of the house and out of her sight.

'Mum?' Neil called out.

'Shut-up,' Alan roared.

Desperately she tried to get away from him and run after Neil.

'I'm calling the police,' he warned, holding on to her jacket.

'I don't care.'

'You'll care when you're thrown in prison for kidnapping.'

'You bastard.' She spoke through clenched teeth.

Lien appeared at the doorway, and hurried down, berating Alan.

'Let go of me.' Claire shook him off.

Whatever Lien had said to him seemed to have some influence, as he did let go of Claire.

'Get out of here.' He shoved her towards the gates.

'I'm not going without Neil,' she said.

'Just leave, before the police arrive. You're trespassing. My father has already called them.'

'I don't believe you.'

'Go.' He thrust her away from him.

'Claire, it will be better if you do as he says,' Lien advised.

'I want to see Neil.' She was very upset, crying.

'Go now,' Lien encouraged.

'I'm not going without Neil. He wanted to come with me, I know that.' She looked around but couldn't see Neil.

'It will cause much problem,' Lien said.

'I don't care about that. I just want my son.'

The large black car appeared at the side of the house.'

'Kim will drive you.'

'No.'

'Please?'

Claire stared at her and could see the appeal in her dark eyes.

The woman's obvious sincerity persuaded Claire to agree. Logically she knew there was no point continuing to argue with Alan, he was an unmoveable force.

He shouted at his mother and she hurried up the steps and they both disappeared inside. But Claire decided that she wasn't going to give in. She would stay there. Obstinate. Until she chose to leave herself. She wondered what was going on now. Strained her ears to hear voices in conflict. Alan berating his mother in much the same way as he had done herself probably. She had an immediate urge to ring the intercom again. Her finger pressing hard on it until it was almost numb. The incessant sound echoing like her own screams of anguish as she lost the soft hand of her precious boy.

The car was still parked, the engine ticking over, but she walked past it, went out the pedestrian entrance and hailed a taxi.

Back at the hotel, she took out her phone and called Tony at the Embassy. Still upset now, she just wanted to talk to him.

'I'm here in Beijing and wondered if you would like to meet later for a drink. Just to have a chat?'

Chapter Thirty-two

The driver, Kim, brought Neil into the kitchen, but he managed to escape the man's grip and rushed upstairs into the hall, his feet clattering on the wooden floor. He had held the warm hand of his Mum until Kim pulled him away. His heart was racing. 'Mum, Mum?' he called out as loud as he could, and met his father coming towards him but he shoved Neil backwards with a quick punch in the chest. He couldn't breathe properly for a few minutes, but he still managed to keep shouting that he wanted his Mum.

'She's gone,' his father said abruptly.

'She isn't,' he insisted. 'And you told me she was in America.'

'She's going back.'

'Neil, come with me,' Nai Nai said.

He didn't listen and rushed at Alan. 'You hit Mum, I saw you.' He punched him with his fists. 'I hate you. I hate you.'

'Don't you speak to me like that.' Alan hit him.

Neil stared at him. His hand on the side of his head which throbbed. Tears flooded his eyes.

'It is time for your lesson,' Nai Nai reminded.

'I'm not doing my lesson.' He burst out.

'You will do as you're told,' Alan ordered.

'I won't. You can't make me,' he yelled.

'You will feel my hand again if you don't.' He raised it. 'Now prepare yourself for meeting the Master.'

'No.' He turned, ran upstairs to his room and flung himself on the bed. This was the first time he had seen his Mum since he had come here and he hadn't been allowed to talk to her. And she wasn't in America. And she wanted him to go home with her. So she did still love him and it wasn't the way his father said. And he hadn't done anything wrong so that she would hate him. She loved him still. He had just heard her say it. Knowing that gave him the strength to stand up to his Dad.

He looked out the window. Searching for her. But the road was empty. He wanted to go out now and find her. But he didn't know where she had gone. He was frustrated.

His door was flung open. His father stood there. 'It's time for your lesson, the Master has arrived.'

He didn't answer.

'Go straight down, he is waiting.'

'No.'

'You are disobeying me?'

Neil lowered his eyes so that he didn't have to meet his father's gaze. But he knew he was refusing to obey him and didn't care. 'I'm not practicing anymore,' Neil said.

'I tell you what to do. And you must do it.'

'It is time, Neil,' his Nai Nai said from outside. 'Come.'

Somehow, he had to obey her.

He finished his piano lesson, and put away his music. Master Xin nodded with satisfaction. Neil had played his very best and if his Mum could hear him he wanted her to know that it was for her. When the Master had left, Nai Nai came into the room and sat beside him.

'I hate Dad. He hit Mum and pulled her hair, and wouldn't let her stay here, and he hit me. Why did he do that?' He burst out.

She put her hand on his.

He looked at her, his brown eyes wide and anxious.

'I am sure he is sorry,' she said gently.

'He didn't say that.' His lip trembled. 'Mum told me she loved me.'

'All mothers love their children.'

'Do they?' He looked down. Through glimmering tears, he could just about see her brown crinkled skin which moved as she rubbed his hand.

'Mothers never stop loving.'

He still had tears in his eyes and felt embarrassed about that.

'I am a mother also and I love my son and I love you, my grandson, too. So much.' She drew him closer to her and lay her face on his head.

They sat there for a while.

He felt comforted.

His heart pumped. 'Mum,' he whispered. Wishing so hard that she was here with him and that it was she who was holding him so close. He wanted to turn and put his arms around her and hold tight. So that he would never let her go.

'Do you think I'll ever see Mum again?' He turned to Nai Nai, holding tight on to her hand.

'Of course, you will.'

'I know she's not living in America.'

Lien nodded.

'Is she here in China?' he asked. Longing for an answer that he could believe.

'I do not know.'

'Could you phone Mum and tell her that I want to see her?' he asked hopefully.

'I do not have her phone number.'

'I had it in my phone but I left that at home in Dublin when I came in the summer and I can't remember it. Maybe you could send her a Christmas card?' he suggested excitedly. 'And I could write the message and tell her everything?'

Lien shook her head.

Or maybe we could invite her to come to us for Christmas. Do you think she would like it?'

'We don't really celebrate like you do in Ireland.'

'That doesn't matter.' Neil was all excited. 'We can show her places, and I can buy her a Christmas present. Would you take me out to the shops?'

'I must ask your grandfather and your father, they would have to agree.'

Neil's heart dropped. Somehow, he knew that his Dad would never say yes. He had been so angry today, Neil had been afraid of him.

Chapter Thirty-three

Claire looked around for Tony who had arranged to meet her in the foyer of the hotel. Almost immediately, he stood up from where he had been sitting. 'Claire, how are you?' he smiled, walking towards her. 'I was so surprised to hear from you. I didn't know you were coming to Beijing again.'

'I'm just here until tomorrow,' she said.

'It's not the best time of the year, the weather can be very cold.'

'I don't mind. Let's go into the bar, I invited you, remember?'

'Thanks.' He took her arm.

They walked in and sat down.

'What would you like? Your usual?' she smiled.

He grinned. 'Thank you.'

'A whiskey and a gin and tonic.' she ordered. 'I know it's early, but I feel I must have a drink.'

'Well, how's it going?' he asked.

'Not too bad.'

'Are you busy?'

'Yes, this time of the year is crazy. It's Christmas, so it's all go back in Dublin,' she admitted.

'I'm really glad to see you.'

'How's life in the Embassy?'

'All the usual socialising going on. It's a pity you won't be here, you would enjoy all the Christmas celebrations.'

'It would be nice,' She sipped her drink.

'Have you seen Neil?' he asked.

She nodded. 'I went to the house today, but Alan arrived and he became very violent,' she tried to explain what had happened without breaking down.

'That sounds like assault,' Tony seemed shocked. 'Did he hurt you?'

'It's a bit sore, but I'll live,' She pressed the side of her face.

'Did your mother in law intervene?

'She did, but doesn't seem to be able to stand up to Alan or her husband, Neil's grandfather.' It was a relief to talk to Tony.

'I'm sorry.'

'Don't worry. The fact that I have built up a relationship with her in recent times may help in the future. But at least I saw Neil today, and he came with me without any hesitation holding on to my hand until the man took him away. That meant so much.'

'Never give up, Claire, anything could happen.'

'There's something else, I was wondering if I could meet Alison, just to show her Neil's photo so I could be sure that their son Robert is friends with my boy. Then I would know what school he goes to.'

'I'm sure we could organise that. When are you going back?'

'Tomorrow night.'

'I'll give Peter a call and see what can be arranged in the short time left.' He picked up his phone.

The following day as she checked out, Tony was waiting at the hotel and drove her to Peter and Alison's apartment. They had been invited for lunch and the couple's welcome was warm. After a delicious meal, they talked about their son, Robert, who had a friend called Neil in college.

'I have a photo of my son.' She handed it to Alison.

'He's very like Robert's friend, yes I'm certain.'

'That is such a coincidence isn't it?' Peter asked with a grin.

'It's astonishing.' Claire found it hard to prevent tears welling up.

'I'm sure you could go to the college and meet him coming out some day.'

'I'll take a note of the name.' Claire made a note on her phone. 'It will be next time. I have to go home to Ireland this evening.'

'That's a pity.'

'I'm very busy at this time of the year and over Christmas so it could be some time before I'm back.'

'We look forward to seeing you then.'

'What time is your flight?' asked Peter.

'Six-thirty.'

'I suppose we'd better head.' Tony stood up.

'I'll get a taxi,' she said.

'I'll drop you off at the airport,' Tony offered.

'Not at all, that's too much trouble. I'll just get my bag from your car.'

'I'm taking you, so no argument,' he smiled.

'Thanks,' she accepted gracefully.

'Next time you're here, you'll have to come for dinner, I look forward to seeing you then.' Alison kissed her. And they both came out to the lift with them.

Claire was very grateful to Tony and felt quite emotional when she arrived at the airport.

'Have you thought of trying to bring him back yourself?' he asked.

'Up to this I wasn't sure where he was, but now that I know the college he is attending that does make a difference. Next time I'll know where to go.'

'Do you think he wants to go back home?'

'Yesterday, when I held his hand and we both ran towards the gates, he didn't hesitate to come with me.'

'Your ex-husband has gone against the agreement you made in

court when you divorced.'

'I have custody.'

'If you bring Neil back home, you may still need your ex-husband's permission.'

'And that could be difficult. Impossible, knowing how Alan feels.'

'But he has kept Neil out of the jurisdiction without your permission?'

'I gave it originally for a month.'

'You wrote a letter?'

'Yes. I copied it from an online version and I just filled in all the details, although I never thought for one moment that Alan wouldn't come back with Neil.'

'Have you kept a copy of the letter?'

'Yes, it's on my laptop.'

'I think you could apply to the District Court in Dublin and they can issue you with a letter of permission to bring Neil back.'

'I hadn't realised that the District Court would do that.'

'I suggest you talk to your solicitor back home about making the application, just in case the opportunity presents itself at some future date.'

'Is it something I could do myself?'

'I think you can do most things these days, although it's not always recommended.'

'The cost could be prohibitive,' she said. 'And I'm not exactly flush at the moment.'

'If you do it yourself it may not cost so much.'

'I'll look into it,' she said vaguely.

'Be prepared, that's my advice.'

'Thanks so much, Tony, for all your help.'

'Any time.' He kissed her lightly on the cheek.

'I'll keep in touch.'

On the flight, she really couldn't relax, her mind kept her in

Beijing with Neil, particularly today when she had been so close to him, so near, so far. So much hope when she travelled here, and so much disappointment on this return journey. Alan's violence had shocked her. This was a side to him that she had never seen before. He was so vindictive she couldn't understand how she had ever loved him. Now she hated him.

Chapter Thirty-four

Claire had to face into the mad Christmas rush immediately on her return, and in some way that helped her deal with the loss of Neil this year which was very difficult. While they closed on Christmas Eve, she only had the following day to catch up with her parents and her sister Suzy who had come home from Edinburgh, and she was back at the store on St. Stephen's Day. She threw herself into work with her usual enthusiasm. Liz was still convalescing and Claire dealt with the crowds of people who came in to see what bargains they could find, some of them even queuing outside the store from three in the morning. Well wrapped up, they sat on chairs, and kept themselves going by drinking flasks of tea or coffee, and eating sandwiches. Luckily, the weather wasn't too cold and everyone had umbrellas just in case.

Claire and some of the staff were there by six o'clock, and were waiting for the hoards to descend on them at nine. It was mad. Even though they only allowed twenty people in at a time, they still fell over each other in an effort to grab whatever item they had spotted earlier, some of them even arguing as to who got there first. The whole week after Christmas was like that, and she only had a chance to spend time with Suzy on New Year's Eve, sorry that she was heading back to Scotland the following day. Although the party they attended with friends of Suzy was great, Claire was glad she had a chance to spend some time with her sister.

Claire longed to visit Beijing again in the hope of seeing Neil, but she couldn't justify going since Liz had been so generous to allow her the time off before Christmas. But she was hoping that it would be possible to go back perhaps in February. Every evening, she couldn't wait to check the post when she came home, praying that there might be a letter from Neil. But to her dismay, there was nothing, and she was certain that as before, he had never received the cards or presents.

Tony called, and she wondered why he had phoned.

'Have you booked your flight to Beijing yet?' he asked.

'No.'

'That's good.'

'Why do you say that?'

'There's something happening over here.'

'What do you mean?'

'There are rumours,' he said.

'About what?' She was suddenly worried.

'That there is a mystery illness.'

'Where?'

'It's quite a distance from Beijing. I just wanted to mention it and suggest that perhaps you shouldn't come over at the moment.'

'What type of illness is it?'

'A flu of some sort. They don't know much about it.'

'Who's they?'

'The Authorities.'

'Is it in Beijing?' Her mind took a leap.

'I think there may have been some deaths.'

She was suddenly very concerned.

'I think you shouldn't travel for a while,' he suggested.

'But I do want to go over in February.'

'I understand that, but I'll let you know how things are over here.'

'Would you, please?'

'Certainly.'

'Thanks for calling me, Tony, I appreciate it.'

'Not at all.'

Claire put down her phone. She was desperately worried. What if Neil caught this flu? He was just a young boy. He could be susceptible to it. Questions swept through her mind. How serious was it. Would it kill people. Would Alan look after him. He was a doctor. He could diagnose and prescribe medication. But if Neil was ill she should be there too. She was the only one who could take care of him. She was his mother.

The Chinese Spring Holiday was due to take place in a couple of weeks' time and usually Claire took Neil to various events which were held by the Chinese community in Dublin, just to give him a flavour of what it was like in China itself. He always enjoyed it, and she would have loved to have him home with her now so that they could enjoy themselves this year again. But she was becoming more and more worried about the virus and prayed that Neil wouldn't contract it and become really ill. Tears filled her eyes. She felt helpless and longed to put her arms around her son, hold him close, and tell him that everything would be all right.

Claire searched the internet for flights to Beijing. In spite of Tony's warning she wanted to be ready to go at a moment's notice and was glad that her visa was still in date. The following morning, she called him in Beijing just to find out how things were on the ground there.

'Sorry to bother you, but I'm still hoping to come over if I can get a flight,' she explained.

'There are just half a dozen of us holding the fort. As you know it is Spring Holiday here, and quite a few went to various places both inside and outside of China and so they're stuck there and can't come back.'

'I see shots of the streets on television and they seem to be deserted. It's frightening.'

'Lockdown. That is what the Authorities call it. People are very afraid of catching the virus so they're staying at home. Schools won't reopen after the holiday, and the teachers are planning to give lessons to students online so they don't miss out. And people are working from home as much as they possibly can.'

'Are most of the factories closed?' asked Claire.

'Yes, there is no production so that is very serious. It will really hit the economy.'

'I'm worried about Jim.'

'Yes, he does a lot of business over here.'

'Are you being informed about what is going on by the government?'

'Not really. The advice is just to stay in and only inform the health clinics by phone if you feel ill. Have you been in touch with your family?'

'No, I don't know what's going on.'

'That's a pity.'

'I'm worried about them.'

'You must be.'

'Alison said she would let me know what's happening at the boys' college.'

'Why don't you call them and ask if the Neil is taking classes online, I could let you have the contact details?'

'I might, thanks,' Claire agreed with his suggestion, but in her heart she knew she wasn't going to do that. 'Thank you so much, Tony.'

Now all she did was to listen to news reports about China. Noting the figures of those who had died from the Coronavirus, or Covid 19 as it was now called, and the numbers who had fallen ill. She watched the steady increase of those figures all the time wondering was her darling child among them.

Chapter Thirty-five

Neil practiced his music, and his Dad stood listening. When he had finished the piece, he asked him how he was feeling. Neil looked at him, surprised. 'I'm fine.'

'There's a bad flu around so let me know if you are starting a cold.'

Suddenly, Neil thought of the driver, Kim, and how he seemed to be feeling ill yesterday. But he didn't mention that to his Dad.

'That was very good, Neil. I think you are doing well, Xin will be pleased when he comes back to us. Now practise the scales. It's important to exercise,' he said and left the room.

Neil didn't like the scales. But although the room was soundproofed, he always knew that his Dad could still hear him, as if he had some secret way of picking up the notes of the piano from outside. He continued for a while, but then went back to one of his favourite pieces. Music was the brightest thing for him.

Later his father would oversee his schoolwork. Revising lessons which he had done since Christmas. And after lunch, he would study Mandarin with Yeh Yeh. He enjoyed that and was getting much better at drawing the characters. The scroll of the curves and sharper lines were beautiful, but there were so many of them he couldn't imagine ever learning them all. When he managed to draw one which was to Yeh Yeh's satisfaction, the old man would tap on the floor with his ebony walking stick.

All the time he remembered that day his Mum was here before

Christmas. Now he knew she had come back from America, and maybe was even here in Beijing. He had remembered every word that she said and hung on to it when he went to sleep at night and it was always there in the morning when he woke up. It brought her closer to him.

He walked down the stairs into the kitchen. Between studying, and practicing piano, if he had a few minutes to spare, he often went there. It reminded him of being at home with his Mum. Sometimes she let him help when she was cooking. They would make the dinner, or maybe bake scones or an apple tart which he would bring over to his Gran and Grandad the following day.

The cook had already gone home for Spring Holiday as had one of the maids, and Ayi too. The other maid, Siu, now had to prepare all the meals for the house and do the cleaning as well, and she wasn't too happy about it.

The back door banged and Kim, the driver, came in carrying two large bags.

'How many people were in the market? Did you manage to get everything we need? That doesn't look like much.' Siu took the bags from his hands.

'There is more in the car. I will get it when I warm myself up.' He rubbed his hands together and shivered, standing in front of the oven. The maid handed him a mug of tea and he sipped it.

'Are you feeling all right?' she asked.

'Yes I am,' he barked at her.

Neil sat at the table and crunched his cookie. They were always arguing, Siu and Kim. He wondered why.

Kim went out and returned after a few minutes carrying more bags.

'What is short?' she asked.

'A few items.'

'Lien won't be pleased.'

He shrugged.

'Can I have another cookie?' Neil asked as he finished the one he was eating.

'We have none left, but maybe Kim bought some.'

'You are very lucky.' He wagged his finger at him.

Neil grinned.

Lien appeared at the top of the stairs and came down. 'Neil, you are to take a lesson with your grandfather now.'

He slid off the chair. When his grandmother spoke, he obeyed immediately and went to Yeh Yeh's study. He knocked.

'Come in.' He could hear his grandfather's voice and went inside.

'Neil, I am feeling tired, maybe we will leave our lesson until tomorrow.' He ran his hand over his forehead which glistened.

'Can I get you anything? I could go down to the kitchen.'

'Ask your Nai Nai to come to me please.'

Neil hurried downstairs.

'Nai Nai, Yeh Yeh wants you, he said he's tired.'

Immediately she hurried upstairs without a word. Neil followed. She went into his grandfather's study for a moment and rushed back out again. 'Neil, ask Siu to come up quickly.'

He ran downstairs and returned with the maid. He waited by the door, listening to them talking.

'Neil, hold the doors open please?' Lien asked.

Immediately he did as he was told, so that Nai Nai and Siu could help Yeh Yeh upstairs to his bedroom. All evening they were going up and down to him, so much so dinner was late which was very unusual. No one took much notice of Neil and he went into the music room to practice.

The door opened. His father came in. Neil's eyes followed his father's figure as he stood in front of the bookshelves staring at the books. Alan smoothed his dark hair back on his head. It was a habit he had when he was annoyed.

Neil wanted to ask him more questions about the flu that

everyone was so afraid of, but he knew that he wouldn't answer. His Dad never looked at him if he was in that sort of mood. Always looking somewhere else. Sort of hiding from him.

Neil took his fingers off the keys.

'We have a problem,' his Dad said.

'What is it?' Neil asked, puzzled.

'Yeh Yeh is not well.'

'What's wrong with him?'

'He may have the virus, like the flu.'

'He said he was very tired today.'

'I know, so I am going to take him to hospital and I will stay there to help. They need doctors because there are a lot of people with the virus.'

Neil stared at him. He was very worried about Yeh Yeh.

'As we were all in contact with him, we will have to be in quarantine.'

'Quarantine?' he wasn't sure what that meant.

'You will stay in your own room and so will your Nai Nai, and you will have no contact with each other until we are sure that you do not have this virus.'

He nodded.

'Go upstairs now and stay there. You have everything in your room. Clothes and books. Siu will bring your meals up to you.'

'Will you be gone for long?'

'I hope not.'

Neil didn't know what else to say. Since his Dad had hit him he was afraid to say very much to him.

'I must go now.' His Dad left the room.

Neil put away the music. Then touched the notes of the piano. Softly he continued playing that last piece he had been practicing. If he had to stay in his room he wouldn't be able to play the piano, and that made him feel sort of lonely.

He loved playing and couldn't imagine how he would get

through the days locked up in his room. But after a moment he closed the lid of the piano and went upstairs. He stood at the window. But there was no-one to be seen. He looked across at the houses opposite. Were all those other people going to be sitting alone in their rooms like he was? He ran his finger across the glass in the window. He breathed on it and wrote his name. He should be in school by now, but it was closed because of the holidays. He missed seeing his friend Robert. Being stuck here was boring. He never thought of it as home. This was just a house where everything had to be kept in its own position. And he always had to take great care because if he upset anything he knew he would be in trouble.

Suddenly, there was the sound of a siren coming closer. He was able to see the gates into the estate slowly open, and an ambulance with flashing lights drive in and up the side of their house. It must be for Yeh Yeh. His heart beat. He could feel it in his chest. He couldn't see what was happening around the side and waited nervously until the ambulance drove out the gates again and disappeared.

Neil hoped that his grandfather would come home soon. His Ayi had gone to see her family, and he was glad about that, but best of all his piano teacher Master Xin wouldn't be coming to give him lessons. Now he was glad of that. Maybe he would never come back.

He kicked his paper football against the wall and practiced shots against his wardrobe goal for a while. Then he sat at the table and set out his chess pieces on the board. It was only a few weeks since his father had decided to teach him how to play and while he didn't feel very confident, he now made an attempt and tried to remember the moves his Dad had taught him. King. Queen. Rooks. Bishops. Knights. Pawns. But he didn't think he was going to be very good.

There was a knock on his door, and after a minute or two, he opened it and saw the covered tray on a trolley. He looked around hoping to see Siu but the landing was empty and he was disappointed that she hadn't waited. He missed having someone to talk to. But now he was hungry, and glad to see she had made rice with pieces of chicken and her own special sauce. He liked that, picked up the chopsticks and ate quickly, enjoying the flavour. He put the tray outside the door again, and only then remembered that his father had told him to wash his hands after he had eaten and rub his hands with the stuff in the plastic bottle which he had given him. He sighed but did it anyway. He didn't want to catch the virus which sounded much worse than the flu. He took his makeshift ball from the wardrobe and began to kick it around again. Bouncing from wall to wall. Enjoying the goals he imagined scoring. But then he stopped. Thinking he heard someone outside. It must be Siu. He listened at the door holding on to his ball afraid she would come in. But there was no sound now. He kicked again. Continuing the football game he played in his head.

He had scored two goals already. He was captain of the team. And now he was lining up for another shot, with a wild shout he aimed at the goal and kicked, seeing the ball go straight into the net winning the match. The crowds rose to their feet. Yelling and shouting. He and the other players grabbed each other and hugged, and then made a victory run around the pitch, waving to the crowd. He threw himself on the bed, a wide grin on his face. In his mind he had seen his Mum there on the side line cheering him on, and would have given anything to rush over into her arms and feel her hugging him tight.

Chapter Thirty-six

Jim was very worried about the supply of components for his clients who were already on to him daily asking when their orders would arrive. All he could do was to reassure them that he would expedite delivery as soon as was possible. In the meantime, he was frantically making contact with other firms with details of his requirements. But the biggest problem was cost. It proved to be much higher, particularly from European companies, and his margins would drop considerably. Up to now he had held on to his staff in various departments. Business had been so good for the last few years, he had built up a team of some excellent people, and if he had to let them go it was going to be very hard on him.

He opened up his computer to check emails, dreading the tone of some of them. Clients did not understand what was happening to him in relation to the Coronavirus. He prayed alternative companies could actually manufacture the components he needed to the very high standard he required and that they would pass the rigorous testing. If they malfunctioned in a machine he was finished.

His business was at a crucial point and if the virus continued and prevented the factories in China for supplying what he needed, then collapse was staring him in the face. He saw an email from Tony in Beijing and immediately opened it. Tony was a very valuable contact and kept him up to date about how things were going in China.

But to his disappointment, there was nothing positive in it, but then he saw a mention of Claire and he was concerned to read that she had been on to Tony talking about the problems she had with her ex-husband and her son Neil. He took a chance and just sent a brief text to Claire offering his help.

The day was like any other. He spent all his time at the factory in Ennis, very much aware of the tense atmosphere. And he found it difficult to look the staff straight in the eye and give them any hope of having a job the next week or the week after. But to his delight, later in the evening he received a text from Claire.

Thanks. Would love to chat. C.

As he was about to press in her number, he stopped himself. What was he going to say? He didn't know. Being at a distance made it even more difficult and on that last occasion she had been quite clear that she didn't want to be involved with him. Was he fooling himself? He didn't know the answer to that question.

But he had no choice now. He had gone too far.

'Jim?' she replied immediately.

'Claire, how are you?' he tried to hide his feelings.

'I'm fine,' she whispered.

'Have you made contact with the family in Beijing?' he asked.

'I was there before Christmas.'

'Did you see Neil?'

'Yes,' she said. 'But it was very difficult.'

He could sense she was upset.

'Would you like to meet some time, we could talk?'

'Yes, I'd like that.'

'I can come up on Friday if it would suit?'

She made no response initially and he felt let down.

'Thank you,' she whispered.

'Will I pick you up at the usual time?'

'That would be fine.'

'I'm looking forward to seeing you.' He couldn't help but

express his emotion. 'We'll have dinner at the same restaurant, would you like that?'

She agreed, and he was excited now and needed to let her know that he was thrilled at the thought of meeting her again.

Jim pulled up outside the house, climbed out of his car and walked up the driveway, glad that he didn't have to start explaining his presence to his son. Both Donal and Sophie had gone to a concert in Ennis. He rang the bell and waited until Claire appeared in the doorway. He smiled, stepped forward and kissed her cheek. 'It's lovely to see you.' He handed her the bouquet of red roses he had brought with him and a bottle of wine.

'Thank you so much, they are really beautiful.' She breathed in the scent, closed the door behind him, and led the way into the kitchen. 'Let me put these in water.' She took a vase from the press, and arranged the roses. 'Thank you,' she smiled, fingering the leaves. 'And for the wine too.'

'I've missed you,' he said.

'And I you.'

He moved closer.

In an instant she hugged him, leaning against him, her head on his shoulder.

He held her tight. His arms around her. Unable to believe that he was this close to her. She raised her face to his, and his lips caressed. As before there was a spark between them. Something which seared through him and took him to somewhere magical. A place where only she existed for him. He just wanted her, every part of her, to be his.

He opened the buttons on her blouse, his fingers trembling. Tiny pearls which were difficult to manoeuvre. She helped him open them.

He looked into her eyes. So warm. So trusting. Within a moment, the blouse had slid off her shoulders. Her pale skin glowed. Her black lace underwear was revealing and she slipped out of it until she stood there in the fullness of her beauty.

Feverishly she pushed off the jacket of his suit, and unbuttoned his white shirt, and within a moment both of them were naked. He lowered her to the carpeted floor and they held each other close.

'I love you, Claire.'

They moved rhythmically, until he was even closer to her. He held himself back anxious to give her as much pleasure from their union. His hands held her to him, her body yielding into his, until he finally let go with a groan, their orgasm matching each other as they reached a climax and it was only then he knew her intimately, his Claire. He looked down at her and kissed her again, their lips soft and moist, wanting more and more of each other. They held tight until at last they were exhausted, eyes closed, almost asleep. These moments were exquisite in their intimacy.

Later, they stood underneath the shower and soaped one another. 'I want you so much, you don't know how I have longed for you.' He kissed her.

She laughed and giggled.

He put his arm around her, and they stepped out. She took a bath towel and wrapped it around him. After a time, they retrieved their clothes and dressed again. Then he laughed, his heart thudding with excitement. 'I can't believe this. It's mind-blowing.'

'Believe it, Jim.' She held his hands. 'I'm sorry, since Alan refused to bring Neil back home, I thought I should not involve you in my life, it seemed so selfish. You didn't deserve that.'

'All I want, Claire, is to be involved.' He kissed her. 'If I have you, my life will be complete. Can you understand what I mean?'

Jim stayed with Claire that Friday night and cancelled the dinner booking he had made. Later, she opened the bottle of wine, and they sat and chatted.

'Sláinte,' she smiled, raised her glass and clinked his.

'To us,' he said. 'Let's order in. Do you like Indian or Chinese or Thai maybe?'

'I'd prefer Indian, the Chinese here isn't a bit like what we'd have in Beijing.'

'Right,' he took out his phone. 'Where is the best place?'

She turned on the gas fire in the lounge, pulled the couch in front of it, and drew the heavy curtains over. In the warm atmosphere, they sipped their wine and enjoyed the meal, talking long into the night. She knew so little about the man and now couldn't get enough of him.

They didn't sleep much. For Claire she didn't want to lose one moment of his company. So unsure of herself. Although he had said he loved her, she couldn't quite believe that in a matter of hours her life had changed completely. On the earlier occasion she had held back from any commitment, but now she had given her all to him. And she knew the truth of that could never be taken back. He was part of her. And as they talked of Neil, strangely his love had given her support, and for the first time she was sure that her boy would come back to her. She wasn't alone any longer.

Claire received the call just before she left the store the following day. This evening Jim had rearranged their dinner engagement and she was almost ready. She stared at the read out on the phone, her heart suddenly thumping with anxiety.

'Claire speaking,' she said, trembling.

'This is Lien.' The voice was indistinct.

'How are you, Lien?' She tried to be polite.

'I am well, but my husband has the Coronavirus.'

The blood drained from Claire's face. 'How is Neil?'

'He is well, but my husband has been taken to hospital. Alan

195

has gone with him to help with the patients, there are so many of them now.'

Tears filled Claire's eyes. This was what she had dreaded since she first heard about the virus. While she was still angry with Alan for refusing to return Neil to her, she wouldn't have wished Coronavirus on any of them.

'Is your husband seriously ill?'

'Yes.'

'I'm sorry, I wish I could be with you.'

'It is too dangerous.'

'I would go to Beijing and look after Neil if I could, but there are no flights available.'

'We will be all right.'

'Can I talk with Neil please, Lien?' she asked anxiously. 'Please?'

'It is not possible.'

'Why not?' she raised her voice.

'There is no phone in his room, and we are in quarantine now because of the virus.'

'He is alone?'

'Yes.'

'My poor boy,' she whispered.

'I will take care of him.'

'Tell him that I am always thinking of him,' she burst out. 'And please call me soon so that I will know how he is, and his grandfather too.'

'I must go now.'

'Tell Neil that I love him,' she continued on but Lien had gone. She sat there sobbing. Time passed and she managed to dry her tears. Jim would be arriving shortly and she didn't want him to find her in such a state. She always seemed to be crying when she was with him.

She went into the bathroom, cleaned her make-up off and reapplied it. Looking at herself in the mirror, the signs of the tears had diminished somewhat and she hoped he wouldn't notice. She felt so foolish to be unable to control herself.

He arrived shortly after that, and as soon as she opened the door to him, he gathered her into his arms and held her close. Immediately, she found herself becoming emotional again and struggled to hide it from him. Extricating herself and hurrying back into the office, setting the alarm, locking the door, and closing the shutters with the remote control. Doing everything at twice the normal speed and chattering about inconsequential things to hide her feelings.

He had left his car in the store car park and they walked around to the restaurant. She was glad they had a window table which looked out on the busy street.

The waiter took their coats and she sat down.

'You seem tired, my love.' Jim took her hand in his.

'I received a call from Neil's grandmother, Lien.'

He was immediately concerned. She could see it in his eyes.

'Neil's grandfather has been taken to hospital, and Alan has gone to help as well,' she tried to explain without losing it.

'What about Neil?'

'He's all right, but isolated in his room.'

'I'm so sorry to hear that, there is a lot about the outbreak in China in the media.'

'I pray that Neil doesn't catch it.'

'If he's isolated he should be all right.'

'Lien is looking after him.

He took her hand and held it.

The waiter handed them the menus.

'What would you like to eat?' Jim asked. 'Are you hungry.'

'Not really.'

'Just have something light perhaps?'

'Yes,' she smiled. 'Maybe salmon.'

She made a quick decision.

'I'll have hake, would you like a starter?'

'No thanks, the main course is fine.'

The waiter came to take their order.

'What else did Lien say?' Jim asked.

'Not very much. She's a very quiet individual.'

'But you must be relieved that she rang you.'

'Oh yes, in one way it means everything but on the other hand the thought of the virus being in the house is terrifying. Neil could die.' She shuddered.

'I'm sure he will be fine.'

'I hope so, but I can't bear the thought of it. He must be so lonely on his own.'

The waiter brought their food.

Jim was very sympathetic and his attitude helped Claire.

'At least Lien has told me what is happening, although last time, I left presents and cards for Neil from myself and my parents, although I wonder if she gave them to him at all.'

'Perhaps she couldn't.'

'Alan doesn't want him to have anything to do with me,' she said bitterly.

'Neil will be all right,' he reassured.

Claire shook her head in confusion. 'I want to go over there now but I can't.'

'Unfortunately.'

'If I could only talk to him.'

'Well, at least you heard from Lien and she told you about Alan and his father. You are a little more informed than you were before that phone call today.'

'If the virus is passed from one person to the other, then what are the chances of Neil catching it?' Claire asked him worriedly.

'He won't catch it,' he reassured.

'I can't bear the thought of it. I just want to be there with him.'

Chapter Thirty-seven

Neil had seen an ambulance stop at the house opposite and the men carry out someone on a stretcher. They were all dressed in white gowns, with masks and gloves so you couldn't see anything at all, they were like spacemen. He was wondering could the flu blow over from the other houses and in his window? But there was no one to ask that question.

He picked up his paper ball and wished he had more paper to wind around it and make it bigger and stronger so that he could strike higher but in this house there was nothing ever left around. His Dad read a paper every day, the Beijing Daily News. But since his father had gone to the hospital with Yeh Yeh, there were no papers.

He kicked the ball and it bounced against the wall. Then he took a jump and landed heavily on the floor. There was a creak from the floorboards. It sounded like an animal underneath protesting that he had stood on its back. It was so quiet in the room every sound echoed. Outside it was very quiet as well. He couldn't see the main road from here but there was hardly any drone of traffic. He wondered why that was. But then remembered that all the cars were still in their driveways and probably in the garages as well and none of them had moved in days. And the maids were not walking the dogs either. And children didn't run out to get into cars which would take them to school and bring them home in the evening. So he wasn't the only student at home. The whole of Beijing was at home.

He wondered how Robert was doing, and he was reminded of his friends at home, Tommy and Calum. They were always around his house at the weekends. Either kicking football in the back garden, or the three of them gathered in Neil's bedroom, playing computer games, only coming down when his Mum called them.

'Boys, pizza's ready,' she would shout up the stairs.

Then there would be a thunder of footsteps as they came down, always hungry.

But there was no pizza in this house.

He went back to the window. The road outside was still empty. There was an eerie silence. It was the same each day. He repeated the word. Eerie. He knew it meant ghostly, or spooky. It frightened him.

He sat on his bed but couldn't understand how a sickness caused this to happen. What sort of sickness was it? He looked at his hands. There was no difference between each one. They were still white and looked the same as usual. What if he caught this sickness? His Mum had always taken care of him if he was sick. She always understood what was wrong with him, and if he needed to go to the doctor she took him. Now there was no one to tell what might be wrong. No one to trust.

His Nai Nai opened the door slightly. Through the crack, she had asked if he had a sore throat, or a cough, or couldn't breathe. 'Stay over by the window, we should not be too close to each other,' she said.

He moved backwards. 'I am feeling all right.'

'I am glad, Neil. But you must remember to tell me if you don't feel well.'

'I will.'

'You promise me.'

'Yes, Nai, Nai.'

'I don't want you to be ill.'

'I will keep washing my hands.'

'You know what your Mum would say if she thought you hadn't told me you felt unwell?'

'She always told me to obey you.'

'And she is a good woman. She knows right from wrong. As I do myself,' Lien said.

'Have you talked to her?'

'No, I have not.'

He was disappointed. 'Where is she?'

'I am not sure.'

'Has she gone back to America or is she still here?'

She shook her head.

'I want to see her.' When he was younger he could always get around his grandmother but now when he wanted an answer he couldn't get it from her and wondered if this was part of being thirteen. A teenager.

'I want to go home.'

'It's not possible.'

'Why?'

'Your father and grandfather want you here.'

'I don't understand that.'

'It's important to Chinese men. They want sons. To continue on their legacy.'

'But I'm just one boy. What use am I?'

'You are his blood. The blood of Wang Li. And of his father, Wang Li Jian.'

'Am I not of your blood also?'

'Yes, but blood of a woman is not considered important.'

'Why?'

'It is the way of Chinese culture.'

'I don't understand.'

'There is no need for you to understand.'

'I want to,' he argued with his Nai Nai for the first time. He had never done this before.

'It is not your place,' she said.

He listened to her. And wanted to understand every word that she said. But there was something else he wanted to know.

'Nai Nai, can the virus blow over here from other places?' he called after her, but she had already gone downstairs.

Neil stared out his bedroom window again. That was all he did. No one came into his room now and he left his used clothes out on the landing every day and collected fresh ones. Today he would have given anything to run down the corridor and shout, just to be free of his room which made him feel like he was in prison. But Nai Nai had given him strict instructions that he was to stay in his room at all times.

Kim the driver and Siu the maid had both gone home, and Nai Nai had to do everything in the house. He had chores to do as well. Change his bed twice a week, clean his bathroom with the disinfectant she left outside in a bucket, wash the tiled floor. He began to enjoy it in a way. It kept him busy and reminded of how he used to help his Mum at home. It took his mind off the boring routine of study and reading which was all he could do.

He heard his grandmother outside with his lunch but had to wait until she had gone down the stairs again. He opened the door and stared along the landing then lifted the tray and carried it in. As he ate the curried pork and drank the glass of milk, he thought about his Dad and Yeh Yeh and wondered how they were. How long would it be before they came home? He had seen another person go to hospital yesterday. This happened almost every day now. He could hear the sound of the siren of the ambulance again and immediately he watched as it stopped outside the house next door. Wide eyed he saw the men climb out and open the doors. Their figures almost blended with the snow which had fallen during the night and he could just about see them as they went into the house carrying two stretchers. He would have given anything to go out and play in the snow. Build a snowman like he would have done with Tommy and Calum if there was a snowy day back home.

He was upset. The family who lived next door were friends with his Nei Nei and Yeh Yeh and he knew that they would be sad that their friends were sick. He put the tray outside again, and then opened his books. He knew if he didn't study then when his Dad and Yeh Yeh came home he would be in trouble if he couldn't show how well he had done. But his mind wouldn't let him. It kept jumping from one thing to another. Mostly about his Mum. He wondered what she was doing now. He lay his head on his arms and tears welled up in his eyes. For once he didn't care if anyone knew he was crying. What did it matter up here? He was all alone. No one could see him. Angry at himself he looked down at his copy book where he had been writing his Mandarin characters but was upset to see that he had smudged the last character he had painted. He was disappointed as he wanted them to be pristine so that he could show them to Yeh Yeh when he came back from hospital. Now he knew he wouldn't be pleased with him and threw down his brush in disgust.

'Your father called and was asking for you,' Nai Nai said from outside the door.

He leaned against the jamb so that he could hear her. 'What did he say?' he asked.

'He is worried about you.'

'How is he?'

'There are a lot of people who are sick and he is helping them.'

'And Yeh Yeh?'

'He isn't well.'

He listened, a feeling of dread inside him and couldn't think of anything to say.

'Neil?' Nai Nai asked. 'Are you all right?'

'Yes,' he whispered. 'I hope Yeh Yeh will be better soon.'

'I will tell your Dad to say that to him.'

He nodded.

'I will be up to talk to you later,' she said.

'Can I come downstairs?' he asked hopefully.

'No, not yet.'

'Will it be soon?'

'I do not know.'

'Are many people sick?'

'Yes.'

Neil's heart dropped.

He woke up and stared around him. The moon in the sky threw a slanting gleam of light which cut through the shadows. The characters he had written danced around him, and he stifled a scream. For a few seconds he didn't know where he was until the shadows took on the shapes of the furniture again and he began to realise that he was still in his room. But he felt that the walls were about to squash him into something very small. He was afraid and didn't know why.

Chapter Thirty-eight

Claire walked quickly through the store and threw her arms around Liz. 'It's wonderful to see you.'

'It's like first day at school,' she smiled.

'How are you feeling?'

'Fine, back to normal thank God.' She seemed in good form this morning.

'Come on in, I've got coffee on.' Claire took her arm and together they walked into the office.

'The store is looking wonderful, and all the spring designs are so pretty.' Liz sipped her coffee.

'There's been a lot of interest. The clients love the pale colours, the lemons and blues, lilacs and greens. There's something delicious about them.'

'How is the shoe range selling?'

'It's going very well.'

'You know we were planning a reception for our clients to introduce the new designs, I'm wondering now if perhaps we should hold back for a while until we see what happens with the spread of the Coronavirus or Covid 19 as they're calling it now.' Claire suggested.

'Why don't we put up all of the designs on our website, let people see what's come in this year. We've a lot of clients who will be planning family events, weddings, celebrations of all sorts, and it will do no harm to broaden the website. If things get any worse, we might find ourselves having to sell more on line.'

'You're right, we should be looking ahead. Let's do that. We'll get our photographer in as soon as we can and make a start on it.'

'If we're posting items or sending by courier, we should maybe look at new packaging as well, what we have at present is rather bulky. I'll do some research into it.'

The door opened, staff began to arrive, and they were delighted when they saw Liz.

'It's great to be back,' she hugged and kissed them. 'Now the day has begun. I can't wait to go around my store, go from floor to floor and enjoy.'

'I'll come with you.' Claire followed, and they went through the departments.

'Our decisions in Paris and London were spot on, Claire, I can see that now.' She held out a shimmering silk gown in the evening wear department.

'We've already re-ordered this particular designer a few times, she's really popular.'

'And it's a pity the autumn shows in Italy have been postponed because of the Coronavirus, it has infected many people there.'

'It's terrible that it has spread so rapidly from China.'

'At least there is only one case in the North of Ireland, and that was someone who came from Italy.'

'There is complete lockdown in China, I hate the thought that Neil is confined to his room all on his own. It must be so lonely for him.'

'It's probably the only way to make sure that he doesn't catch it. Who is in the house?' Liz asked.

'His grandmother. I'm praying I'll hear from her soon. Although it won't stop me worrying.' She tried not to show too much emotion. It hovered barely below the surface these days and when anyone showed sympathy tears were inevitable.

'You'd think she would give you her phone number so that you wouldn't have to wait until she wishes to talk to you. It's peculiar that, a sort of manipulation in a way. Like they want to keep you at a distance.'

'I've been controlled by that whole family. Alan, his father, and Lien too. And now I feel like she just wants to drip feed me. Little by little. Keep me hanging in. If I didn't go to China I wonder would she have ever called me, or would they have forgotten me completely as if I'd never existed, and Neil had always been theirs.'

'Very strange.' Liz pressed the lift button for the next floor.

'She seemed to understand how I feel. You know, woman to woman. I was so hopeful that last time when I met her in China.'

'Maybe things will change because of the virus?'

'I don't know. God forbid it won't spread as rapidly as it has in Italy. I don't know how we would cope if it did.'

'There's a terrible death toll.'

'And it's in some other Asian countries as well. South Korea and Singapore. Some of them deal with it better than others.'

'It's frightening.'

They stepped out of the lift on the top floor. There were no clients in yet and they had the place to themselves. In each department, Liz had positioned a table, with comfortable chairs and there was always hot water, coffee and snacks available. They sat down at the window.

'What a view over the city,' Claire murmured. 'It's beautiful.'

'Dublin is our Dublin. Nowhere like it,' Liz added. 'I'm always glad I came back to live here. Never thought I would, you know. I enjoyed the bright lights of Paris and Rome too much.'

'There's something so special about Paris. It's such a romantic place. City of honeymoons, and affairs.'

'It's the French thing, affairs. Most French men have mistresses,' smiled Liz. 'I knew many of them when I lived there, and I was one too.'

Claire looked at her, eyes wide, taken aback.

'He was my first lover.'

She didn't know what to say. An instant realisation that this probably meant a lot to Liz. She had never talked very much about her past and certainly not her love life, and didn't deserve a glib jocose remark by way of response. Claire waited for her to continue and the silence widened between them.

'I met him on my first summer working in Paris. I was working in a design atelier. Helping in different departments and gaining experience. I particularly enjoyed millinery. And I could work with a needle and thread thanks to my mother who taught me how to sew. It was part of life then. She made all her own clothes and mine too until I began to do that myself,' she said with a wry smile 'I'll fill you in about Jean Claude next time we have a glass together.'

'I can't wait,' Claire laughed, standing up. 'Time to go to work.'

'I'm looking forward to meeting our clients.'

'Come on,' Claire led the way across the salon.

Chapter Thirty-nine

Jim just managed to catch one of the last flights out of Soeul in South Korea. He had spent the last couple of weeks in Asia trying to get new suppliers for his components. While some of the companies were still open, there was always the chance that regulations could change suddenly in various countries and lockdowns applied.

Conscious of the Coronavirus, he had worn a mask and gloves all the time, and the flight happened to be half empty. He worked on his computer for most of the journey. Sent some emails, including one to Claire. He hadn't seen her in the weeks since he had left Dublin and really missed her.

He looked out the window of the plane into the night sky and wished he could explain how deeply he felt about her. But that was almost impossible. He had so little opportunity. That first night they made love he had told her how much he loved her. He longed for her to know what it meant to a man in his forties to meet a beautiful woman and fall in love with her. To tell her how special she was. How lovely. Deep blue pools told of untold depths he wanted to explore. Lips painted soft peachy pink. Blushed cheeks. Lashes thick, black, shadowed. He longed so much to say the words which would explain to Claire the depth of his feelings but the chance to say it out loud now drifted away into the distance where it echoed, a hollow empty sound.

He knew there would be no chance with Coronavirus controlling their lives. He wondered what she was thinking about him. How would she go down that road with so much on her mind. The loss of her child paramount. Could he really understand. He had lost Marina so he should. But if he didn't have empathy for Claire would her grief ease? The same question re-occurred. Again and again. Without the return of Neil, was there any future for himself and Claire? He felt helpless. If only he could go back to Beijing and see if he could help find her son. But it wasn't something she wanted him to do. She didn't want him to cross those imaginary lines which she had drawn. Lines which prevented him from moving any closer to her. He was reminded of the lines which shops in the East had drawn keeping customers at a distance from the staff who served them, and wondered if this happened in Ireland then it was very likely he would be kept apart from Claire as well.

'I've missed you, I'd give anything to talk to you.' He phoned immediately he had landed in London.

'Where are you?'

'Heathrow. I'm heading to the hotel now.'

'Was it a successful trip? Did you meet some companies who could supply what you need?'

'Yes and no, they're all unsure about the future.'

'As we are.'

'It's pretty bad over there, countries locked down, cities deserted, you wouldn't believe. And a lot of flights have been cancelled.'

'I've seen television footage and it's horrifying. Like a biblical holocaust.'

'That's some description.'

'Maybe it's some sort of germ warfare.'

'I've even heard rumours of that already.'

'I suppose it's fake news.'

'Whatever, the world has to try and find a vaccine. Once we have that, then we have a chance. Without it …' he stopped talking. 'I'm sorry, I'm being too negative.'

'It's hard for everyone.'

'I wish I could see you, it seems ages since we've been together,' he said. 'But I'm going to have to self-isolate for two weeks when I get back. I can't take the risk of passing on the virus to anyone. I could already be carrying it.'

'That's difficult. What about Donal?'

'He'll stay with my sister here.'

'He seems to be doing well at college, he's enjoying it.'

'And madly in love with Sophie,' he laughed softly.

She smiled to herself.

'We were all like that once.'

'Yeah.'

'Must go,' he said. 'I'll call you. Take care. Love you.'

'See you.'

She put down the phone.

Once again, he felt as if he had been pushed out there on to the edge of her life, and now found he was struggling to hold on to her, like she had fallen off a cliff.

The following day his worst fears regarding Covid 19 were realised as the first case was announced in the Republic of Ireland.

Chapter Forty

Claire was disappointed that Jim couldn't call to see her. It sounded as if he wanted to, although her confidence always wobbled and she was never quite sure. He said he loved her, and she had told him that she felt the same, but he was away so often she wondered whether he really meant it. Now he was quarantined and although he rang every night she could tell he was very worried about his business. Events were moving so fast he wasn't able to keep up with them. She was sympathetic, but couldn't help unfortunately. By now Liz was becoming very concerned also. Although her designers were still producing product, all runway shows had been cancelled. Airlines had cancelled flights as well.

'I'm worried Claire, what if we go the same way as China? Where will we find ourselves?' Liz asked.

'I don't want you to worry too much. It won't do you any good. And you're vulnerable since your operation.'

'But they've closed the universities and schools for the next two weeks.'

'I know, and my two lodgers have gone home. At least they are sensible and I'm glad about that. The medical information is that we should stay two metres apart any time we meet.' Claire was concerned about being able to pay her own mortgage, although there was talk of the banks offering a moratorium to people who might fall behind in their repayments. 'There are cases here, although it hasn't spread as fast as it did in Italy.'

'At least, business is good at the moment. Since I've got back all our old clients are coming in, buying like mad, as if clothes were going out of fashion.'

'They know you're here, and our spring collection has been really successful, they love it. And having all of the ranges online now is a good idea because clients can look up the web site when they go home and make a final decision about their choice without having to come back to the store.'

'But if the shows don't happen then how will we see the autumn and winter collections?'

'Online I suppose.'

'It won't be the same.'

'We can still see the designs and place our orders,' explained Claire, anxious to placate Liz. She didn't want her to worry too much.

'I suppose, but I was looking forward to New York and Milan, but now it looks as if those shows will be deferred or cancelled altogether.'

'I'll check with them and see what programme they've set up,' Claire reassured.

'Would you?' Liz asked, seeming relieved.

'I will, relax, don't get your knickers in a knot,' she laughed.

'I don't know myself these days, I can get upset so easily.'

'We all can, but we won't let ourselves be dominated by it. We'll hang in there, like we always have,' she smiled at Liz.

'We have our website already set up and if the government decide to close down businesses, like they've done in Italy, then we must be prepared.'

The reaction to Covid 19 by the government suddenly exploded. It was announced that with the exception of supermarkets, and pharmacies, most businesses, venues, and facilities were closed. A few days later, the Government banned all non-essential travel, except people working in critical services.

Otherwise people were told to stay at home, with all travel banned beyond two km from their homes. And people over seventy were advised to stay indoors.

When Claire heard that she immediately went over to her parents.

'Lockdown?' Her father couldn't get his head around it.

'It's for your own safety.'

'And how will you go to work?' Peggy asked.

'I won't be working at the shop, it's closed. I've already been on to Liz and we'll be selling on line. Both of us brought home stock so that we can fulfil the orders. I can't move around my house there is so much in it.'

Her parents were very worried.

'I will do your shopping for you every couple of days, and take Rusty for a walk,' Claire explained, talking to them from the end of the drive.

'I'm going to miss my walk,' her father's face was downcast.

'I hope it won't last that long, but I don't want either of you to catch Covid 19, so be very careful. You know that the over seventies are more likely to catch it. Your immune systems are lower than younger people.'

'But I thought it was like flu?' her mother asked.

'It's far worse than flu, so please don't take any risks.'

'I hate the thought of it.' Peggy looked at Michael.

'But think of the numbers of people who will lose their jobs if all the companies are closed,' Claire said gently. 'All our staff will have to be let go as well and Liz hates doing that. She's going to keep paying them for the moment until something is arranged but I suppose it depends on how long this pandemic will last. But if you phone me in the morning with your shopping list then I'll go to the supermarket, pick them up for you and drop them back. Then you let Rusty out and I'll take him for a walk.'

Her Mam and Dad were very grateful.

Clare suddenly realised that her own situation was going to prove difficult. But at least she would be working at home and hoped Liz would manage to pay her. But if they were getting the orders in then the company would still be viable. But on top of that she was worried about her mortgage repayments and how she was going to manage to keep up to date now that Donal and Sophie had gone home.

Jim checked in on a Zoom call.

'How is everyone these days,' she asked, so happy to see his smiling face on the computer screen. 'There is so much happening with Covid 19, I don't know how we will cope. Are you managing to keep your business viable?'

'Not really, we've been closed down as our usual products are not considered essential. Although we are adapting our production lines to manufacture perspex products at the moment. They are needed for cough screens for front line staff, and there will be different types for supermarkets and shops which will replace our normal range, so it's a complete turn around.'

'That is fantastic, you're lucky to have some products which can be made. There is such a need for all types of PPE.'

'We have to keep going, I want to keep on my staff. They're very experienced.'

'Hope your business will survive.'

'Has Liz closed up the shop?'

'Yes, unfortunately. Although our website is looking good now and we're hoping that it will do well with people out of work and confined to home.'

'Everyone is online all the time.'

'Although we're not sure how successful we will be.'

'The two kilometres prevents us travelling, which means I cannot see you, although I hope it doesn't last for long, I've missed you so much since I've been away.'

'If it's anything like China, God knows what lies ahead of us although the numbers who have been infected there have reduced.'

'Let us hope we can keep it under control.'

'The government are taking advice from the medical people, and I suppose they know what they're at.'

'This is lock-down.'

'There's something so final about that description. I hate the word.'

'Have you heard from Lien in China?'

'No.' Her heart was heavy. She had not heard from her mother in law in weeks and did not know what was happening to Neil.

'I'm sorry to hear that.'

'I'm hopeful that he is still all right and hasn't caught the virus.' She didn't want to let him see how upset she was. These days her grief had to be borne without a murmur. And she had become conscious of mentioning Neil's name. Talking too much about his loss. Expecting people to be sympathetic, although it wasn't always what she wanted or needed. Her parents mentioned him regularly, although it was as if he had gone to some really good place and was enjoying himself. For herself, she still sent him cards every week, and presents too, but found the lack of response always difficult to deal with. Calculating how many days it would take for the post to arrive, and how many for his reply, if any, and noting that in her diary, always on edge, waiting. It never changed.

'I'm sure Lien would have been in contact with you if anything happened to Neil,' Jim said gently.

'I hope so.'

'As the Coronavirus has taken a grip on Ireland, China seems to be gradually coming out of it. Let's hope it will be the same for us.'

'I wish.'

'His grandfather is in the most vulnerable age group, as most deaths occur in those over seventy. It's very frustrating for you, I wish I could be there with you.'

'So do I.'

'Let's hope it will be soon, my love.'

'I'll see you on Zoom tomorrow night, look forward to that.'

'I'll be here.'

Chapter Forty-one

Neil ran out of enthusiasm for kicking the paper football in his bedroom. He searched in the wardrobe for something else which might be more interesting. There were some things he used to play with when he came on his holidays. But now the problem was to reach up to the presses at the top. He remembered that Ayi kept a stepladder in a cupboard on the landing and now he opened the door and peered out. There was no sound. The house was silent. Like it was completely empty. He could see the cupboard and hoped that it wasn't locked. But he was worried about Nai Nai. She would be very angry with him if he left his room. He knew that, but decided to take a chance. He was going to get that stepladder no matter what.

He took off his shoes and darted across the shining wooden floor in his socks almost slipping in haste, sliding towards the wall and banging up against it. He grabbed the round handle of the door and pulled it open, delighted to see the ladder. He reached in and carried it across to his room. Then he ran back and closed the door quietly.

Excited, he lifted it over to the wardrobe and climbed up. In this position he just managed to reach the top door and opened it. He was faced with a treasure trove of games. Draughts, Monopoly, and many others. Then to his delight he saw the box that held his old keyboard underneath everything. He yelled out loud and hoped Nai Nai hadn't heard him. If she told him not to play he would be really sad.

He put his arms around it, and took it down. Opened it up and ran his fingers along the keys. But he had to plug it in and wondered what Nai Nai would say when she heard the sound. Although he wanted to play immediately, he decided to wait until she came up with his lunch and ask. But the wait was too frustrating and he began to play softly. His heart lifted but crashed down again when there was a knock on the door. Only then he remembered he should have put on his headphones.

'Neil? What are you doing?' Nai Nai asked from outside.

'I found my keyboard in the wardrobe.'

'How did you reach so high?'

'I stood on the desk.' He lied. Reminding himself not to forget to replace the ladder later.

There was silence from outside.

'Will I leave out my bedclothes for washing?' he asked.

'Yes, you can do that,' she answered although he thought she sounded very strange, as if she didn't believe him.

'Is the keyboard too loud?'

'No, I like hearing you play.'

'Thank you, Nai Nai.' He was delighted that she didn't tell him to stop.

That made a huge difference to his day. And when she left up the fresh bedclothes, she included a bundle of his sheet music as well. He chose all his favourites and played for the evening, enjoying himself so much he almost forgot he couldn't leave his room.

The following morning, as usual, she asked him how he was feeling and he said he was fine.

'I have been speaking to your father and he tells me that if you are still feeling all right then we can be together again soon.'

'And I can go downstairs?'

'Yes.'

'Can I come out now?' he asked, excited.

'I will give you a thermometer to take your temperature. If it is normal then we can have dinner together.'

'What is normal?'

'I will tell you.'

'That is great Nai Nai, I hate my room.' He meant that too.

'Play some music for me,' she asked.

'What would you like.'

'Anything. I am sitting here waiting.'

He placed his fingers on the keys. He was so glad that his grandmother had come up to talk to him. Normally, she came up and down the stairs but never stayed.

'Would you like Mozart?'

'Beautiful.'

He began. Loving the sound of the notes as they rippled. He let the music take him to another place. To play for someone meant everything.

When he had finished, he went to the door again and could hear the echo of her hands clapping. He smiled, delighted. 'Did you enjoy it?' he called.

'Yes, I did. It was very good. Your Dad and Yeh Yeh will be so happy when they hear how well you have done.'

'Is Yeh Yeh better yet?'

'No, he is still very sick.'

He was sad to hear that.

'I will tell your Dad to say to Yeh Yeh that you are thinking about him.'

'I am.'

After that he waited anxiously for her to tell him when he could come downstairs. Every time she left his food, or clothes, he asked her, but she never said yes.

220

Chapter Forty-two

Claire's phone rang as she lay sleeping and she just managed to reach for it before it went on to voicemail. 'Yes?' Her voice was husky.

'It is I, Lien.'

'How are you?' she gasped breathlessly pushing herself up.

'I am well.'

'I am glad to hear that. And Alan and his father?'

'My husband has died.' Her voice sounded weak.

'I am so sorry,' she whispered, feeling genuinely sympathetic for the woman.

'And Alan is ill with the virus.'

She couldn't think of what to say at first.

'Is it very serious?'

'I do not know, I was not able to speak with him.'

Claire was shocked into silence for a moment.

'When is the funeral for your husband?'

'It will be a cremation but I must stay indoors to protect Neil.'

'That is very sad for you. How is Neil, is he all right?'

'Yes, he is.'

An enormous sense of relief swept through her.

'Does he know about his grandfather and Dad?' she asked that vital question.

'I will tell him about his grandfather soon, but not about his Dad. He would be too upset.'

'Does he ask about me?'

'Sometimes.'

Tears brimmed.

'Will you send him back to me?'

'It is not possible now.'

'But if the virus disappears, will you send him then?'

There was silence.

'When the flights begin, will you?' She waited a moment before speaking again. 'It would be much safer here in Ireland, we do not have very high numbers of Covid 19.'

'It is not my decision, I have explained this to you when we talked before.'

Claire hated the stilted nature of conversing with Lien. There was no warmth about her.

'What does he do all day?'

'He plays his keyboard and is supposed to study but I am not sure how much he does of that.'

Claire was surprised at the mirth she could detect in her voice.

'And he kicks a football around, although he thinks I don't hear him.'

'How can he play in his room?' she smiled at the thought of it.

'He has some sort of ball. There is a lot of noise sometimes from there.'

'He is very resourceful, my son,' Claire said. 'And I'm glad that he plays football. I believe the schools are opening soon in Beijing, he will be happy to go back I'm sure.'

'I will let him come downstairs soon.'

'Tell him that I love him. Please?'

'I must go now,' Lien said.

'Thank you for calling. It means a great deal to me to know what is happening to my son.'

'I understand. You are a mother.'

'Call me soon?' Claire begged. 'And give Alan my regards, I hope he will be well soon. And my sympathies to you on the death of your husband.'

She didn't sleep for the rest of the night. The vision of Neil in his bedroom day after day cut through her. A sudden thought then. Would children begin to catch the virus? Would it mutate into something altogether different? How would he manage on his own? If only she could have him home. Then together they would get through this pandemic. Tears drifted and the pillow was damp under her face.

The light filtered into the room. She pushed herself out of bed and had a shower. The water was refreshing and she felt somewhat better as she stepped on to the softness of the bath mat and wrapped herself in her robe. Sipping a cup of coffee, she looked out into the garden pensively. The sun shone and the sky was a blue arc above her. The weather had been unusually good over the last few weeks, long sunny spring days. She wondered what the weather was like now in Beijing, and looked it up on her phone surprised to see it wasn't all that different in March, but there was a big increase in temperature in April and on into the summer when they experienced much warmer weather, high humidity and even rain.

She thought about Jim, but hoped that he wouldn't call her on the phone as he often did in the morning. Now she needed time to herself. To absorb what Lien had told her. She would have given anything to book a flight to Beijing, but that was impossible as the Chinese government had suspended the entry of foreigners into China so she had no chance at all of seeing Neil until the pandemic had died off, and there was no longer the fear of catching the virus across the world. It was a terrifying prospect.

Chapter Forty-three

'Nai Nai, when can I go downstairs with you?' Neil asked when he heard her walk on the landing, and that clink as she placed the breakfast tray on the trolley.

She didn't answer.

'Nai Nai?' he called out, his voice louder, afraid that she might already have gone down without speaking to him.

'Neil?'

'I can't hear you.'

'Eat your breakfast and I will come for you.'

'Today?'

'Yes, today.'

Finished his breakfast, he showered and put on clean clothes. Combed his straight black hair which was longer than usual because he couldn't go to the barber. Then he made his bed and tidied around the room, stood at the door, and waited. But she didn't come.

Later there was a knock on the door.

He stood up.

'It is me, my Neil.' The door opened and Lien appeared wearing a mask. She handed him one also. 'Come, but follow me from a distance. We must not be close to one another.'

She led the way down into her study, that place where she read books, and painted pictures, and told him to stand at the door.

'You are feeling well?' she asked, smiling, her voice soft,

brown eyes meeting his.

He nodded.

'I have something to tell you,' she said. 'It is not good.'

'Not good?' He repeated the words, puzzled.

'It is our loss.' She bent her head. 'Your grandfather has died.'

'Of the sickness?' he gasped.

'Yes.' She clasped her hands together.

Tears moistened. He took a sharp breath.

'Let us pray to Buddha. I am wearing white, the colour of death.' She opened a narrow door in the far wall and went inside. There was a large golden statue in an alcove at the far end. 'Kneel just here.' She pointed to a flat cushion on the floor and went up closer to the statue herself.

He had never been in this room before and was amazed by the size of the Buddha which reached almost to the ceiling. Nai Nai knelt in front of it, took a taper and lit long narrow candles. The light flickered and sent shadows across the carved shape. She lit the incense burner. The scent wafted into the air and tickled his nose and almost made him sneeze. Then she held her hands in prayer and bent in respect. He did the same. She began to sing. A strange moaning sound. He listened and knew that she was singing for Yeh Yeh.

They stayed there a long time. Her singing became faint and after a while he could hardly hear her at all. Neil was afraid to move. His mouth was dry. His knees sore from the hard cushion. Slowly she rose up. He did the same and she ushered him ahead of her into the study.

'Can I go to the funeral for Yeh Yeh,' he asked.

'There will be no funeral.'

'Why?'

'Because of the virus it is not allowed.'

He was puzzled about that. Before he came out to Beijing last summer, he remembered going to a funeral for his uncle and there were a lot of people in the church and back at the hotel afterwards. His Mum had tears in her eyes as they stood around the grave at the cemetery. And now he could feel tears in his eyes because there was no funeral for Yeh Yeh. He looked at Nai Nai and could see that there were tears in her eyes as well.

Lien allowed Neil to come down the following day.

'We will have to be very careful that we are not too close to each other,' she said. 'And we must wear our masks at all times, and our gloves.'

He didn't ask the question, but giggled to himself as he wondered how he would eat with it on.

'Would you like to go back to school?'

'I would,' he said with a wide grin. School. At last.

'When?'

'Monday.'

'That is fantastic, I'll be able to see Robert again. I thought it would never happen.'

'The authorities are easing things. People are going back to work. More shops are open. But we will have to live in a different way now.'

Immediately he ran to the window. It was still deserted outside. Cars parked in driveways. But knowing he was going back to school on Monday made all the difference.

For the first time Lien drove him to school. Insisting that he sat in the back seat as far away from her as he could be. He walked up the steps, but was stopped by a man dressed in a blue uniform over his clothes. He wore a mask similar to the one he wore himself, and he had a plastic visor over that. He took something and held it in front of Neil's forehead. Then he looked at it and told Neil to go ahead.

In the foyer, Neil looked around for Robert, but he couldn't see him. It was very strange. All the students were wearing masks, as were teachers, and he didn't recognise anyone. As he stood at the door, another man dressed in a blue uniform prevented him from moving towards his classroom until the girl before him had gone on ahead. There were white lines on the floor creating a pathway and he was told to follow that. When he arrived in his classroom, he immediately looked to where Robert sat and was delighted to see him there. He smiled, but realised when Robert didn't smile back that it was because he was wearing a mask too. The desks were now placed much further away from each other, and there were plastic screens at either side of it. He wondered how he would talk to Robert, and only then was aware of how quiet it was in the room. Normally, the boys and girls would be talking to each other loudly, but today no one spoke very much.

It was the beginning of a strange time. The only way he could talk to Robert was when they had a break and even then it was difficult because they had to stand two metres apart and only remove their masks when they had to eat or drink something. He found that first time extremely funny and could not stop laughing, as did Robert.

'I'm glad to be back,' Neil said.

'So am I.'

'I had to spend so much time on my own, it was weird.'

'I was with my mother and brother. Dad had to stay in work. And we had to do online study which was a pain.'

'I could do what I wanted and I have no computer so no classes online.'

'Lucky you.'

They laughed again.

Neil was so glad to be back in school and enjoyed the fun he and Robert had.

But he had to catch up with the time he had lost and the teachers were anxious to make sure that all the students reached the standard they should have achieved by this time of the year, so there was a lot of extra work each day. Previously he used to stay and study in the evenings, but now Nai Nai collected him earlier as she never liked to drive in the city at a late hour. And Kim wasn't here to drive him.

'When will Dad be home?' he asked her.

'I do not know.'

'Where is the hospital?'

'It's a new one built especially for looking after people with the virus.'

He nodded. 'Could I go to see Dad?'

'No, you might catch Coronavirus.'

'But Dad could catch it like Yeh Yeh.'

'He is very careful.'

'I hope so.' He wished his Dad would come home soon. He missed him even though he was still a little afraid of him. But he wanted to tell him that he was thinking of him.

'How was school today?' she asked.

'I have lots of homework.'

'We will have something to eat and you can begin your study.'

'I hardly have time to practice the piano at all now,' he said to her.

'Maybe there will be time when you have finished your studies at the weekend.'

He missed playing the piano and that night when he had finished his homework he played his keyboard. Afraid to disturb Nai Nai, he put on his headphones. So long since he had played the piano downstairs, the keyboard was a good substitute. He hugged his own bedroom now. In that place he could choose when he might play. He liked that he could make his own decisions.

He wondered did his Mum know about the virus? Could she see

228

on the television that there were people being taken to hospital. He wished he could talk to her. Tell her what it was like now that Yeh Yeh had died. And that there were no servants in the house and he and Nai Nai were alone. Did she know that his father was at the hospital now and he didn't see him at all. If everyone was sick there with the virus then maybe he would catch it as well. Neil wondered what he would do then?

Chapter Forty-four

Life changed drastically. Claire couldn't get her head around it. The city was deserted. Hardly any traffic. Buses and trains empty except for a couple of passengers. All shops, pubs, restaurants and other businesses were closed, except for supermarkets and pharmacies. She felt that Dublin must be the same as Beijing. According to Lien, Neil was isolated in his room. Knowing that made her feel that he was imprisoned. Like a butterfly incarcerated, wings clipped. He was held against his will by this family, and Claire was certain that he must be feeling the same way as she was herself. Losing her boy and never hearing his voice left her out there in the wilderness. But more than anything she had to deal with the loneliness which came in waves. Her moods dark and unpredictable. She struggled to hide how low she felt.

Every day she drove to see her parents, always worried about them too. But they didn't like that Claire had to do their shopping for them and missed their daily trip to the shopping centre where her Dad bought his Irish Times and they picked up a small amount of groceries. It was a social occasion, and as they had a wide circle of friends and acquaintances they often met them for coffee. But now they were *cocooning* and completely confined to the house and found that difficult, really missing their choir practices, and bridge nights. Driving over to them Claire was stopped by the police occasionally, and asked where she was going, but they were always very understanding.

Always a busy person around the house and garden, her mother managed the restrictions quite well, but her Dad was less able, and he was the one who found the constrained nature of life these days very hard. Although Claire took the dog for a walk every couple of days, Michael insisted on throwing the ball over and over and walking him up and down the garden, through the side passage and around the front and back again. It was tedious although the dog didn't seem to mind. But Peggy wasn't too happy. Her garden was her pride and joy and her flowerbeds were still full of daffodils and narcissus and other spring flowers which were in danger of being knocked over by the ball.

Claire was glad she was able to visit them. Always anxious to remind them about hand-washing, using the sanitiser she bought, and telling them to make sure that any people who called stood at least two metres down the path. Her parents were not avid television watchers, and it was usually the news or soaps they enjoyed. She had heard of people being literally addicted to news reports about Covid 19 which could be depressing.

She Zoomed Liz every day and they discussed business. When the lockdown had happened, Liz and Claire called all of the clients they had on their database, just to make contact and find out how they were doing. Everyone was confined to their homes except for the two kilometre distance, but worse than that was the restriction advised to people over seventy. Their clients were of every age, and most of them were delighted to know that Liz was still open and they could make contact with her and talk through the new designs. It was a very personal business and their clients really appreciated the friendship she had with each and every one of them. While they were really keen on the new ranges, to Liz and Claire's surprise, most of them were asking for a supply of masks which would complement their clothes. So that was a very successful new line they carried.

'How will you manage financially if you are intending to pay the staff?' Claire asked Liz.

'I have reserves, and hopefully I can pay them a certain amount, and with the government subsidy on top of that, they should reach their normal salary levels. But I don't want you to worry about your mortgage repayments, I will continue to pay your full salary, as you are probably working even longer hours than you would normally. And I know that Donal and Sophie have gone home so your financial position is affected.'

'Since you gave me such a substantial raise at Christmas, I've managed to keep to the payment schedule so I'm not as worried as I was, and it's all thanks to you. I'm praying that we will do some really good online business and that will help to keep us afloat as long as the Covid 19 restrictions are in force. I'll call into the store just to have a look around this afternoon. I need to check for leaks or anything like that.'

'You'll be more than two kilometres,' pointed out Liz. 'Hopefully, the Gardai won't stop you. Although I should really be doing that.'

'I want you to take care of yourself. You are vulnerable because of your operation, so you should stay in the house. I'll drop off your shopping when I'm doing it for my parents, just give me a list. And I'll make a few dishes so that you can put them in the freezer and you won't have to cook.'

'Thank you so much, you always look after me,' she smiled.

'You need someone.'

'I appreciate your care, you're almost like a daughter to me particularly since I've been ill.'

'Any time. You've been so good to me, and paying my full salary too, you're very generous. I could still apply for the Covid 19 payment if you like which would reduce the amount you pay me?'

'Not at all, I'll manage.'

'Thanks.'

Claire was missing Jim. While she had told him that she didn't want a relationship in the beginning now it seemed that she had got her wish. But on that first night they had made love she had committed herself to him. Physically and mentally. Now she had lost him again through this lockdown. While they talked on the phone, texted, and Zoomed, she didn't feel close to him and in the back of her mind worried that she might lose him altogether. She needed to hold him close. To hear him say he loved her.

Working on her own, she actually missed Donal and Sophie. She woke up earlier than usual in the mornings and the day stretched ahead of her, long and empty. But immediately she was filled with a need to shape it, and went online to see the orders which might have come in overnight. It was only then that she had something to do. But the thought of returning to the night again was always there lurking in the background of her days.

She Zoomed Lucy and Elaine regularly, but it wasn't the same as having a good chat.

'Everyone's baking and someone made sourdough bread and it exploded in the hot press,' Lucy laughed. 'Would you believe that?'

'I tried to make it but I wasn't successful either,' Elaine said, laughing.

'I haven't had time to bake.'

'We have to keep the kids entertained.'

Lucky you, she thought in her head.

'We play it like it's a game. School activities mixed in with crafts.'

'How do they like the online classes?'

'They enjoy them. The teachers are great. So full of enthusiasm and ideas.'

'I hear them on the radio sometimes talking about what they're doing.'

'It's hard to get the kids to concentrate for any length of time.

'I'm trying to do my work but then I have to leave it and deal with them. Most nights I'm still working at ten.'

'Sounds tough.'

'It is.'

'Not so bad for me obviously,' she admitted.

'How is your online business?'

'Very good. The orders are coming in all the time, although I have to do the packaging as well which means it takes that much longer.'

'It's great you are doing so well.'

'Hopefully, in a few weeks we will be allowed to travel in our own county, and in the next phase of the plan we'll all be free. Can you believe that we'll be able to go to the hairdressers?'

'It's like being released from prison.'

'My hair is a disaster, I'm looking forward to having a proper cut, my own attempts haven't been great.'

'So am I, it's far too long.'

'We're nearly there. Then we can celebrate.'

Claire usually called Tony on the phone around lunchtime. 'I hear that you haven't had any new cases in Beijing for some time now.'

'Yes, we're getting back to normal.'

'Every night the HSE announce the numbers who have caught the virus and those who have died. I find that a bit difficult.'

'Have you any news of Neil?'

'He's fine, but his grandfather died and Alan has caught the virus.'

'That's such a pity.'

'I'm praying he recovers. Neil needs him.'

'That's very generous considering you and Alan are divorced and he took your son.'

'It's not fair on Neil to lose both parents, and I don't know what it will do to him in the long run. I'm still sending cards a couple of times a week but I haven't received any replies.'

'How odd.'

'I wondered if I should write to Lien now that Alan is at the hospital. As she is the only person at home perhaps she might feel she could respond to me. Would you mind if I gave her your name and number?'

'Not at all.'

'Thank you. I could suggest that she make contact with you if there was any chance that she might be able to send Neil back if circumstances changed or become too difficult.'

'I'd be only happy to help if she did decide that. But in the meantime, you would need to send me various documents. You know, birth certificates, yours and Neil's, marriage, divorce, custody etc.'

'I'll begin that now.'

'I would advise it.'

'If only I could fly to Beijing,' she sighed. 'But I can't even get a visa now.'

'The virus is making your situation even more difficult. It's affecting everyone.'

'I'm so glad that the spread of it has eased with you, at least you can go outside now and live normally. That must feel so good.'

'All the bars, restaurants and clubs have opened, and the streets are full of people again. It's amazing to see it. But we are all still being very careful.'

'I'm glad to hear that.'

'And hopefully there won't be a second spike here, that is the big worry.'

'Now the streets are deserted here, it's strange and eerie.'

'It was the same here, but as we're coming out of it, so will you no doubt. I'll let you know how things go.'

'Thanks Tony. Stay safe.'

There was something reassuring about chatting with Tony. She felt he knew her. Understood what she was about. And was grateful for that.

She talked to Jim that evening.

'When I introduced you to Tony on that first night in Beijing, I was sure he fancied you big time.'

She giggled.

'I was so jealous that you would respond to him and not me,' he spoke softly and smiled at her from the computer screen. She could immediately see what had attracted her to this man in the first place.

'No, Jim, there was no chance of that,' she reassured. 'Although I do like him, like,' she emphasised.

'I'm glad to know that.'

'He has offered to help bring Neil back if there's any chance of that happening.'

'Could he do anything?'

'I don't know.'

'I hate to think that you are so alone, I wish you were close to me now,' he said.

'So do I.'

'Let's hope Covid 19 diminishes soon and life returns to normal. By the way, how are your parents? Are they keeping well?'

'They're fine, I make sure they follow all the rules.'

'I'm sorry I have to run twenty-four hour shifts, it means that I must be on site most of the time.'

'How much sleep do you get?' she asked, concerned.

'Not a lot, but I manage.'

'Look after yourself.'

'And you.'

Claire hated Zoom. She wanted to hug Jim so tight he would

never get away, but couldn't tell him exactly how she felt only seeing him on a computer screen. That would have to wait.

That night she wrote to Lien, and gave her Tony's name, and phone number as he had agreed. Then she spent a couple of hours searching through her files for the various documents he needed.

'I am so tired of this lockdown. If we didn't have so much to do with our online business I think I'd go mad altogether,' Liz groaned when Claire called to leave the shopping with her later, taking care to keep a good distance between them.

'I know, it's very hard on you. But you have to protect yourself. After your heart operation you're very vulnerable.'

'But life is so dull. I miss meeting all our clients every day. And socialising with friends. I can't even go out for a decent walk. I'm hemmed in by these four walls.' Liz seemed genuinely worried.

'It's very hard on you, although at least we've managed to stay in business.'

'Thanks to your efforts, Claire, couldn't do it without you.'

'It won't last much longer, the government are speeding up the progress of the various stages, so that we'll have almost everything open by the end of June hopefully. And the numbers of people who can gather inside and out will have increased which will be a big relief for everyone.'

'We'll have to arrange for screens so that we can have social distancing between our staff and the clients.'

'Jim can supply those.'

'Maybe you'd ask him to call me. Doing that makes me feel that we'll be open even sooner.'

'Next time I'm in the store, I'll check the measurements and send Jim photos of the reception desks.'

'Thanks. There are so many aspects to the restrictions. The clothes will have to be sprayed in between clients.'

'We'll have to allow them to fit them on.'
'And we'll have no bathroom.'
'That's not going to be easy.'
'And we should supply masks and gloves too.'
'There will be a lot of hassle.'
'We'll get used to it.'
'And all of that will be *normal* after a while.'

Chapter Forty-five

Neil sat down at the table and waited while Nai Nai placed his dinner plate in front of him.

'You have finished your homework?' she asked sitting down herself.

'Yes.'

'That is good.'

He scooped rice from a bowl with his chopsticks, and then picked some chicken. He didn't really like the meals his grandmother cooked for him, every day being much the same, and very boring too. But he knew she had to depend on the shop owner to deliver whatever he had. And she had explained that there wasn't a big selection because of Covid 19.

'My friend Robert is going back home to Ireland,' he said slowly, hating the thought of losing him.

'When will this happen?'

'Soon, he told me today.'

'He will go with his family?'

He nodded.

'Would you like to go home too?'

'Yes, I would.' His eyes brightened. He was surprised she had asked him that.

'To see your mother?'

'I would love to see Mum but I don't know where she is. Do you know if she has gone home?'

'I'm not sure of that.'

'She wanted me to go with her on that day she came.'

'I told you that mothers always love their children.'

He nodded. 'I would give anything to go home,' he whispered.

'You prefer it to Beijing?'

'There I have my friends and Gran and Grandad.' He felt guilty saying that. 'But I like it here too,' he added, afraid he might upset his grandmother.

'I am glad.'

'You could come and visit us,' he said.

'It is a very long way.'

'We could go together. Please Nai Nai?'

'I would miss my life here too much,' she said.

He was quiet after that, not sure what to say.

The next day in school he asked Robert when he was going home.

'I'm not sure, we are waiting to book the flight, Mum said.'

'Is your Dad going too?'

'Yes, and my brother. Is your Mum still in America?'

'I think so, although I'm not sure.'

'Doesn't she call you?'

Neil shook his head.

'Why don't you ask your Dad if you could come home with us?'

'He's working at the hospital, helping with the virus.'

'You could phone him.'

'I'm not allowed.'

'Will I ask my Dad to talk to yours?'

'Would he?'

'If I ask him.'

Neil listened to Robert. How exciting it would be if his Dad said he could travel home with Robert.

'We would have such fun on the journey.'

'Yes, it's so long and boring.'

He imagined how he would race up the driveway to the front door. Ring the doorbell. Bang on the knocker. Like a mad person. Calling out. Mum? Mum? But then the thought that his Mum might not be at home when he arrived occurred to him. There would be no one to meet him at the airport. And how would he get into the house. He didn't have a key. And there were other people living there now. A chill swept through him and he decided he didn't want to live at home if his Mum wasn't there.

'I was thinking I mightn't go if my Mum is in America,' Neil told Robert.

'Can you ask your Mum to come home to Dublin from America?'

'No.'

'Maybe your Dad can.'

'They don't speak much.'

'Are they divorced?'

Something surged and tightened around his chest. But he couldn't explain that to Robert.

'The parents of some of my other friends are divorced as well,' his friend said.

'I wish my Mum and Dad were still together and then I wouldn't be here,' Neil told him.

'My father's job takes us to live in different places. We will go home now for a while and then we'll be living somewhere else in the world.'

'Will he be working in another Embassy?'

'Yeah.'

'Do you like that?'

'No, I'd prefer to stay in one place.'

'Here?'

'No, Dublin.'

'Like me,' Neil laughed.

'If we were both living in Dublin we could play football on the

same team.'
    'And go to the cinema.'
    'Matches.'
    'Swimming.'
They laughed out loud.

Chapter Forty-six

Claire was excited. Jim was coming up with his staff to fit the screens.

'I just want to see you for a moment. I can't wait. Although we'll still be two metres apart, and I'm going to find that very difficult. It reminds me of those early days when we first met and I had to love you from a distance,' he had said the night before. 'I arranged to come up instead of the salesman who normally oversees the fitting of screens.'

'I'm looking forward to seeing you. Anyway, the government is loosening the restrictions, and the store will open at the end of June.' Claire couldn't believe that life was returning to normal at last.

Both Claire and Liz were already working in the store on that day, wearing masks and gloves as they re-arranged stock.

'We actually haven't got many designs left.' Liz stood looking at the range of clothes.

'Orders will take a long delivery time. But I've noticed that the designs being produced by the French and Italian fashion houses are far more casual than usual and cheaper too.'

'They've been working around the clock.'

'I'm expecting a lot of clients in on the first week so if we reduce the prices, we can clear a lot of the formal cocktail and evening wear. There are no events happening so obviously the casual clothes are becoming more popular.'

'I think that's the best approach. If you think of how people's social lives have changed, if we order in our usual ranges, we may not be able to sell them at all.'

Claire's phone pinged. She read the text.

'It's Jim, they've arrived. I'll open the gates.' She pressed the remote and then took the lift down to the ground floor, and hurried out through the office to open the back door. She stood waiting as a white van came into the carpark, followed by Jim's own car.

'Hi,' she called out, and waved. She could see the two lads in the van but her eyes immediately fastened on Jim as he drew up and stopped behind her own car. She walked towards him, and waited as he put on a perspex shield over a fabric mask, and stepped out of the car. She smiled at him, and looked into his eyes.

'It's great to see you,' he said.

'I'm looking forward to having one of those visors instead of these fabric ones which are not very comfortable,' she walked as far as she could towards him.

'If you're wearing them all day, they are uncomfortable. Although they say the fabric ones are safer than the visors. I'm wearing both today, I can't afford to pass the virus on to any of our clients, you and Liz especially.'

She found it very hard to stop herself from rushing closer and throwing her arms around him.

Jim introduced the men, and after that they immediately opened up the back of the van and began to unload the consignment.

'Would you like a cup of coffee?' she asked.

They said no thanks, and continued with their work.

'We stopped and had something on the road,' Jim added.

'Sorry we have to stay so far apart. I find it very difficult to remember, I keep straying towards people and then have to remind myself that I shouldn't do that.'

'We must,' he said and stood back. Claire walked into the office and he followed.

'Liz is upstairs on the top floor.'

'Just as well, I don't want to come too close to either of you, but particularly Liz, she is vulnerable.'

'Where will the lads start working. We have desks on the different floors but they're all the same size.'

'I'll go through everything before we finally install them. I hope they're suitable.'

'I'm sure they will be.'

'Give me a few minutes. I'll talk to the lads.'

'I'll go on up to Liz, we're just sorting out stock.'

'Well, how is it going?' Claire asked Liz.

'We should have enough to open, and maybe some of our new orders will have arrived by the opening day. Is Jim here?'

'He's downstairs with the men who are going to fit the screens.'

'I'm looking forward to meeting him.'

'It's a pity we can't spend any time together.' Claire was disappointed. All morning she had waited for Jim to arrive. Her heart tight, quivering in anticipation. As if she was waiting at an airport, or station, praying nothing had happened to her loved one on the journey. She had missed him so much over the last couple of months in lockdown, to be forced to hold herself aloof from him proved difficult now. She could taste him. Sense the touch of his hands. And longed to draw him into her arms, and never let him go.

'Claire?' He appeared at the head of the stairs.

'Let me introduce you to Liz.'

'It's lovely to meet you at last.'

They stood at a distance.

'I've heard a lot about you,' Liz said.

'Not all bad I hope,' he said with a grin, glancing at Claire.

'That would be telling.'

'Would you like to come down and have a look at the first screen, we've just fitted it.'

They followed him down to the ground floor.

'It looks fine, although I hate the thought of talking to clients through it.' Liz shuddered.

'We have no choice unfortunately,' Claire murmured.

'And as for wearing masks ...' Liz grimaced.

'I can never find anything in my handbag if I'm looking, they do seem to ride up. Look, even now it happens.' Claire adjusted hers.

'I brought a box of visors as an extra, you should really wear both. And let me know if you need more.'

'Thanks, Jim, we really appreciate it.'

'My pleasure.'

'And hopefully next time we meet this will all be over,' Liz laughed.

'It dominates all our thoughts.'

'At least in the early days of lockdown the weather was wonderful and that helped,' Liz said.

They laughed.

Claire watched them chat together. Glad to have a chance to hear him talk to someone else, and see his enthusiasm and interest in what Liz was saying, quite obvious from the expression in his eyes.

Their voices echoed in the high-ceilinged room. Suddenly Claire felt excluded and wanted to be part of that conversation. But couldn't move any closer. Frustrated by having to keep at a distance from him. She urged him to look around. Meet her eyes and tell her he loved her. She needed that assurance. A smile crossed her lips behind the mask she wore. It was strange. Now she could feel his lips soft on hers and let herself revel in his tenderness.

'I'd better see how the men are doing,' he said.

'That screen looks great,' Liz smiled.

'I'm lucky to have such good workers,' he said. 'I'll check on the rest of the screens.' He turned and took the stairs down.

'Wow, he's a nice guy,' Liz commented.

'Yes, he is.'

'Lucky you,' she laughed softly.

The men finished their work, and Claire followed Jim out to his car.

'It's been wonderful to see you,' he said. 'At least I have a chance to talk to you now that the lads have gone.' He glanced after the white van which had just exited the car park.

'I thought I would never see you. I hate staying apart and wearing masks,' Claire said.

'In spite of that, you're still looking wonderful. It's very frustrating to be confined to Zoom.'

Liz appeared in the doorway.

'Jim, thanks for delivering the screens, they look really good.'

'And will keep you safe.'

'Send on the invoice and I'll settle it immediately.'

'There's no hurry, Liz.'

'Thank you.'

'I'll head off. We've to fit more screens today,' Jim smiled at them both.

'Thanks again. Lovely to see you.' Claire watched him reverse the car out through the gates and drive away. A pang of regret darted through her.

'You must miss him,' Liz murmured.

Claire nodded.

'It's tough on you. With the loss of your Neil and now to have no contact with Jim,' Liz murmured, as they walked back into the store.

She nodded in agreement, but couldn't say anything.

By July, the figures of Covid 19 deaths, and new cases, had both reduced considerably, and the Irish government eased the lock-down. Although pubs were still prohibited from opening which wasn't popular. Everyone was relieved, Claire, Liz and all the staff were back at work. Business wasn't quite as hectic as pre Covid and while a lot of their clients came back into the store, there were still quite a number who preferred to order their clothes online.

'Some of our older clients have said that they won't be shopping again until there is a vaccine. They are quite worried.'

'That is understandable.'

'The pace of business is much slower than it was before with all the distancing etc. and then having to spray the fitting rooms between each person, and the clothes as well takes a lot of time.'

'Keep the fingers crossed that the spraying process doesn't harm the fabrics,' Claire commented. 'Our garments are very delicate.'

'So far they seem to be fine.'

'Hope the clients don't comment.'

'No one has said anything to me,' Liz added.

'I suppose everyone else has the same problems. We'll just have to live with it.'

'Still, it's great to see people on the streets, sitting out in the sunshine in restaurants eating, drinking, and enjoying themselves,' Claire murmured. 'Let's pray we have seen the last of Covid 19.'

Mostly she was thinking of her parents, and Liz too, who were vulnerable, and prayed they wouldn't catch the virus. Although she had to admit that she had heard of quite a few younger people who had contracted it. And that worried her. They were wearing the visors and cloth masks in the store, and felt confident enough. But they also had the cotton face masks and sanitisers available around the store, and there was a staff member always at the entrance to welcome in the clients.

She talked with Jim every evening and was able to unburden herself to him. He was a good listener.

'I wish I could help you,' he said last night. 'I should be able to do something. And I can't even come to see you. That's the most exasperating part of it. When we met at your store that last time we had to stay two metres apart and it was like there was a wall between us blocking any communication. 'I'd give anything to be together again,' he murmured. 'You know you are my life.'

'So would I.' She moved closer to the screen of her laptop. 'Just to touch you.'

'Kiss you,' he whispered.

'I love you.' She put her hand on the screen.

'I love you.' He did the same.

'But I'm afraid.' She had to admit. 'I have been thinking that I have nothing to give you. Without Neil I am only half a woman. I can't get that out of my head.'

'You are everything I want,' he insisted. 'If only I could persuade you of that.'

'It's not fair on you. I'm too caught up …' She found it difficult to explain to him exactly what she meant, and felt her love for Jim was dry. Empty. Full of dust. All he could touch was superficial and without depth. She could see an image of herself on the screen. Was she the person Jim wanted? He was silent. She could see disillusionment in his grey eyes. Was there any more living to be done? She asked herself. Had she anything left to give? Hemmed in by loss. She didn't know where this sudden feeling of inadequacy had come from. Was it her reaction to Covid 19?

There was still a hint of tears in Claire's eyes. Still a trembling lip. Longing to hold Neil close to her heart. Soon it would be his fourteenth birthday. He was becoming a young man. Moving further away from her motherly embrace all the time. Panic provoked a rush of emotion which triggered guilt.

She reproached herself for what she must have done for Alan to have kept her child from her. Blaming her for unknown wrongdoing. As time passed and Covid 19 continued to spike in various parts of the world, she began to think she would never see Neil again. She had no future with her son. He lived on the other side of the world.

'I'm sorry, Jim.'

They finished talking. Just left it there. Without further explanation. She didn't want to be persuaded that she should feel as much as he did. Didn't want to make promises that didn't include Neil.

Chapter Forty-seven

Neil was studying when Lien walked into the room. He stopped and looked at her. There was something strange about her, he thought.

She walked closer to him.

'What's wrong, Nai Nai?' he asked, noticing that there were tears in her eyes.

'I have more bad news,' she said slowly.

'What news?' His heart began to thump.

She pulled a chair over and sat down. 'Your Dad has died too.'

Tears flooded his eyes and he couldn't see clearly.

'The doctors couldn't save him.'

'But he should have been able to save himself, he's a doctor,' he burst out.

'There is no medicine for the virus.'

'If my Mum was here she could have looked after him, and Yeh Yeh too, she always looked after me. Can we go to the hospital?'

'No.'

'But why?'

'The government does not allow it.'

'They wouldn't let us see Yeh Yeh either.' Neil was very unhappy.

'No.'

'But I want to see Dad.'

'I understand.'

'No one told me that he was so sick,' he said angrily.

'It was sudden.'

'What am I going to do?' he appealed to her.

'I will look after you.'

'I want Mum.' he burst out crying.

His door was opened. 'Neil, it is time for your breakfast.'

'I don't want any.'

'I am waiting for you.'

Tears dribbled down his cheeks. They tasted salty. He was all alone. His Mum wasn't here or his Dad either. And now he didn't know whether he would ever see them again. He turned in the bed and buried his face in the pillow. Hot tears soaked the crisp cover.

'Neil?' his grandmother called again.

He couldn't answer, and was glad when she went away.

Nai Nai came back up during the day but he just pulled the covers over him to block out the daylight. He felt so alone. Longing to hear the voices of his Mum and Dad calling out for him. But he couldn't hear them. They had deserted him. There was a knock on the door. He rushed out of bed and pulled it open. But it was only Nai Nai. For a long moment he stared, crushed with disappointment.

'My Neil?'

'Where are Dad and Mum?' He looked at her. Praying that she would have a different answer for him. His Dad hadn't died and his Mum hadn't disappeared.

'I am so sorry.'

'Where are they?' he shouted.

'I cannot tell you.'

'But you must,' he insisted.

She looked into his eyes.

And he knew at that moment that she didn't have an answer.

'Come and eat. You must be very hungry.'

'I'm not hungry.' He retreated into his bedroom.

'I have made some cookies for you'

'I don't want any,' he snapped. Annoyed that she was trying to persuade him to eat when he didn't want to.

'Please, Neil, I am worried about you. You cannot go so many days without eating.'

'Will there be a funeral for my Dad?'

'No, I am sorry Neil.'

He banged the door closed and threw himself on the bed. That's all he did now. Just lay on the bed and thought of his Mum and Dad.

Lien was very persistent. Coming up and down to his room and begging him to have something to eat. He was annoyed with her.

'You must go to school too,' she reminded.

He said *no* in his head.

'Do you not miss your friend Robert?'

At her mention of his name, he suddenly realised that his friend would be going back to Dublin soon and that he might not see him again. Instantly, he decided that he had to go back to school, he couldn't miss saying *goodbye* to Robert before he left for Ireland.

That evening he decided to eat the dinner Nai Nai had prepared for him. He still wasn't very hungry but he made an effort to swallow some of the curried pork, and drank the large glass of water she poured for him.

'If you eat normal meals tomorrow also then you can go back to school the following day,' she said.

'Why can't I go tomorrow?' he asked.

'You are not well enough, let it be Tuesday.'

He wanted to argue but had to accept that. His Nai Nai knew best.

'Where have you been?' Robert asked as soon as he saw him.

'My Dad died from the virus,' Neil explained.

'I am sorry.' Robert was sympathetic.

He bit his lip but said no more. He couldn't talk about it, and struggled hard to prevent himself from bursting into tears. But he was glad he was wearing a mask which shielded his expression. 'When are you going back to Dublin?'

'I don't know yet. There are no flights.'

'I hope it won't be too soon.' Neil didn't want to think about losing his best friend. He had already lost his friends Tommy and Calum at home. He would have given anything to go home with Robert, especially now that his Dad had died.

'What will you do for the holidays?'

'I don't know. I'm on my own now with my grandmother. There is no-one else in the house, and we have to stay at home. She is afraid to go to anywhere else because of the virus.'

Chapter Forty-eight

Claire's phone rang.

She picked up the phone.

'Hallo?'

'It is I, Lien.'

'How are you?' a trembling breath swept through her.

'I am well but ...'

'But?' Her heart raced.

'I have something to tell you.' The woman's voice was wavering.

'Is it Neil?'

'No.'

A huge sigh eased the coiled spring inside.

'It is your husband. He has died from Coronavirus.'

Claire's lips twisted. Tears moistened her eyes.

'How is my boy?'

'He is very upset.'

'Can I talk to him?'

'He is at school.'

'I need to talk to him.'

'I will call you.'

'Thank you, Lien, thank you. I will be waiting.'

'Mum?'

'Neil?' Claire couldn't believe she was hearing his voice after all this time.

'Dad died, Mum, he was in the hospital when Yey Yey was sick, and he died too,' Neil said. 'I am very sad.'

She could sense his emotion.

'I'm so sorry my love.'

'I wish you were here Mum, are you still in America?'

'No, love, I'm at home.'

'In Dublin?'

'Of course.'

'Dad told me you lived in America and there were other people living in our house.'

'No, I don't live in America.' A flash of anger sped through her. How cruel of Alan to say such things to her boy.

'He said you didn't want me.' Neil's voice quivered.

'He wasn't right,' Claire said. 'I'll always want you, and will love you for ever.'

'Will you, Mum?'

She could tell how he felt. And remember that look in his eyes when he didn't believe what she was saying.

'Yes. You are my boy, Neil, and I've really missed you.'

'I want to come home, Mum.'

'And I want you too, Neil.'

'When will you be coming for me, Mum?'

'I'm not sure yet.' She had to admit that to him. 'I have to get a visa and book a flight.'

'How long will that take?'

'I'm not sure.'

'It could be a long time.' There was disappointment in his voice.

'I hope not.'

'I'll be waiting for you, Mum,' Neil whispered.

'Bye until I see you, pet. Can I talk to Nai Nai again please? I'll just arrange things with her.'

The other woman came on the line.

'Lien, I want you to send him home to me.'

'I will,' she agreed.

'Thank you.'

'I will call Mr. O'Keeffe at the Embassy and ask him to help.'

She couldn't believe what Lien was saying. 'Can you travel to Ireland with Neil?' she asked.

'It is too far.'

'But how will Neil travel alone? I can't go to China, I have no visa. Please, would you think about it,' she begged. 'I will pay for your flight.'

'It would be impossible for me.'

'I will contact the Chinese embassy and see if I can get a visa.'

'Yes, that would be best.'

'Can you give me your phone number so that I can let you know when I am coming?'

'I will text it to you.'

'Thank you, I am so grateful to you, Lien.'

'I am sad to lose my grandson.'

'You understand how I felt?'

'I do now.'

'I am sorry that you lost Alan and your husband.' As she said it, she realized how equally hard it must be for her mother in law to lose both to this terrible virus.

'Qishu …'

She knew what Lien meant – it was *fate*.

Chapter Forty-nine

The first person Claire called was Tony, but his phone line was engaged. She left a message but kept trying his number until eventually he answered.

'My ex-husband has died and my mother in law has agreed to send Neil home, I can't believe it,' she said.

'Lien has just been on and told me, and I was going to call you,' he said. 'I'm sorry about your husband but I'm sure you must be happy that Neil is coming home.'

'It's a dream come true, Tony. But there is a problem, I want to go to Beijing to bring Neil back but I have no visa and I won't get one now.'

'I have been checking various possibilities.'

'Thank you, Tony, if you could do anything to help, I'd really appreciate it.' She was very anxious.

'Peter and Alison will be returning to Dublin via Paris as soon as flights begin again and they have offered to bring Neil back with them. The two boys are good friends.'

'What? Say again?' She was unable to grasp his meaning at first.

'Relax, Claire,' he laughed.

'You have arranged this?'

'They are delighted to bring him home.'

'I was so worried about getting a visa.'

'Now you can forget about that.'

'I'll have to pay for his flights.'

'Don't worry, that will be arranged.'

'You've done so much for me, Tony, I can't thank you enough.'

'My pleasure, Claire, I'm delighted to help although I'm sorry Alan has died.'

'I'm sorry too, particularly for Neil.'

'He will miss him.'

'He said he was sad.'

'Poor kid.'

Next, Claire called Jim. A mixture of emotions within her. Now that Neil was coming back, she was so looking forward to seeing her son that she could think of nothing else. When she thought of her last Zoom meeting with Jim, and what she said to him, she felt guilty. But until Neil came home, and she settled back into normal life again, or as near as normal as possible because of Covid 19, she couldn't see how she would give Jim the love he deserved.

'I'm so happy for you. It's what you want more than anything. I know that, my love.'

'I'm sorry for how I spoke to you last time, but I just began to doubt myself.'

'Don't worry, my love, just think about Neil.'

'Thank you.'

'I just hope everything goes well for you, how soon do you think Neil will come back?'

'I'm not sure about that, I don't think there are any flights yet, but Tony will let me know the details as soon as he has made the bookings.'

'It's wonderful to have got this far, I'm glad Tony is helping you. He's a decent guy.'

'He's been amazing really, so anxious to help.'

Her eyes were bright, almost feverish. In that moment, she realised how much Jim meant to her.

Suddenly, the wounds which had pierced her heart since Alan had taken Neil began to heal just a little. Although she knew that this was only the beginning.

'I'm sorry that Alan has died, it's very sad for a young boy to lose his father, and especially so for Neil.'

'I hope he can deal with the grief.'

'Children are surprisingly strong,' Jim murmured quietly.

She could hear the compassion in his voice.

'Will my love be enough to replace his love for his father?'

'He will be very happy when you are reunited, I'm sure he's been longing to see you. Be confident, sweetheart, everything will be all right,' he reassured.

Chapter Fifty

'You are going to be late into school today,' Nai Nai told him.

'Why?'

'We have an appointment.'

'Where?'

'You will see,' she smiled.

He wondered where Nai Nai was taking him. When they arrived and got out of the car, he instantly recognised the sign on the building. 'This is the Irish Embassy, where Robert's Dad works,' he said excitedly.

'Your friend in school?'

'Yes, why are you bringing me here.'

'To meet a man who knows your Mum.'

He had that feeling of being somewhere he knew. He remembered that Robert had told him that his father said that Irish people should always feel safe in the Irish Embassy.

'Nai Nai, do you think Robert's Dad might help me get back to Ireland?'

'I don't know if that is possible.'

'But why are we here?'

'Stop talking,' she said sharply. 'And put on your mask.'

He obeyed her, but still wanted answers to the many other questions which whirled around his mind.

Nai Nai spoke to a man at the desk.

He made a phone call.

They sat on chairs. Neil was nervous.

Soon a man appeared. He smiled and bowed to Nai Nai. Then he turned to Neil and shook his hand.

'It's really nice to meet you both.'

'I have the papers,' Nai Nai said.

'That's good.'

She handed him an envelope.

'I will make enquiries and let you know what I have arranged,' he replied.

'My friend's father works here,' Neil said.

'Does he?' the man smiled.

'His name is Peter.'

'And his son is Robert, I know him.'

Neil was glad that the man knew Robert, but felt Nai Nai would be cross with him if he said any more, but he did anyway.

'You know my Mum?'

'I do indeed.'

Neil's eyes brightened.

'She is a good friend of mine.'

Lien stood up, and tipped Neil on his shoulder.

'It has been very nice to meet you,' the man said to Neil.

'I will call you, Lien.'

'Thank you, Mr. O'Keeffe.' She bowed.

He did the same.

They left.

'Why did we come here?' Neil asked as soon as they were outside.

'It is because your father has died.'

'You will miss Robert when he leaves?' Lien asked when she collected him from college that evening.

He gulped.

'Would you like to go home too?'

He turned to look at her.

'Would you?'

His mouth was dry. He opened it and closed it again with a sort of snap.

'Yes.' His reply was just a squeak. But instant. And sure.

'Would you like to travel with Robert and his family?'

'Could I?' He burst out, thrilled.

'It is being arranged.'

'Will you come too?'

'No, I cannot.'

'But then you will be all alone.'

'I am hoping some of our servants will return.'

'But if they don't, how will you do everything yourself?' He was concerned for his grandmother.

'As I do now, I suppose,' she smiled.

'I feel guilty leaving you. Dad wouldn't have wanted it.'

'Your mother loves you, I have promised to return you to her, it's your rightful place.'

Happiness spread through him. He could see his mother's face waft in front of him. She was smiling. Reaching for him. And holding him close.

'The man in the Embassy, Mr. O'Keeffe, will make the arrangements.'

Neil was torn in two. Guilty at leaving Nai Nai and joy that he was going home to his Mum. The very sound of the word *home* sent his heart soaring.

That evening before he went to bed, Lien handed him a bundle of envelopes. 'Your mother sent these.'

'When?'

'During the time you were here.'

He stared at them.

'And there were presents too. I will bring them.'

He picked up a card. 'It's addressed to me. Why didn't you give them to me? I used to wait for Mum to write to me but I thought she never did.'

'It was your father's decision.'

He bit his lip. A flare of anger deep within him that his Dad hadn't given him his own letters.

'I am sorry.'

'It's not your fault.'

She bent her head to him. 'Read them before you sleep.'

That night Neil opened the parcels and read all of the cards. And for the first time, his tears were not for himself, but for his Mum.

Chapter Fifty-one

'Claire, the flights will begin in August,' Tony told her.

'At last, I can't believe it,' she said, wanting to scream out loud with excitement. 'Thank you, Tony.' Claire couldn't get her mind around the wonder of seeing her darling Neil again. She was thrilled. The uncertainties she had expressed to Jim were still there, but she had tried to eliminate them, reluctant to dwell too deeply now that Neil was coming home to her at last.

'Let me make a note of that.' She picked up a pen, and wrote down the details. Neil would be flying with Alison and Peter and their boys from Beijing to Paris, and then there would be some hours delay, and they would catch a flight to Dublin. When they arrived, he would have to self-isolate with Alison and Peter and their boys at their home.

'I can't believe that Lien decided to send Neil home. Although she did promise me last time I was over there that she would do her best.'

'The most important aspect of it is the fact that your ex-husband died. She gave me Neil's passport and other papers and had managed to obtain a death certificate for Alan quickly. That family have a lot of influence.'

'It's sometimes the same here.'

'Anyway, all is sorted.'

'I can't thank you enough, Tony. I don't think I ever expected to see Neil again, and now because of your help, he's coming home.'

'You never gave up.'

'I've been so lucky to have such good friends.'

'Always be here for you, Claire. Never forget that.'

After her call with Tony, Claire knocked quickly on the door of Liz's office and burst in.

'Sorry, Liz, but I just want to tell you …'

Liz looked at her. 'Something wrong?'

'I've got the date at last.'

Liz stood up. 'When is it?'

'Neil will be arriving on Thursday week. I can't believe it Liz.'

'That's wonderful.'

'And then he'll be in quarantine for two weeks so if I could have some time off after that I'd really appreciate it. He's coming home at last,' she said excitedly, sank into a chair and burst into tears.

'Of course you'll have to spend time with Neil. That's vital. Take as long as you like. It's wonderful to think he'll be with you soon. I'm really looking forward to meeting the young man.'

'I can never thank you enough, you've been wonderful to me.'

Claire was at the airport early. There were very few people there, and at Arrivals she stood waiting, anxious to catch a first glimpse of Neil. She knew she couldn't throw her arms around him, and was forced to keep a distance which was extremely frustrating.

His flight from Paris was on time. She tried to judge how long it would take for him to walk off the aircraft and then through to the baggage terminal. After he had picked up his bag, he would come straight through the doors into Arrivals. And she would be there waiting for him.

Suddenly he appeared with two other boys, Peter and Alison. She couldn't believe it was Neil. Immediately she wanted to shout, wave and dance so as to draw his attention. Although she had to be careful to stay apart from the small number of other people there.

'Neil?' she called.

He looked up. Dark eyes searching for her. 'Mum?' He waved excitedly.

'I can't go too close because of Covid, but I'll see you very soon.' Her voice echoed across the terminal. 'Do you understand?'

'Yes Mum. I'll be staying with Robert.'

'I'll come over and talk to you through the window.'

'We'll all be there together for two weeks. Then I'll be home.'

'I'm really looking forward to seeing you.'

'So am I, Mum.'

Claire was running along in parallel with Neil, but then held back as the group moved towards the exit doors. 'Bye, see you soon.' She called out.

They waved to her as they went through, her heart bursting with love as they disappeared.

Chapter Fifty-two

When Neil saw his Mum waiting for him in the airport, his heart jumped. She was just the way he remembered, and he knew her instantly even though she was wearing one of those visors and a mask. He was wearing a cloth mask too. He had been worried that his Mum wouldn't be able to recognise him but when she waved he knew that she did and was delighted. He longed to run across to hug her but stopped himself, aware that it had to be fourteen days before he could do that. But he waved madly and she did the same, and she crossed her arms which he knew meant a virtual hug.

'Right lads, let's pick up our rental car.' Peter set off pulling the bags behind him and Neil had to follow, although he kept looking around to keep Claire in sight.

'Your Mum is following us,' Robert said.

'Yeah,' Neil grinned.

They stood at the desk of the car company, but Neil continued looking at his Mum as she stood some distance away, still waving. He waved again as Peter turned a corner and he had to follow and lost sight of his Mum.

Claire came to Alison and Peter's house every day during her lunch break and stood in the garden looking at Neil through the window.

'There's your Mum again,' Robert called Neil.

'Mum?' he rapped on the glass.

She smiled at him. 'How are you?'

'I'm well,' he shouted.

'Are you enjoying yourselves?'

'Yes, we are.' They both nodded.

'It's only eight more days, Mum,' Neil said, a wide grin on his face.

And then it was seven, six, five, four, three, two and one. And none of the family or Neil had shown any symptoms of Covid 19.

'I think Robert will miss Neil a lot,' Peter said.

'And vice-versa. But he can call over as often as he likes,' Claire suggested.

'Thank you, and the same goes for Neil,' Alison added.

When the day finally came, Claire couldn't contain herself as she drove over to the house. So glad to be able to walk up the driveway and ring the doorbell. Standing there, heart racing, she waited until the door opened and Neil threw himself on her, and she wrapped him in her arms. They stood silently, her tears wet on his dark hair, and when he looked up at her she could see that his eyes were full of tears as well.

'I love you, my Neil,' she whispered.

'I love you, Mum,' he said. 'I thought you had forgotten me.'

'No, never, Neil, that would be impossible.'

He tightened his arms around her.

'I must thank you for bringing Neil home,' she was very grateful to Alison and Peter.

'It was our pleasure, the boys all enjoyed the journey.'

'It was great fun, Mum,' Neil added.

'And they took our temperatures every time we went on the plane,' Robert grinned.

'You know one of those they point at your forehead,' explained

Neil.

The boys giggled.

As Claire drove home, Neil was in great form. Pointing out things he saw on the journey. When she opened the front door, he immediately dashed up the stairs into his room, and she followed.

'Everything is just the same,' he shouted. 'Look at all my posters.'

'And we must get some more.'

'Can we?' he turned to her, delighted. 'Dad wouldn't let me have any at the house in Beijing.'

She put her arm around him and hugged.

'And all my games are still here too.' He picked up some of them.

'I thought we might call Nai Nai and let her know that you are out of quarantine in Ireland and safe at home.'

'Let's,' he smiled.

He chatted to his grandmother, and she seemed to be very happy to hear from him. Claire felt a lot of sympathy for the woman who had lost her husband and her son to Covid 19, and now her grandson had returned to his home. Claire was grateful to her, and had every intention of going back to China to thank her in person as soon as Covid 19 had been defeated.

In the afternoon, they went to visit Neil's Gran and Grandad. It was a wonderful reunion. Both Peggy and Michael were overjoyed to see their grandson. But Claire and Neil kept to social distancing guidelines and walked around the side of the house into the garden.

'Sorry we can't give you a big hug.' Peggy was tearful.

'I'll give you a virtual hug, Gran,' Neil grinned, and crossed his arms over his chest.

270

'That was lovely,' she smiled at him.

'Me too,' his Grandad said.

Immediately, the dog, Rusty, leapt up on him and Neil rubbed his coat, delighted to see him.

'It's such a nice day so let's sit out here. We'll have tea and apple tart.' Peggy went into the kitchen, and Claire carried out the tray and set the table under the parasol, the chairs well apart for safety.

Claire was so happy to be with her family and celebrate Neil's return. She could hardly believe it was happening.

That night Jim Zoomed as usual, and was very anxious to know how she was now that Neil was home.

'I can't believe he's actually here. Safe and sound in his own bed.' She was emotional as usual and didn't even bother to hide it.

'I'm so happy for you,' he said, smiling. 'And I look forward to meeting the young man as soon as I can.'

'And I want to see you too. Touch you. Love you. It's been too long, but we're restricted to Zoom,' she said, her voice dull.

'How do we make love on Zoom?' he asked, with a smile.

'All I want is to hear the sound of your heart.'

'All I want is the taste of your lips,' he whispered. His face moved closer and she could see the features which characterised this man she now loved so much.

'When will this end?' she asked. 'I have my Neil back but I've lost you.'

'Soon my love,' he reassured.

'If only …'

'Don't lose faith. Promise me?'

'Promise.'

Chapter Fifty-three

The melody echoed around the room and Neil was very happy to be playing his own piano again. It was so different to being taught by Master Xin and having his knuckles tapped by a chopstick if he made a mistake. Now he just wanted to play for his Mum, and didn't make any mistakes at all.

'Thank you, Neil, that was beautiful,' Claire smiled. 'I have been very lonely for you and your music.' She was sitting beside him and she put her arm around him. He hugged close.

'I used to think I was playing for you,' Neil said.

'I used to imagine I could hear you.'

'My teacher, Master Xin, was very cross.'

'Do you want to go back to your music lessons?'

'Yes I do,' he said enthusiastically.

'He hasn't put you off altogether?' she smiled.

'Dad wanted me to be a concert pianist.'

'You can decide what you want to be yourself.'

'Can I?'

'You could do anything, Neil, if you want to study music that's great, or if you want to study something else then you can do whatever that is. It will be your choice.'

'Thanks Mum.' He was delighted she told him that. 'But I'm not sure what I want to do.'

'There's no hurry. You could be a professional footballer if you want. You can go back to the football club and you might even be spotted. You've plenty of time,' she reassured.

After dinner, they sat on the big red velvet couch together. 'It's a pity I didn't have a party for my birthday this year,' Neil said.

'We'll have a special party when all this is over. I'm so glad you're here, I've really missed you.' She hugged him.

He felt warm and loved.

'I'm looking forward to seeing Tommy and Calum tomorrow. They won't think that I have Covid because I came from China, will they?'

'No, I was talking to Lucy and Elaine, and the boys are all excited that you're home. And you'll all be going to school together soon. But you must tell me if you feel ill, that's very important.'

'Dad said that to me.' He felt a pang of sadness that he wasn't here anymore.

'I'm sure you must miss him,' she said softly.

'I do.'

'And I feel the same.'

But there was something which upset him and he hadn't explained that. 'Mum?'

'Yes, my love?'

'There was no funeral for Dad or Yeh Yeh either.' He found it hard to prevent tears moistening his eyes, and was embarrassed to let his Mum see how he felt.

'I know that, Lien told me.'

'Remember we had a funeral for Uncle Bill?'

'I do.'

'I thought it would be the same for Dad.'

'It's difficult with the virus.'

He nodded.

'But some time we might have a special service in memory of your Dad, although he wasn't a Catholic.'

'Could we?'

She nodded.

'Thanks Mum. Nai Nai said prayers at her shrine of Buddha for Yeh Yeh and Dad too.'

'We can do that as well,' Claire said. 'We have a small statue of Buddha upstairs.'

'Thanks.'

And there was something else he wanted to ask his Mum. So many questions going around his head. And he was sure that his Mum would answer all of them for him.

'Once Yeh Yeh said I had more Chinese blood than Irish.' He was silent for a moment. 'That I looked more like my Dad and ...are you my real Mum?'

Claire put her arm around him.

'Of course I'm your real mother.' She kissed him.

He stared at her, eyes wide. He had been really worried about that.

'You've been with me since you were born. A little baby.' She held out her hands to give him an idea of his size. 'You were just seven pounds, two ounces. Imagine that?'

'Seven pounds, two ounces?' he smiled.

'That's all. And I've loved you since you were that tiny.'

He hugged closer to Claire. 'It's good to be home, Mum, I never want to leave again.'

TO MAKE A DONATION TO
LAURALYNN HOUSE

Children's Sunshine Home/LauraLynn Account
AIB Bank, Sandyford Business Centre,
Foxrock, Dublin 18.

Account No. 32130009
Sort Code: 93-35-70

www.lauralynnhospice.com

Acknowledgements

As always, our very special thanks to Jane and Brendan, knowing you both has changed our lives.

Many thanks to both my family and Arthur's family, our friends and clients, who continue to support our efforts to raise funds for LauraLynn House. And all those generous people who help in various ways but are too numerous to mention. You know who you are and that we appreciate everything you do.

Grateful thanks to all my friends in The Wednesday Group, who give me such valuable critique.

Special thanks to Vivien Hughes who proofed the manuscript. We really appreciate your generosity.

Special thanks to Martone Design & Print – Brian, Dave, and Kate. Couldn't do it without you.

Special thanks to Workspace Interiors.

Grateful thanks to Transland Group.

Thanks to CPI Group and thanks to all at LauraLynn House.

Thanks to Kevin Dempsey Distributors Ltd. and Power Home Products Ltd., for their generosity in supplying product for LauraLynn House.

Special thanks to Cyclone Couriers and Southside Storage.

Grateful thanks also to Permanent TSB. Febvre & Company Limited. Supervalu.

Many thanks to Elephant Bean Bags – Furniture – Outdoor.

Special thanks to CarveOn Leather – Custom Engraved Leather Goods.

And in Nenagh, our grateful thanks to Tom Gleeson of Irish Computers who very generously service our website free of charge. Nick Long, Website Designer. Walsh Packaging, Nenagh Chamber of Commerce, McLoughlin's Hardware, Cinnamon Alley Restaurant, Ger Gavin House of Gifts, and Caseys in Toomevara.

Many thanks to Ree Ward Callan and Michael Feeney Callan.

And much love to my darling husband, Arthur, without whose love and support this wouldn't be possible.

MARTONE DESIGN & PRINT

Martone Design & Print was established in 1983
and has become one of the country's most pre-eminent
printing and graphic arts companies.

The Martone team provide high-end design
and print work to some of the country's top companies.
They provide a wide range of services including
design creation/development, spec verification,
creative approval, project management, printing, logistics,
shipping, materials tracking and posting verification.

They are the leading innovative all-inclusive solutions
provider, bringing print excellence to every market.

The Martone sales team can be contacted at

(01) 6281809 or sales@martonepress.com

CYCLONE COURIERS

Cyclone Couriers – who support LauraLynn Children's Hospice – are the leading supplier of local, national and international courier services in Dublin. Cyclone also supply confidential mobile on-site document shredding and recycling services and secure document storage & records management services through their Cyclone Shredding and Cyclone Archive Division.

Cyclone Couriers – The fleet of pushbikes, motorbikes, and vans, can cater for all your urgent local and national courier requirements.

Cyclone International – Overnight, next day, timed and weekend door-to-door deliveries to destinations within the thirty-two counties of Ireland.

Delivery options to the UK, mainland Europe, USA, and the rest of the world. A variety of services to all destinations across the globe.

Cyclone Shredding – On-site confidential document and product shredding & recycling service. Destruction and recycling of computers, hard drives, monitors and office electronic equipment.

Cyclone Archive – Secure document and data storage and records management. Hard copy document storage and tracking – data storage fireproof media safe – document scanning and upload of document images.

Cyclone Couriers operate from
Pleasants House, Pleasants Lane, Dublin 8.

Cyclone Archive, International and Shredding, operate from
11 North Park, Finglas, Dublin 11.

www.cyclone.ie. Email: sales@cyclone.ie Tel: 01-475 7000

SOUTHSIDE STORAGE
Murphystown Road, Sandyford, Dublin 18.

FACILITIES

Individually lit, self-contained, off-ground metal and concrete units that are fireproof and waterproof.

Sizes of units : 300 sq.ft. 150 sq.ft. 100 sq.ft. 70 sq.ft.

Flexible hours of access and 24 hour alarm monitored security.

Storage for home
Commercial storage
Documents and Archives
Packaging supplies and materials
Extra office space
Sports equipment
Musical instruments
And much much more ....

Contact us to discuss your requirements:

01 294 0517   -   087 640 7448
Email: info@southsidestorage.ie

Location: Southside Storage is located on
Murphystown Road, Sandyford, Dublin 18
close to Exit 13 on the M50

ELEPHANT BEAN BAGS

Designed with love in Co. Mayo, Ireland, Elephant products have been especially designed to provide optimum support and comfort without compromising on stylish, contemporary design.

Available in a variety of cool designs, models and sizes, our entire range has been designed to accommodate every member of your family, including your dog - adding a new lounging and seating dimension to your home.

Both versatile and practical, our forward thinking Elephant range of inviting bean bags and homewares are available in a wealth of vivid colours, muted tones and bold vibrant prints, that bring to life both indoor and outdoor spaces.

Perfect for sitting, lounging, lying and even sharing, sinking into an Elephant Bean Bag will not only open your eyes to superior comfort, but it will also allow you to experience a sense of unrivalled contentment that is completely unique to the Elephant range.

www.elephantliving.com

THE MARRIED WOMAN

Fran O'Brien

Marriage is for ever ...

In their busy lives, Kate and Dermot rush along on parallel
lines, seldom coming together to exchange a word or a kiss.
To rekindle the love they once knew, Kate struggles to lose
weight, has a make-over, buys new clothes, and arranges a
romantic trip to Spain with Dermot.

For the third time he cancels and she goes alone.

In Andalucia she meets the artist Jack Linley. He takes her with
him into a new world of emotion and for the first time in years
she feels like a desirable beautiful woman.

Will life ever be the same again?

Available now online
McGuinness Books
www.franobrien.net

THE LIBERATED WOMAN

Fran O'Brien

At last, Kate has made it!

She has ditched her obnoxious husband Dermot and is
reunited with her lover, Jack.

Her interior design business goes international and TV
appearances bring instant success.

But Dermot hasn't gone away and his problems encroach.

Her brother Pat and family come home from Boston
and move in on a supposedly temporary basis.

Her manipulative stepmother Irene is getting married
again and Kate is dragged into the extravaganza.

When a secret from the past is revealed Kate has
to review her choices ...

Available now online
McGuinness Books
www.franobrien.net

THE PASSIONATE WOMAN

Fran O'Brien

A chance meeting with ex-lover Jack throws Kate into a spin.
She cannot forgive him and concentrates all her passions on
her interior design business, and television work.

Jack still loves Kate and as time passes
without reconciliation he feels more and more frustrated.

Estranged husband Dermot has a
change of fortunes, and wants her back.

Stepmother, Irene, is as wacky as ever
and is being chased by the paparazzi.

Best friend, Carol, is searching for a man on the internet,
and persuades Kate to come along as chaperone on a date.

ARE THESE PATHS TO KATE'S NEW LIFE OR
ROUNDABOUTS TO HER OLD ONE?

Available now online
McGuinness Books
www.franobrien.net

ODDS ON LOVE

Fran O'Brien

Bel and Tom seem to be the perfect couple with successful careers, a beautiful home and all the trappings. But underneath the facade cracks appear and damage the basis of their marriage and the deep love they have shared since that first night they met.

Her longing to have a baby creates problems for Tom, who can't deal with the possibility that her failure to conceive may be his fault. His masculinity is questioned and in attempting to deal with his insecurities he is swept up into something far more insidious and dangerous than he could ever have imagined.

Then against all the odds, Bel is thrilled to find out she is pregnant. But she is unable to tell Tom the wonderful news as he doesn't come home that night and disappears mysteriously out of her life leaving her to deal with the fall out.

Available now online
McGuinness Books
www.franobrien.net

WHO IS FAYE?

Fran O'Brien

Can the past ever be buried?

Jenny should be fulfilled. She has a successful career,
and shares a comfortable life with her husband, Michael,
at Ballymoragh Stud.

But increasingly unwelcome memories
surface and keep her awake at night.

Is it too late to go back to the source
of those fears and confront them?

Available now online
McGuinness Books
www.franobrien.net

THE RED CARPET

Fran O'Brien

Lights, Camera, Action.

Amy is raised in the glitzy facade that is Hollywood.
Her mother, Maxine, is an Oscar winning actress, and
her father, John, a famous film producer. When
Amy is eight years old, Maxine is tragically killed.

A grown woman, Amy becomes the focus of John's
obsession for her to star in his movies and be as
successful as her mother. But Amy's insistence
on following her heart, and moving permanently to
Ireland, causes a rift between them.

As her daughter, Emma, approaches her eighth
birthday, Amy is haunted by the nightmare of
what happened on her own eighth birthday.

She determines to find answers to her questions.

Available now online
McGuinness Books
www.franobrien.net

FAIRFIELDS

1907 QUEENSTOWN CORK

Fran O'Brien

Set against the backdrop of a family feud and prejudice
Anna and Royal Naval Officer, Mike, fall in love.
They meet secretly at an old cottage
on the shores of the lake at Fairfields.

During that spring and summer their feelings for each
other deepen. Blissfully happy, Anna accepts Mike's
proposal of marriage, unaware that her family have a
different future arranged for her.

**Is their love strong enough to withstand
the turmoil that lies ahead?**

Available now online
McGuinness Books
www.franobrien.net

THE PACT

THE POINT OF THE KNIFE
PRESSES INTO SOFT SKIN ...

Fran O'Brien

Inspector Grace McKenzie investigates the
trafficking of women into Ireland and is
drawn under cover into that sinister world.

She is deeply affected by the suffering of one
particular woman and her quest for justice
re-awakens an unspeakable trauma in her own life.

CAN SHE EVER ESCAPE FROM ITS
INFLUENCE AND BE FREE TO LOVE?

Available now online
McGuinness Books
www.franobrien.net

1916

Fran O'Brien

On Easter Monday, 24th April, 1916, against the
backdrop of the First World War, a group of
Irishmen and Irishwomen rise up against Britain.
What follows has far-reaching consequences.

We witness the impact of the Rising on four families,
as passion, fear and love permeate a week of
insurrection which reduces the centre of Dublin to ashes.

This is a story of divided loyalties, friendships,
death, and a conflict between an Empire
and a people fighting for independence.

Available now online
McGuinness Books
www.franobrien.net

LOVE OF HER LIFE

Fran O'Brien

A man can look into a woman's eyes
and remind her of how it used to be
between them …once upon a time.

Photographer Liz is running a successful business.
Her family and career are all she cares about since
her husband died, until an unexpected encounter
brings Scott back into her life.

IS THIS SECOND CHANCE FOR LOVE DESTINED

TO BE OVERCOME BY THE WHIMS OF FATE?

Available now online
McGuinness Books
www.franobrien.net

ROSE COTTAGE YEARS

Fran O'Brien

The house in the stable yard is an empty shell
and Fanny's footsteps resound on her polished floors,
the rich gold of wood shining.

Three generations of women, each leaving the home they loved.
Their lives drift through the turmoil of the First World War,
the 1916 Rising, and the establishment of the Irish Free State,
knowing both happiness and heartache in those years.

Bina closes the door gently behind her.
The click of the lock has such finality about it.
At the gate she looks back through a mist of tears, just once.

Available now online
McGuinness Books
www.franobrien.net

BALLYSTRAND

Fran O'Brien

The future is bleak for Matt Sutherland when he is released from prison after being convicted of murder. He faces life in a changing world and rehabilitation begins in a homeless shelter.

His sisters, Zoe and Gail, anticipate his return with trepidation and are worried that their father will react badly.
When Matt calls to see them on Christmas Eve, this visit precipitates events which change their lives.

A letter is found. A secret is revealed. An unexpected meeting causes Matt to reach the limit of his endurance.

WILL IT TAKE ANOTHER DEATH TO
RIGHT THE WRONGS OF THE PAST?

Available now online
McGuinness Books
www.franobrien.net

VORLANE HALL

Fran O'Brien

TWO WOMEN LIVE OVER
TWO HUNDRED YEARS APART.

STRANGELY THEIR LIVES SEEM
TO MIRROR EACH OTHER.

Beth Harwood, passionate about history, is invited by
Lord Vorlane to research his family archive at Vorlane Hall
in Kildare, where against her better judgment
she is attracted to his eldest son, Nick.

In 1795, Martha Emilie Vorlane lived with her husband
on his sugar plantation in the British Virgin Islands.
In her journal she described her love affair with an
army captain and the pain and loss she suffered.

Reading Martha Emilie's journal captures
Beth's imagination and leads her into a situation
which changes her life dramatically.

Available now online
McGuinness Books
www.franobrien.net

CUIMHNÍ CINN

Memoirs of the Uprising

Liam Ó Briain

(Reprint in the Irish language originally published in 1951)

(English translation by Michael McMechan)

Liam Ó Briain was a member of the Volunteers of Ireland
from 1914 and he fought with the Citizen Army of Ireland
in the College of Surgeons during Easter Week.

This is a clear lively account of the events of that time.
An account in which there is truth, humanity and, more
than any other thing, humour. It will endure as literature.

When this book was first published in Irish in 1951,
it was hoped it would be read by the young people of Ireland.
To remember more often the hardships endured
by our forebears for the sake of our freedom
we might the better validate Pearse's vision.

Available now online
McGuinness Books
www.franobrien.net